P9-DCY-351

THE
HARBINGER
II

JONATHAN CAHN

FRONT
LINE

Most Charisma House Book Group products are available at special quantity discounts for bulk purchase for sales promotions, premiums, fund-raising, and educational needs. For details, call us at (407) 333-0600 or visit our website at www.charismahouse.com.

THE HARBINGER II by Jonathan Cahn
Published by FrontLine
Charisma Media/Charisma House Book Group
600 Rinehart Road, Lake Mary, Florida 32746

Septuagint quotations are taken from Lancelot Charles Lee Brenton, *The Septuagint Version of the Old Testament: English Translation* (London: Samuel Bagster and Sons, 1870).

Visit the author's website at jonathancahn.com and booksbyjonathancahn.com.

Library of Congress Cataloging-in-Publication Data:
An application to register this book for cataloging has been submitted to the Library of Congress.
International Standard Book Number: 978-1-62999-891-6
E-book ISBN: 978-1-62999-892-3

20 21 22 23 24 — 9 8 7 6 5 4 3 2 1
Printed in the United States of America

Contents

Part I: THE RETURN

Part II: THE UNREVEALED

Part III: THE MANIFESTATIONS

Part IV: THE COMING

What you are about to read will take the form of a story, but what is revealed in the story is real.

Part I

THE

RETURN

Chapter 1

The Return of Nouriel

"W HERE DO WE begin?" he asked.

"How about at the beginning," she replied, "with the seal. You come into possession of a small clay seal with ancient inscriptions. You have no idea what it all means. You begin searching. In the midst of your search, you come across a mysterious man. You don't know his name or where he comes from. You don't know how he knows things he shouldn't or couldn't have known. You speak of him as 'the prophet.'

"He tells you the meaning of the seal. And so the mystery begins. How am I doing so far, Nouriel?"

"Perfectly. I don't think you have any need of me."

"He gives you a second seal in exchange for the first. You have to try to unlock its meaning until you see him again. Your encounters with the prophet happen by what appears to be coincidence or some supernatural agency. But one way or another, he's always there at the exact time and place. And in each encounter the full significance of the seal is revealed. Each seal leads to another revelation, another puzzle piece in a still larger mystery. All together there are nine seals, nine mysteries, and nine revelations."

"Keep going," he said.

"The mystery centers on nine harbingers, nine warnings of coming judgment, calamity, and destruction, the signs that appeared in the last days of ancient Israel. But the mind-blowing thing is that those same nine harbingers have now reappeared in modern times...on American soil, some in New York City, some in Washington, DC, some involving objects, events, utterances, even American leaders, and with eerie precision and without anyone orchestrating them. And as in ancient times, they give warning...now to America."

She paused for a few moments, waiting to see if he would interject. But he was silent, so she continued.

"At the end of all the encounters, mysteries, and revelations, the prophet reveals that you were born for a purpose now to be fulfilled. He charges you to spread the word, to reveal the mystery, to sound the alarm."

"The call of the watchman," he replied.

"And that's where it left off, what you told me that night."

"Yes."

"And you did what the prophet charged you to do. You spread the word of it. You committed the revelation to writing…in the form of a narrative."

"The narrative was *your* idea, Ana…to change the names and details of what happened until it became a story through which the mystery would be revealed and the warning delivered."

"And you had never written a book before."

"No. I had no idea how to do it. But it was as if the book wrote itself. The words just flowed onto the pages."

"Most books never get published, but yours did. I never heard how it all happened."

"The week I finished the manuscript, I was scheduled to fly out to Dallas. The flight had a layover in Charlotte, North Carolina. While waiting for the connecting flight, I closed my eyes, bowed my head, and prayed for God to intervene, to send the message to the world."

"And what happened?"

"I opened my eyes. There was a man sitting to my left. He wasn't there when I closed my eyes. He turned to me and said, 'So what's the good word?'"

"A bit mystical for an opening line."

"A bit mystical of an encounter," he replied.

"So what did you talk about?"

"It was small talk…at first. But then his tone changed. He stared intently into my eyes and spoke with a sense of intense urgency. 'Nouriel,' he said, 'God has given you a message…and a book. It's from Him. And He'll send it forth to the nation and to the world. And your life will be changed. And you'll be known.'"

"It sounds like your encounter with the prophet," she said. "It's what you wrote about in the book, at the beginning of the story. You're sitting down in a public place with a man sitting to your left. He turns to you and starts a conversation. Then he speaks to you prophetically. And it leads you to bringing a prophetic word to the nation."

"Yes, except this happened *after* the book was written."

"And he couldn't have known?"

"No," said Nouriel. "No one could have known. No one had read it yet."

"So who was he?"

"A man of God, a believer, who just happened to have been scheduled to be on the same flight and who just happened to sit down next to me the moment I prayed that prayer."

"But how could he have known what he knew?" she asked.

"How could the prophet have known what he knew?"

"Did he ever tell you why he gave you that word?"

"He told me that when he sat down next to me, the Lord told him to give me a message. He was reluctant but finally spoke."

"And what happened next?"

"Not long after that encounter, I received a communication from the president of a publishing house. He told me that the man at the airport had shared with him of the encounter and of the book I had just written. He had no idea what it was about, but he was interested.

"And that's how the book went out to America and the world—not by the hand of man, but by the hand of God."

"So it was by a supernatural encounter that the revelation became a book and went forth to America. So how many people read it?"

"Many."

"How many?"

"I've been told millions."

"And everything changed for you, Nouriel, just as the man at the airport told you it would. Suddenly you're known. You're speaking across the nation. You're being interviewed. You're appearing on television and all over the web. You're in Washington, DC, speaking to leaders in government. Pretty heady stuff. It could make one forget his humility."

"No," he said. "I know it's not my doing. If anything it humbles me."

"That's good," she replied, "because it doesn't just happen. A man who doesn't know how to write books writes a book about nine harbingers of judgment, and millions read it. It doesn't just happen."

"None of it just happens," he replied.

"But it had to," she said. "It was what the prophet told you would happen. It had to happen because the word had to go forth as it did in ancient times."

And then she was quiet, as was he. She reached over to grab a cup of coffee that was resting on the edge of her desk, brought it to her lips, and began sipping on it. But she didn't take her eyes off of him. She was hoping to see some reaction, some trace of an expression that would convey more than she was getting. There was a cup of water on his side of the desk, but he wasn't touching it. He was staring into the distance as if in deep thought. And then, finally, he spoke.

"OK, Ana, why?"

"Why what?"

"Why did you ask me to come? In all the years since I first came here to tell you what happened, you've been reluctant to broach the subject."

"I didn't want to get in the way."

"What do you mean?"

"The whole thing was so beyond anything I had ever heard of. It was like dealing with a sacred object. I felt I shouldn't touch it. But I watched everything from a distance. I read your writings. I watched you on television. I searched for you on the web. I just felt I couldn't approach it."

"All the more, it begs the question 'Why now?'"

"Because," she said, "I had to know."

"You had to know what?"

"You did what you were supposed to do. You completed the charge. The word went forth.... So what now?"

"What now?"

"The book revealed the signs and warnings of a nation in danger of judgment. It was the beginning. There has to be more. Where are we now?"

"You want me to reveal what's *not* in the book?"

"Have there been other revelations?"

"Nothing other than what the prophet told me."

"And you haven't seen him since then? And there've been no more mysteries, no more revelations?"

He didn't answer that, but put his left hand below his chin and looked downward. His lack of response intensified Ana's interest. She held back from saying anything, waiting instead for a response. But instead of answering her, he got up from his chair and walked over to the huge glass window, through which the light of the afternoon sun was streaming in, and just stood there, staring out at the skyline of the city.

"So there've been no more revelations?" she asked again.

"I didn't quite say that," he said without turning his gaze from the window.

"Have you heard from him, Nouriel? Since you finished writing the book, have you heard from the prophet?"

It was then that he resigned himself to the possibility that telling her might be part of the plan.

"One might say that," he replied.

"One might say that you've heard from him?"

"Yes."

"How?" she asked.

Finally, he turned to her.

"He returned."

Chapter 2

The Girl in the Blue Coat

"Come, Nouriel," she said as she got up from her chair. She led him out of the office and down the hall. At the end of the hall was a door that opened into a large meeting room with a long table of dark brown wood in its center. Its outer wall consisted almost entirely of glass, and beyond it, a vast panorama of skyscrapers.

"Please," she said, motioning him toward the seat at the head of the table, "sit down." So he did. She took the seat to his right, with her back to the panorama.

"It's more secure in here," she said. "It's soundproof. May I get you something to drink?"

"Just water," he replied.

She pressed the button on the intercom at the head of the table.

"A glass of water and a cup of coffee, please."

A minute later a woman appeared with a cup of coffee and a glass of water.

"Thank you," said Ana. "Hold off all calls...no interruptions."

"For the remainder of the meeting?" the woman asked.

"For the remainder of the day or until I say otherwise. No interruptions."

Ana didn't touch her coffee but just sat there and watched as Nouriel drank his water. When it looked as if he was done, she spoke.

"So, Nouriel, how did it begin?"

"It began at a book signing."

"I imagine you've done many."

"I have. This one was at the end of a speaking engagement. I was sitting in back of a long table. Most of the time when I do a signing, everyone waits in a line with their books. But this time was different. There was no line. It was chaotic. The table was surrounded by a thick crowd of people handing me their books in no particular order. I signed them and handed them back, hopefully to the right person.

"I was about halfway through when a girl appeared in the midst of the crowd, directly in front of me on the other side of the table. She had to have been about six or seven years old. She had wavy blonde hair, blue eyes, and a light blue coat. There was something about her."

"What?"

"For one thing, there didn't appear to be anyone accompanying her, no mother or father, just a little girl standing in a crowd of people on her own. And there was something about her that I couldn't put into words. As the others pressed in to get their books signed, she just stood there as if separate from the rest of the crowd. She never pushed for me to sign her book but stood there, looking at me, with a gentle smile.

"I realized if I didn't say anything, she would end up the last to get her book signed."

◆◆◆

"Would you like me to sign your book?" I asked.

"That would be good," she answered.

Stretching her hand across the table, she handed me her book. I opened it to the title page and lifted my pen to sign it.

"Your name?"

"You don't have to put down my name," she replied, "just yours."

So I signed it.

"Here you go," I said, handing it back to her.

At that, she gently took hold of my right hand, turned it so my palm was facing upward, and placed in it an object.

"And here *you* go," she said.

◆◆◆

"What was it?"

"A small circular object of reddish-golden-brown clay . . ."

"A seal."

"Yes."

"An ancient seal?"

"It appeared to be."

"Like the seal the prophet gave you?"

"Yes," said Nouriel, "just like the seals of the harbingers."

"Maybe she read the book and made the seal to look like those in the story."

"No. It was too exact; it was identical to the seals of the prophet...in every detail."

"But how?"

"I don't know how."

◆◆◆

No one around the table realized what was going on. I imagine they figured the girl had given me a gift, a token of appreciation. And then she spoke.

"Nouriel," she said, "you've done what you were entrusted to do. You have delivered the message with which you were entrusted." The words were no longer those of a little girl.

"What do you mean?" I asked.

"You've given warning. And now the time is coming to an end."

"And what does *that* mean?"

"Your time of not seeing...and the first part of your mission."

"Why are you saying this?" I asked. "Who told you to say it?"

She didn't answer.

"Where did you get the seal?" I asked. "Who gave it to you?"

"A friend," she replied.

"What friend?"

She didn't answer.

"Prepare yourself, Nouriel."

"Prepare myself for what?"

"For the time," she said, "for the revelation."

"What does that mean?"

"He's coming."

"Who's coming?"

"He's coming back."

"Who's coming back?"

"He's coming back...but not as you expect."

"I don't expect anything."

"Then all the more so he'll come as you don't expect. Prepare yourself, Nouriel...for the return. And this is how it begins."

"How *what exactly* begins?"

"How it *all* begins," she said, "with the seal."

I looked down at the seal as if I would find something that would make sense of what was happening. I looked back up at the girl, and she was gone, or almost gone. I could just see the last trace of her blue coat disappearing into the crowd.

I got up from my chair, made my way around the table to the place from which she had disappeared, and then into the crowd to catch up with her. The book signing was thrown into confusion. When I emerged at the other side of the crowd, there was no sign of her. She was gone.

◆◆◆

"And there was no one with her?"

"No one."

"And nobody who knew who she was?"

"I asked around, but no one had ever seen her before."

"Who do you think she was?"

"I can only guess."

"And how did she get the seal?"

"I had my guesses, but I couldn't say for sure. But I knew it wasn't that she just happened to show up there. She was sent. She was a messenger."

"By whom?"

"That was the question."

"So what did you do?"

"I went back to the table and finished the book signing. But my mind was elsewhere. I couldn't stop thinking about what had just happened and what it might mean."

"Then what?"

"That night, alone in my hotel room, I took out the seal to look at it. As with the seals that the prophet had given me, there was an image engraved on it."

"Of what?"

"The figure of a man, ancient, bearded, and robed. He was turned to the right and holding, in his left hand, a ram's horn, set to his mouth...as if he was sounding it, or about to."

"The watchman," said Ana, "the watchman sounding the alarm. It's what the prophet told you when you last saw him; when he told you to spread the message, you were being given the charge of a watchman, to sound the alarm."

"Yes."

"And now you were given another seal and with the image of the watchman, which is where it all left off when you last saw the prophet— so it meant that you were about to receive another revelation. So the seal was a sign of a coming revelation... and that it was about to begin again... from where it left off."

"It was."

"And every seal you were given led to another encounter with the prophet. That's what the little girl was alluding to... to prepare yourself for the return. The return was of the prophet."

"Yes," he replied, "the prophet would come... but in a way I would not expect."

Chapter 3

The Return of the Prophet

S o what did you do?"
"The only thing I could think of was to go back to the place where I last saw him and when he first told me about the watchman."

"Which place?"

"The same place where he *first* appeared to me, where we first met, on the bench overlooking the Hudson River. So I returned there."

"And?"

"And all I found was a bench. I sat down and waited for about half an hour, but nothing happened. About a week later I went back, and again, nothing. After examining the seal, yet again, hoping to find some clue or revelation, and finding nothing, I went to bed.

"That night I had a dream. I was walking through New York City toward the west side, to the Hudson River. It appeared to be late afternoon. It was a windy day, and the sky was filled with clouds. And in the distance ahead was the bench."

"The same bench?"

"The same bench. I made my way over to it and sat down. I reached into my coat pocket and took out the seal to examine it."

"The seal with the watchman."

"Yes. And it was then that I noticed I wasn't alone. Sitting to my left was a man."

◆◆◆

"Looks like a storm," he said as he gazed out into the water.

It was the prophet. He looked just as I had remembered him, dark hair, Middle Eastern features, and a closely cut beard and wearing the same coat he always wore when I had encountered him.

"What do you have in your hand?" he asked without turning his gaze to look at me.

"A seal," I replied.

"An ancient seal?"

"Yes."

"May I see it?" he said.

I handed it to him.

"The watchman," he said as he examined it. "What did the watchman do?"

"He stood on the city walls, in the watchtowers, looking into the distance for the first sign of danger, an enemy, an approaching army."

"And if he saw in the distance the first sign of danger, what was he to do?"

"Blow the trumpet, the ram's horn; sound the alarm."

"So those in the city would know…so that those who had ears to hear the warning could be saved."

They were the same words he had used when he gave me the charge, the last time I saw him. They were the words that led me to write the book…to sound the alarm.

"So," he said, still gazing into the water, "has the watchman given the warning?"

"Has he?" I asked. "You tell me."

"Has he sounded the alarm?"

"I believe he has."

"And the people, have they heard the sound?"

"Many have. Many have not."

"And have they taken warning?"

"Many have…but most have not."

"Then they're still asleep," he said, "and in danger. Then the call of the watchman isn't finished."

"What does that mean?" I asked.

It was only then that he turned to me.

"It means that your calling isn't finished, Nouriel. Your mission isn't over. It means that there's more," he said, "more to be given, more to be received, and more to be made known."

"You look exactly as I remember you."

"I suppose that's good," said the prophet, "though this is a dream. Were you not told that I would come to you in a way that you didn't expect?"

"By the girl in the blue coat?"

"Yes."

"I was."

"And did you expect me to come to you in this way?"

"No...but did you really come?"

"What do you mean?"

"Am I dreaming of you, or are you coming to me in my dream?"

"Does it make a difference?"

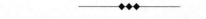

"So which was it?" asked Ana. "Was it from your thoughts or from beyond your thoughts?"

"Time would tell."

"Tell you which?"

"That there was no way I could have come up with what I was seeing. It was definitely beyond me."

"Then from what?"

"In the Bible, revelations were sometimes given through dreams."

"What about the prophet?"

"The revelations given in a dream or vision could sometimes come through the words of angels, messengers of God, even from God Himself. So it wasn't so much that the person was dreaming of an angel speaking or of God speaking, but that God or a messenger of God was actually speaking through the dream."

"So was the prophet speaking to you through the dream?"

"What the prophet said was that perhaps it didn't matter if the prophet was speaking in the dream."

"But he said that in the dream."

"I believe that that was the point. Whether a revelation comes through a prophet, a dream, or a prophet within a dream, it doesn't matter. It's not about the means through which it comes—it's about the revelation. And the revelation could not have possibly come from me."

"So what happened next?"

"So you returned," I said, "because..."

"Because it's time," he said, "and there's more to be revealed."

"More?"

"But first we must set the foundation. Why is it that a nation is given warning?"

"Because of the danger," I replied, "of judgment."

"And what nation is it that stands in danger of judgment?"

"A nation that wars against the will of God."

"And what nation more specifically stands in such danger and is more accountable?"

"One that has especially known the will of God, the ways of God, and the blessings of God...but turned away and now wars against them."

"And what ancient civilization was dedicated, from its inception, to the will of God?"

"Israel," I said, "ancient Israel."

"And what other civilization?"

"America."

"And what else joins the two?"

"The pattern," I said. "America was founded after the pattern of ancient Israel."

"And what happened to ancient Israel?"

"It fell away. It turned against the ways of God."

"And in the case of America?"

"It also fell away and, likewise, turned against the ways of God."

"And what happened to ancient Israel?"

"Judgment happened," I said. "It was destroyed."

"And why does that matter now?"

"Because the fall of ancient Israel reveals the template and progression of a nation heading to judgment."

"And what happened, specifically, in that template?"

"God called them, sent prophets and messengers to warn and plead with them to come back. But they wouldn't return; they wouldn't listen. They hardened their hearts to the point where the only way to reach them was through a shaking."

"And how did that shaking come?"

"The nation's hedge of protection was lifted up, and an enemy was allowed to strike the land...to wake them up that they might return."

"And what about America?"

"America likewise hardened its heart to the voice of God, and likewise came the shaking; the hedge of the nation's protection was lifted up."

"When?"

"On September 11, 2001. The hedge was lifted, and America was struck by its enemies, a wake-up call, that the nation might return."

"And did it?"

"No."

"And according to the template, what happens next?"

"After the shaking, the nation is given a chance to turn back, a window of time, years of grace in which to return to God."

"And what happened to ancient Israel in that window of time?"

"They never returned, and the window came to an end. The judgment fell. The nation was destroyed."

"Now remember, Nouriel," he said, "judgment is not the heart of God, not for a nation or a soul. Judgment is His necessity. But redemption is His heart. He wills that none should perish and longs to save, to grant mercy and forgiveness, to heal and restore. It is the necessity of good to bring evil to an end, that judgment must come—but it is the heart of good to bring salvation, to call back, to warn, and to even allow the shaking of nations that those who would hear His calling would come back and be saved."

"So what now?" I asked. "America hasn't turned back."

"It's not over," he said. "There's more to be revealed, more for you to be shown, and more that must be done."

"More to be revealed of what?"

"Of that which was...of that which was not but now has been...and that which is yet to come."

"*Of that which was*...meaning, the first shaking...9/11?"

"Yes."

"But didn't you already show me that when you revealed the harbingers?"

"You were only shown a piece of the larger mystery. More than what was revealed to you was that which was unrevealed."

"Why didn't you reveal it then?"

"You couldn't have been shown everything at once. And even if you could, it would have been too much for you to receive. And it wasn't for that time to be revealed—but for now."

"And *that which was not but now has been*...meaning what has happened since then, since 9/11?"

"Yes, and particularly that which has happened since we last saw each other...up to the present day."

"So are there more manifestations, more signs, more harbingers?"

"You will have to see."

"And *that which is yet to come*...the future, of course."

"The future, of course," he said, "and the future of the course."

"The course, can it be changed?"

"We shall see," he said. "But for now, remember one thing, Nouriel."

"What's that?"

"Record it."

"What?"

"When you wake up, remember to record what has been shown you."

————◆◆◆————

"So when you woke up," said Ana, "you wrote it all down."

"I recorded it. I kept the same recorder by my bed that I used in my conversations with the prophet in our first encounters. I've always kept it with me since that time, just in case."

————◆◆◆————

"When I see you again," he said, "we will begin uncovering that which has not yet been revealed."

"What wasn't shown me from the beginning?"

"The mysteries hidden from the beginning but that are now to be revealed."

"Why now?"

"Because they hold the keys to where we've been, where we are, and what is yet to come."

"For America."

"For America and more than America. America is the head of nations, the center of the present world order. It stands for many nations, for a civilization, a world, and an age. What happens to America will, in the end, touch the nations."

"So what would you call them, the other mysteries?"

"*The unrevealed.*"

Part II

THE

UNREVEALED

Chapter 4

The Gate

S o YOU WOKE up and recorded the dream. And what happened?"
"Nothing," said Nouriel, "nothing for some time. And I had no
idea what I was supposed to do, if anything. The prophet didn't leave
me with any direction. The only thing I had to go on was the seal. But I
couldn't glean anything from it that would point me to what was next."

"And then?"

"And then it came…in the form of a dream. I was standing in front of
two colossal golden doors. To the right and left of the doors were walls
made of large sand-colored stones. The doors were closed and bolted
shut. I knew that I was standing on the outside of an ancient city and,
judging from the size of its doors and walls, a great city. Adorning the
two golden doors were engraved images."

"Of what?"

"On the right side of the doors," he said, "a representation of hills, a
land of hills, and on the left, what appeared to be a giant torch. Above
the flame of the torch was the sun, a stylized image with rays that looked
more like spikes than light. Separating the sun and the torch from the
land of hills was a series of curved lines, waves, that I took to represent
water."

"What do you think it meant?"

"At the time, I had no idea. I was staring up at the colossal image,
trying to make sense of it, when I heard a voice."

◆◆◆

"So what do you make of it, Nouriel?"

I turned to my left, from where the voice was coming. It was the
prophet…the same appearance, the same coat—everything was the
same as in the first dream except we were in an ancient setting.

"I have no idea," I replied. "I would think you could help me with that."

"It's a gate. The great cities of the ancient world were walled, and within those walls were gates to allow their inhabitants and visitors to go in and out. The gate was the city's portal to the rest of the world, the center of trade, through which commerce and merchandise poured, the place of markets, of buying and selling and trading. The gate was also a place of power, where the elders sat, where decisions were made, and cases judged. The gate thus became the symbol of a city's power or a kingdom's greatness. And so the gates were often adorned and embellished with the symbols and signs of power, wealth, and greatness...the gates of Nineveh...the gates of Babylon. The gate would become the embodiment of the city itself or the kingdom, empire, or civilization by which it stood."

It was just then that I heard a faint, distant rumbling.

"What do you hear, Nouriel?" he asked.

"A rumbling."

"Listen more closely."

"It's the sound of hoofbeats...horses...and chariots."

"Approaching hoofbeats," said the prophet. "The sound of an invading army, an enemy attack."

The moment he said that, in an instant, we were transported. I was now standing with the prophet on top of the wall, on the rampart by the gate.

"Look, Nouriel," he said, pointing into the distance. It was then that I saw the enemy, an ancient army with banners, horses, chariots, soldiers armed with spears, swords, bows and arrows, ladders, platforms, battering rams...siege works. "They're coming to us," he said. "They're coming to the gate. The gate is the most vulnerable place in the wall."

"That's why it was closed and bolted."

"Yes. The attack will focus on the gate."

The army drew near to the gate. What followed was a barrage of flaming arrows, the hurling of boulders, and the pounding of battering rams. I began to fear for our safety.

"Don't worry," said the prophet, "it can't hurt you. We're only watching."

As the onslaught continued, the gate weakened and then, with the final crashing of the battering rams, gave way. The two colossal golden doors fell to the ground. The army entered in. It was all over. The city was lost.

I stood with the prophet, gazing down at what had once been the great gate of the ancient city but was now nothing more than wreckage and smoking ruins.

"What do you think it all means, Nouriel?"

"It has to do with judgment. When judgment came to the nation of Israel, it would most often involve the attack of an enemy. And it would begin with the enemy coming to the gate."

"Yes. For the enemy to appear at the gate meant that the judgment was beginning. And so Moses warned the nation of what would happen if it turned away from God:

They shall besiege you at all your gates...[1]

"The days of judgment would begin when the enemy came to the gate.

...your enemy shall distress you at all your gates.[2]

"So in the days of judgment, the enemy would cause distress at the nation's gate. Through the prophet Ezekiel, the Lord said this:

I have set *the point of the sword against all their gates...*[3]

"And so the gate would become the focal point of the sword, of violence. And after the judgment had fallen on the city of Jerusalem, it would be written:

All her *gates are desolate....Her gates have sunk into the ground.*[4]

"So the destruction at the gate will embody the nation's judgment. Judgment begins at the gate.... A nation's judgment begins at the nation's gate."

"You have to be showing me this because it has something to do with America. But America doesn't have a wall or gate."

"Are you sure?" he asked.

"Yes."

"But it does."

The moment he said those words, everything changed. I found myself standing on top of a ledge on a building, high above ground level, looking out at a vast city, around which was a body of water, a river, and a bay. I don't know why I didn't recognize it immediately.

"You're wrong about America," he said. "It may not have walled cities, but it certainly has a gate."

"What do you mean?"

"This," he replied, pointing to the landscape that surrounded us. "This is the gate."

"I don't see any gate."

"You were looking for a walled city. They don't build them anymore. But gates still exist. This, Nouriel, is the gate of America."

"I still don't see it."

"This city, this river, this bay, this passageway."

"I'm not getting it."

"The island of Manhattan, the Hudson River, the New York Harbor…New York City…is the gate of America…the portal of American civilization. Do you see the land on the other side?"

"Yes."

"Do you know what it's called? It's called the Gateway. As the gate was to the ancient city, so New York City is to America. What was it that took place at the ancient gate?"

"People went in and out."

"And so it is that through this gate, more than any other, the multitudes have come to America. Look over there," he said, pointing to his left. "That's Ellis Island, the gate through which millions of immigrants passed to enter this land. It was even known as the Gate of America. What happened at the ancient gate?"

"Trade," I answered. "Merchandise and commodities, buying and selling, the marketplace."

"And so this gate has been the center of American trade. And within it has resided the central markets, the focal point of the nation's buying and selling. And what else was the ancient gate?"

"The embodiment of power, wealth, and greatness."

"And so too does this gate, New York City, stand as the embodiment of the power, wealth, and greatness of American civilization."

"The image on the golden doors—it was this."

"Yes, the land of hills—that was Manhattan. That's what it originally was—an island of hills. And the water was the Hudson River."

"And the sun and the torch on the other side of the water?"

"Look over there, Nouriel, to the left of Ellis Island. What do you see?"

"The Statue of Liberty! The torch, of course! And the sun with the radiating spikes—the crown."

"Yes," he said, "and the statue was patterned after the ancient Colossus of Rhodes, Helios, the Greek sun god."

"The words of the poem on the statue's pedestal, 'I lift my lamp beside *the golden door!*'"[5]

"Yes, the doorway, the gate to America."

"So the golden doors in the gate of the ancient city—it was all pointing to this."

"And to the mystery," said the prophet.

"The mystery..."

"Of judgment. Judgment begins at the gate. Therefore, it had to be this way."

"What do you mean?"

"The judgment had to begin at the gate. What does that mean?"

And it was then that it hit me.

"9/11," I said. "It began here. It had to begin in New York City."

"And what did the beginning of Israel's judgment involve?"

"The appearance of its enemies at the gate."

"So the days of judgment begin when the enemy appears at the gate. And what happened on 9/11?"

"The nation's enemy appeared at America's gate."

"The terrorists came from across the world, from the Middle East, to manifest themselves in New York City—the enemy at the gate—the sign of judgment. And they did more than appear. Remember the scripture:

> They shall besiege you at all your gates.[6]

"So on 9/11 they struck the gate of America.

> Your enemy shall distress you at all your gates.[7]

"And so on 9/11, distress came upon America from the calamity that began at its gate. And it was not only that they struck America in New York City—but where specifically did the strike take place?"

"In lower Manhattan," I replied.

"Which is the part of the city that most exactly constitutes the nation's gate. And more exactly where? At the edge of lower Manhattan, the edge that overlooks the river, the gateway. The attack began as the first plane crossed the river, the gateway, to its target. The second plane then flew up the New York Harbor, the gateway itself. So the calamity not only took place at the nation's gate but at the very specific entrance of that gate, at the gate of the gate of the nation."

"I remember seeing pictures of the Statue of Liberty on that day overlooking the cloud of destruction at Ground Zero."

"Yes," said the prophet, "at the golden door, the gate of the gate.

> Her gates shall lament and mourn.[8]

"And so as in the days of Israel's judgment, the gates became a place of mourning and lamentation. So what is the warning of the gate?"

"I don't know."

"The gate is the entrance point, the portal through which judgment begins. Remember the biblical pattern: first comes the strike, the warning, and then a window of time. What happens at the gate represents the beginning. What happened on September 11, 2001, was the beginning, the entrance point of judgment. If the nation doesn't turn back…then what began that day moves inexorably to its conclusion."

It was as he said those words that the dream came to an end.

————◆◆◆————

"It's a lot to take in," said Ana.

"Yes, and it was only the beginning."

"So when was the next revelation?"

"They came on their own timing," he replied. "The next one came a week later. It would take up where this one had left off…and would be even more specific."

"How did it begin?"

"With an image from my childhood."

Chapter 5

The Towers

I WAS A LITTLE child in the dream as it began, sitting in a classroom, with other little children. On the table was an assortment of papers— white papers, colored papers, newspapers, magazines—scissors, paste, and glue."

"Arts and crafts."

"Something like that. I found a sheet of paper that had the color and appearance of stone. I cut it up into little pieces, then pasted pieces onto another sheet of paper to create an image."

"Of what?"

"A tower. It was then that I realized what I was seeing. It was from a real moment in my life, when I was a little boy. For some reason I had never forgotten it. But what followed was not from my life. When I finished the picture, I took the sheet and was propping it up on the table to make it appear as if the tower was standing upright. But the paper slipped out of my hands and fell to the floor. I got up from my chair and bent down to retrieve it.

"At that moment, everything changed. The paper was gone, the classroom was gone, and I was no longer a child. I was now standing outside in the middle of what appeared to be an ancient Middle Eastern landscape. In the distance ahead of me was a multitude of people in robes and sandals. They were all involved in a major undertaking, a construction project. Some were surveying and measuring. Others were moving massive stones into place. Others were directing.

"As the project progressed and the building began to rise from the ground, I realized what I was seeing. It was the reason I was taken back to that classroom and reminded of that picture. It wasn't just a tower—it was the Tower of Babel. And what I was now witnessing was the building of the Tower of Babel."

"And wasn't that what appeared on one of the nine seals in your first encounters with the prophet?"

"Yes, the ziggurat."

"And a ziggurat is what again?"

"A terraced or stepped tower made of rectangular sections, each one smaller than the one below it. And that's what was now rising from the earth before me. The tower ascended to such a great height that it looked as if it would soon touch the clouds. But it was then that its ascent came to an end. That's when I heard a voice, the voice of the prophet, who was now standing to my left."

———◆◆◆———

"And they said,

> Come, let us build ourselves a city, and a tower whose top is in the heavens; let us make a name for ourselves.[1]

"Do you know, Nouriel, what the word for *tower* is, in the Bible, in the original language?"

"I wouldn't."

"The word *migdal*. It comes from the Hebrew root *gadal*. *Gadal* speaks of greatness. It literally means to become great, to increase, to be enlarged, or to be lifted up. And even that root word, *gadal*, can be translated as 'tower.'

"And that's the heart of the matter. The people of Babel sought to build a tower to make a name for themselves. They were seeking greatness."

At that, he pointed toward the tower.

"Look, Nouriel."

I looked and saw now other towers rising from the ground. No one was building them; they were just going up...all of them ziggurats, just like the first, but of differing heights and widths and with differing facades. It became a city of towers, a skyline of ziggurats, towers of babel.

"So," said the prophet, "as kings and kingdoms rose to the heights of world power, they built towers to stand as monuments to their greatness. The towers of the ancient world boasted of the powers and glories of the civilizations that erected them. Their heights would bear witness to the heights attained by their builders. They stood as symbols and embodiments of the kingdoms that built them.

"The connection between towers and greatness as revealed in the word *migdal* has continued into the modern world."

"How so?"

"Paralleling America's rise to world power was the rise of its towers. In the twentieth century, when it reached the heights of power and greatness no nation or empire had ever before attained, so too its towers, its skyscrapers, would reach heights no man-made structure on earth had ever before attained."

"The Empire State Building."

"Yes."

"And the Twin Towers."

"Except the Twin Towers were not erected in the age of America's rising, but of its falling. It was as the nation turned away from the moral and spiritual foundation on which it had been established, as it turned away from God and His ways, that it built those towers. And they rose at a time when America's power relative to the rest of the world was declining. But there's something else that the Hebrew for *tower* is linked to."

"What?"

"Pride. And so the towers of the ancient world were also linked to the pride and arrogance of the nations, kingdoms, and civilizations that built them. You see, to seek greatness and power and glory apart from God and in defiance of His will...is pride."

"As in the Tower of Babel."

"And so the towers of nations become monuments as well to their pride and arrogance. And so it was as America fell away from God, that the Twin Towers rose from the earth."

It was then that I noticed two ziggurats of similar height towering over the rest. I knew that they represented the two towers of the World Trade Center.

"In the beginning of a nation's judgment, that which is high and lifted up is brought low. Listen to what the prophet Isaiah wrote of that day:

> For the day of the LORD of hosts shall come upon everything *proud* and *lofty*, upon everything *lifted up*—and it shall be *brought low.*[2]

"And again...

> The *loftiness of man* shall be *bowed down*, and the *haughtiness of men* shall be *brought low*.[3]

"So in that day," said the prophet, "the pride of man is judged. And that which is lifted up is brought low."

It was at that moment that the ancient skyline transformed into a modern one, each ziggurat changing into a skyscraper and the two highest ziggurats, into the Twin Towers.

"Thus a civilization under judgment will see that which it has lifted up and set on high be cast down to the ground."

"The Twin Towers," I said, "were high and lifted up. And on 9/11, they were brought down to the ground."

"In the days of a nation's judgment," said the prophet, "its high places are broken down by its enemies:

> And they shall throw down your shrines and break down your high places."[4]

"So on 9/11," I said, "America's high places were given into the hands of its enemies, the terrorists...and were broken down."

"And the scriptures speak not only of the nation's high and lofty places, but more specifically. In the day of judgment, destruction will fall...

> Upon every *high tower*."[5]

"On every high tower," I repeated, "*the Twin Towers*."

"And it is written," said the prophet, "that on the day of a nation's judgment,

> They shall...*break down her towers*...[6]

"It will be a day of alarm, warned the prophet Zephaniah, 'against the *high towers*'[7]...a day, said the prophet Isaiah, 'when the *towers fall*,'[8] the sign of a fallen nation. When the high towers fall to the earth...a nation's judgment is beginning."

"And it all happened," I said, "on 9/11, the day that America's high towers fell to the earth."

"A most ancient sign," said the prophet. "The same sign that appeared to ancient cities and kingdoms now appeared to America."

"And the whole world saw it."

"Nouriel, why was it that the enemy attacked the gate?"

"Because the gate was the vulnerable part of the wall."

"And do you know what they did to strengthen the gate?"

"No."

"They built towers by the gate. So the gate was the place of the towers. What does that reveal?"

"The gate of America will be the place of its high towers...New York City."

"The city known especially for its high towers," he said. "So at the beginning of a nation's judgment, the enemy will attack the towers of its gate."

"The towers at America's gate."

"And do you know what form the towers of the ancient gate would take?"

"No."

"They would build one tower on each side...two towers...built of the same materials and in the same image. So standing at the gate would be two matching towers...twin towers."

"The Twin Towers."

"Yes," said the prophet. "And so on 9/11, the judgment began as the enemy attacked the Twin Towers that stood in America's gate."

"And what does it mean?" I asked.

"As with the gate," he replied, "it speaks not of the end but of the beginning...of judgment—the warning. The tower embodies the nation. American civilization was founded for the purposes of God. But it ascended to heights no civilization had ever attained. It became a high tower...a great high tower that turned against the foundation on which it was built. And so unless it returns to that foundation...the tower will fall."

————◆◆◆————

"And then I awoke."

"What happened next?" asked Ana.

"The next revelation would take me to the mystery's other ground and its other side, which the prophet had never before opened."

Chapter 6

The Wall

I FOUND MYSELF INSIDE a museum..."

"In reality or..."

"In a dream, in the next dream. I was walking down its corridors, passing ancient artifacts on my right and left. I came to a gigantic stone wall. It had to have been at least fifty feet high. It was covered with engravings. The imagery and style of the engravings looked familiar."

"In your first encounters with the prophet," said Ana, "he met you in a museum in front of a stone relief."

"Yes," said Nouriel, "an ancient Assyrian relief. And that's what I was now staring at."

"You were looking at an image of what?"

"A battle scene. The Assyrian army was laying siege to a walled city. As I watched, the images came alive."

"What do you mean?"

"They began to move, and accompanying the movement were sounds of war. The Assyrian soldiers began shooting arrows and slinging stones over the city walls. The city's defenders, those who stood on the ramparts and in the towers by the gates, were hurling stones and torches down on the invaders. Then the Assyrians began setting ramps against the walls and rolling siege engines up the ramps. As the battle raged on, I noticed more and more battering rams lined up against the city walls, on the ground and on the ramps. They pounded the stone wall over and over again. It seemed, at first, as if the battering was having no effect. Then, suddenly, one of the battering rams opened up a breach. With that, the focus of the attack and the battering shifted to that one breach. And then it all gave way. The wall collapsed. The resulting opening was so great that the entire army was able to flood through. It was then that I knew the city would be destroyed. And then the movement stopped, and everything was again still, frozen in place."

◆◆◆

"The siege of the enemy…the beginning of the end."

It was the prophet, standing beside me.

"What were you looking at, Nouriel?"

"Another siege of an ancient city."

"A city of ancient Israel," he said. "You were watching that of which the nation had been warned. 'They shall besiege you…'[1] It was the fulfillment of prophecy. And what did you see, specifically?"

"The shooting of arrows, the battering of siege works."

"And where did you see them attack?"

"At the gate…at the towers by the gate…"

"And?"

"The wall. They were attacking all along the wall."

"So we have these three," said the prophet, "the gate, the towers, and now the wall…the three focal points of siege—and the first three signs concerning the beginning of judgment. We have opened up the mystery of the gate, and then of the towers. Now we must open up that of the wall. So tell me, Nouriel, what is a wall?"

"A barrier," I replied.

"And to an ancient city, what was the wall?"

"Its defense. Its protection. The walls would protect the city against the attack of its enemies."

"The wall was less vulnerable than the gate, but on the other hand, there was much more of the wall than there was of anything else. So the wall gave the enemy the opportunity to attack from virtually any direction and position. And like the gate, once the wall was breached, it would only be a matter of time before the city's destruction. In fact, the Jewish people have observed days of fasting and mourning to specifically commemorate the dates that Jerusalem's defensive walls were breached. The breaching of the walls was the beginning of the end."

"And what does this have to do with…?"

"It is another sign of a judgment. On the day that begins a city's judgment," said the prophet, "its wall of protection is broken…and not only a city but a nation, a kingdom, a civilization. The day that begins a nation's judgment sees the breaching of its wall of protection…the wall of a civilization is broken."

"I see America's gate. And towers are obvious. But a wall around the nation? It doesn't exist. And without a wall there can't be a breach."

"But there *is* a wall," he said. "You don't see it because it's not of stone. A wall of stone is of little use in modern warfare. But the need for protection is just as critical now as it was in ancient times. And America does indeed have a wall. What was the purpose of the ancient wall? To protect the city or kingdom against danger, the attack of its enemies. So tell me, what would be the walls of a modern nation?"

"Its defense," I said, "its protection against attack and danger."

"The wall of America is its defense, its structures and systems of defense, its military, its weaponry, its intelligence systems, its operatives around the world. The ancient walls of defense have been replaced by modern departments of defense."

"The Defense Department," I said. "That's the wall of America."

"Yes, and where is it headquartered? What is the central structure of that wall?"

"The Pentagon!" I replied.

"And what happened on 9/11?"

"The enemy attacked the Pentagon."

"Because it was the wall," said the prophet. "The Pentagon is America's wall of defense. And so the attack was the third sign of biblical judgment. On the day of a nation's judgment, its barrier of defense, its wall of protection, is broken. On the day of Israel's judgment, its enemies come to its walls. And on 9/11, America's enemies appeared at its wall."

At that, there came a rumbling from the ancient stone reliefs. Cracks began forming in the image. And then pieces of stone began falling off until a large opening was left in the engraving. The opening was of the same size and shape and in the same place as the wall's breach in the engraving. Daylight began pouring in from the other side.

"Come," said the prophet as he led me through the opening.

When I came out on the other side, I found myself standing in the midst of smoldering ruins, except nothing was moving; everything was frozen in time.

"What am I seeing?" I asked.

"9/11," he replied.

"And is this the Pentagon?"

"Yes. Do you know that the Pentagon was built in the shape of a fortress? It bears the form of a fortress of many walls. Look at what the terrorists did, Nouriel. What does it look like?"

I looked up at the destruction the terrorists had inflicted.

"It looks like a gigantic breach in a colossal wall."

"Yes, the symbol of a nation's protection...lying in smoldering ruins."

He gave me time to take it all in.

"Up to this time," I said, "when you spoke of what happened on 9/11, you focused on New York City. This is the first time you've touched on the other side...what happened here in Washington."

"It's all connected," he replied. "Do you remember, Nouriel, the warning Moses gave Israel concerning what would happen in the days of judgment, the enemy who would come to the gate?"

"I do."

"I didn't tell you the rest of it. It says this:

They shall besiege you at all your *gates*..."[2]

"The attack at the nation's gate," I said. "New York City."

"Yes, but then it continues:

...until your high and fortified *walls*, in which you trust, come down..."[3]

"The attack at the nation's wall," I replied. "Washington, DC, the Pentagon."

"Notice," he said, "the two signs of judgment are joined together. And in America, the two signs of judgment were manifested on the same day. The scripture speaks first of the attack at the gate and then of the breaking down of the wall. And so on 9/11, the attack came first, at the nation's gate, in New York City, and then came the breaking down of the wall in Washington, DC. And do you remember Isaiah's prophecy about the day of judgment when every high and lofty thing is cast down?"

"Yes."

"Yes. It says that the judgment will fall...

Upon every high tower, *and upon every fortified wall.*[4]

"So the terrorists came first to the nation's high towers, the World Trade Center...and then to the nation's wall, the Pentagon."

"All three signs of judgment: the gate, the towers, and the wall."

"Yes. The enemy appeared at the gate, the towers, and the wall. He struck all three. The gate was broken into, the towers fell, and the wall was breached. The three signs that signal the beginning of a nation's judgment—and all in one day—September 11, 2001."

"And what does it mean?"

"The breaking down of the wall is that which begins judgment and opens the door for destruction. It was the beginning, the beginning sign, the warning. On 9/11 the wall of American civilization was breached. The Pentagon embodied the wall that protected the nation, that kept it safe from danger. The breaching of the wall is a warning...a warning that the nation is not safe. It's unprotected and lies in danger. A nation that departs from God will, in the end, find no safety in its walls, in the defenses on which it relies. And if it does not return, then it will find, on that day, that the walls in which it placed its trust will come crashing down."

———— ◆◆◆ ————

"The next mystery would be different from the first three."

"How?"

"It would involve a weeping prophet and an act that took place not before the entire world—but in secret."

Chapter 7

The Selichote

I WAS WALKING THROUGH a landscape of devastation. It was night, but under the light of the moon I could clearly discern my surroundings."

"Which were?"

"Ruins...the ruins of fallen buildings, fallen walls, fallen towers, ruins of what appeared to have been an ancient city. I could see billows of smoke rising and fires in the distance. And every so often I could hear the crumbling of a half-destroyed building collapsing to the ground. I knew that whatever it was that had caused all this destruction had just happened.

"As I continued walking, I heard the sound of a man's voice speaking in a foreign language, which I took to be Middle Eastern and, most likely, Hebrew. The tone, volume, and manner in which he spoke were in continual fluctuation. At times it seemed as if he was weeping, and at other times pleading, at other times reciting, and at still other times worshipping. What was beyond natural was the fact that I heard his voice for some time with no sign of his presence. I finally saw him.

"Sitting on top of the ruins was a bearded man clothed in a simple cloth garment that covered his entire body, including his head. His garment was, in turn, covered in ashes and illuminated by the light of the moon. With his arms outstretched, his palms turned upward, and his eyes sometimes closed and sometimes gazing upward into the night sky, he continued his speaking, his pleading, and his weeping as if totally oblivious to my presence.

"I watched him for some time. Then I heard another voice. Standing behind me was the prophet."

◆◆◆

"You don't have to understand his words," said the prophet, "to know what's happening."

"He's weeping," I said, "because of the destruction of his city."

"That's correct."

"Who is he?"

"A prophet."

"Which one?"

"One of several who mourned over Jerusalem's destruction. But they didn't only mourn; they came before God to confess the sins of their nation, to acknowledge the justice of the judgment, and to plead with Him for mercy and restoration."

It was when he finished speaking that the scene began to undergo a transformation. It was still night, and I was still surrounded by ruins, but the ruins had changed.

—————◆◆◆—————

"How so?" asked Ana.

"They were now the ruins of Ground Zero, the massive heap of ruins where the towers had once stood, metal beams and frames jutting up from the heap as if sculptures of modern art, and all of it covered by the haze of white dust and ash. And there, sitting on top of the heap, was the man in sackcloth and ashes, still weeping, still praying, and still pleading with his outstretched hands."

—————◆◆◆—————

"There is," said the prophet, "a series of prayers recited by the Jewish people called the *selichote*. The prayers were committed to writing in ages past and contain scriptures from times still more ancient to be spoken at the appointed times."

"What does *selichote* mean?"

"The word refers to forgiveness, the forgiveness of God. The selichote are pleas for God's mercy in light of the nation's sin, specifically a nation that had known the ways of God but departed from them. So they involve the confession of sin and its pleas for God's mercy. They also involve judgment. Judgment is the context behind their cries for mercy and restoration...the day of national judgment."

"Judgment in the form of what?"

"Calamity," he replied, "national calamity and, most specifically, the attack and devastation inflicted by its enemies. So one might say that the selichote are prayers ordained for the days of national judgment."

"You said they were written down in past ages to be spoken at the appointed times. When are the appointed times?"

"For most of the Jewish world, the appointed times fall in the last days of the Hebrew month of Elul, the days leading up to the Feast of Trumpets. It is then that the first prayers of selichote are spoken."

"How are they spoken?" I asked.

"Certain parts of the prayers require the presence of ten men. But other parts may be spoken in smaller groups or alone. So the ancient words are recited in synagogues, in Jewish homes, and wherever else the Jewish people choose to recite them. It all begins in the days before the Feast of Trumpets, at midnight following the Sabbath, so from Saturday night until dawn or sunrise on Sunday morning comes the first selichote. Then from midnight on Sunday to dawn or sunrise on Monday morning comes the second selichote. The prayers may be recited anytime between midnight and dawn, though they are most often recited at the approach of dawn. The third selichote ends at the breaking of day on Tuesday morning."

At that, he paused.

"Why are you stopping?" I asked.

"The prayers appointed for the day of national judgment...were finished at dawn Tuesday morning...on that day."

"On what day?"

"September 11, 2001. The events of 9/11 happened to fall during the days of the selichote, the days of the prayers appointed for a nation's judgment.

"And so as that day began, the prayers concerning national calamity were lifted up. And it was then that the calamity fell. On the morning of 9/11 they recited the ancient words that concern the striking of a nation by its enemies. And it was that day and that morning that America was struck by its enemies. The words they prayed on the morning of 9/11 concerned the shaking of a nation that had once known God but turned away. And it was that morning that the nation that had likewise turned away from God would be shaken."

"What's that?" I asked. "I couldn't make out what I was hearing or which direction it was coming from."

"Look, Nouriel," he said, pointing to the cityscape that surrounded the ruins. I saw a man standing on top of a building, looking very much like the man I had seen in the ruins at the beginning of the dream, robed and hooded and with his arms lifted up as if in prayer. Then I saw another figure, similar to the first, standing on top of a more distant building, and then another and another, and then through the windows of lit-up apartments, the silhouettes of like figures, all of them as if in the midst of prayer.

"What you're hearing," said the prophet, "are their voices, the voices of those speaking the selichote. New York City is home to more Jewish people than any other city in America. So what would that mean?"

"It would mean that the selichote would be spoken all over the city and throughout the region."

"It means that as 9/11 began, the ancient words were being recited all over the city concerning national calamity, an enemy attack, and the devastation of a city—*before it took place.*"

"What words specifically?" I asked.

"For the Jewish people, it echoed back to the destruction of their city, Jerusalem. But it would now echo forward to speak of what was about to come. The words recited the morning of 9/11 spoke of enemies who would come to the land and seek to bring destruction to the nation's buildings:

> They said: *Raze it! Raze it down to its foundations!*[1]

"On 9/11, the high towers that embodied the glory of American civilization became a desolation. So the ancient words that were spoken on the morning of 9/11 said this:

> Our desires have been devastated and *our glory has been demolished*...our palace *has become a desolation.*[2]

"And the end of that day, as America gazed at the desolation of its crowning city, many were led to invoke the words 'God bless America.' But *before* the calamity had even taken place, the plea for God's mercy was already echoing through New York City:

> My God, incline Your ear and hear, open Your eyes and look
> upon *our desolations and the desolations of the city*...[3]

"By the night of 9/11, the entire nation and much of the world had seen or heard of the devastation. At midnight it was time for the next series of prayers appointed from ages past to be lifted up. They were the prayers of the fourth selichote. They would speak again of the nation's devastation, of the desire of its enemies to raze its buildings to their foundations, and of the demolishing of the nation's glory. But the greatest tragedy of 9/11 was not the loss of buildings, but lives. So the ancient words would now speak of the loss of life caused by the nation's enemies:

> *They cut off our life.... They spilled our blood in order to destroy us.*
>
> ...*violent men drove them to destruction*...[4]

"The calamity of that day began as the first plane crashed into the North Tower of the World Trade Center. Then, as the first calamity was not yet finished, the second suddenly followed as the second plane crashed into the South Tower. The ancient words of the fourth selichote said this:

> *The first visitation of calamity was not yet finished when the second one suddenly followed it*...[5]

"The most iconic image left in the wake of the calamity was that of the massive heap of ruins left in the place where the nation's high towers had once stood. The selichote appointed for that night said this:

> *My city is reduced to a lasting ruin heap and my high places are brought low.*[6]

"And as the nation gazed in shocked horror that night at the dust-covered desolation of Ground Zero, the words of the selichote appointed for that night were recited:

> *Raise up the city that is lowered to the dust...* "[7]

"So it just happened," I said, "that those words were appointed from past ages to be recited on the days of the calamity."

"Or the calamity just happened to fall on the days of the appointed words. So on the morning of 9/11, when the nation's Defense Department had no idea what was about to happen, the ancient words were being recited of the attack of a nation and its city by its enemies. And the words were being spoken especially on the nation's East Coast and in New York City that morning where the attack would take place. The reciting of the selichote was to be completed by daybreak. And so on 9/11, it was in the last hour of the utterance of those ancient words of judgment that the terrorists of 9/11 set the attack in motion. Daybreak came to New York City at approximately 6:30. The prayers appointed for the day of calamity were now completed. Within fifteen minutes of that moment, the terrorists arrived at Logan Airport in Boston, from which they would launch the nation's calamity."

------◆◆◆------

"The next mystery would take me onto a centuries-old ship on a voyage that would uncover the secret of 9/11...in a mystery of time."

Chapter 8

Foundations

I N THE NEXT dream, I found myself standing inside a large house, a mansion. Everything inside the house was large, grand, ornate, and luxurious, the rooms, the furniture, the chairs, the wooden doors and tables, the curtains, the golden chandeliers. I had never before been in such an opulent setting.

"Then I heard a rumbling. The house and everything in it began to shake. And then the floor on which I was standing gave way. Everything collapsed. I went down with the house but in a way that seemed to defy gravity... slowly, as if I were floating down in the midst of a collapse that appeared to be happening in slow motion. As I descended, I became aware that the house had many floors, all of which were collapsing around me.

"Finally, my feet touched the bottom. I was standing at the ground level, at the building's foundation, watching everything else come down around me. And then it was over. I began walking through the ruins. I noticed a piece of stone jutting out. I was drawn to it. I began clearing away the debris that partially obscured it. It was a foundation stone. But it didn't match the rest of the building. It seemed to be from an earlier age. As I continued uncovering it, I noticed letters, words, carved into its surface."

"What did it say?"

"Before I could read it, everything disappeared, the ruins, the debris, everything except the foundation itself. But now the foundation was moving, rocking. I heard the sound of waves and seagulls. The foundation had transformed into the deck of a ship, a centuries-old ship, with sails and wooden masts. Everything was wooden except for the deck, which was still of the stone from the building's foundation.

"I wasn't alone. There were others on board, crewmen, all of whom were dressed in clothing from, I would guess, five or six centuries in the past. The ship was moving slowly through a passageway. I don't know if we were navigating through a river or not, but there was land on both sides.

"Then I heard a voice. Standing beside me was the prophet."

◆◆◆

"What happens," he asked, "when a building is destroyed? What is it that is then exposed?"

"Its foundation."

"So God laid the foundation stone on which Israel rose as a nation. But at the height of its blessings, it turned away and was corrupted. Its cities were filled with immorality, its streets with bloodshed. Again and again, God called the nation to return, but it only grew more defiant and evil. So He said this:

> I will break down the wall you have plastered with untempered
> mortar, and bring it down to the ground, so that its foundation
> will be uncovered.[1]

"The words were first addressed to the lies of the false prophets of Israel who assured the nation that no calamity would come. Their lies would be undone. But so too would be the nation. It would be broken down to the ground. God would undo what He had built. He would strip away all that had risen on top of the foundation He had laid. He would bring everything back to its foundation. It is a principle of judgment: the nation will be brought back to its foundation."

"The falling tower," I said, "was it a symbol of America?"

"Yes, a high and proud tower and far removed from the foundation on which it began."

"And on 9/11, the high tower crumbled back to its foundation. It was brought 'down to the ground.' Its foundation was uncovered."

"But there's more to the mystery. The high tower of America rests on two earthly foundations, its economic power and its military power. Of the two, it was its economic power that was the first to rise. Long before American soldiers could be found in every corner of the earth, the nation's economic power had already encircled the world. And long before there even was an American military power, the foundation on which its economic power would rise had been laid."

"Where?" I asked. "Where was the foundation laid?"

"The center of America's economic power and of the nation's rise to economic superpower was New York City. And when was its foundation laid? When did that which we now know as New York City begin?"

"I don't know."

"In the foundation of the city is ultimately the foundation of that power. The day the one began, so did the other."

"Can we find that day?"

"Perhaps *he* can," said the prophet, pointing to a lone figure in a long black coat standing at the front of the ship, gazing out into the waters.

"Who is he?" I asked.

"The ship's captain."

"Where are we?" I asked.

"On a voyage in search of a passage."

"What ship is this?"

"It belongs to the Dutch East India Company. The captain's name is Henry Hudson."

"Henry Hudson! I learned about him in elementary school."

It was just then that the man in the long black coat pointed into the distance and said something to the crew that caused them to look into the distance.

"And now you'll see," said the prophet, "the mystery of the foundation, the day it all began."

The ship was heading toward the tip of a land mass.

"It's an island," said the prophet.

"Is that it?" I asked. "Is that New York City?"

"It's the beginning," he said, "of what would become New York City, the island known as Manhattan."

"So this is the day of its discovery."

"Yes."

I watched as the ship approached the island and anchored by its shore.

"This, Nouriel, is the day it all began, the beginning of the city, the power, and the rising. This is the day of the foundation."

"And the mystery is…"

"The day itself."

"Which is what?"

"September 11."

"September 11!"

"It all began on September 11. September 11 is the day New York City was born."

"Its birthday...So the city was struck on the day of its birth."

"And the rise of America's economic power—it all began on September 11."

"So on the day of the rising...came the fall."

"And it was this power that was before and behind the nation's other powers and the rise of the nation itself. So all those other powers have their origins on 9/11...as does the rise of America itself. It all began on 9/11."

"So it all converged; it all came back to that same day."

It was then that the captain picked up a large rectangular block of stone that was sitting on the deck and carried it off the ship and onto the shore of the island. The prophet and I followed behind.

"I would think," I said, "that the stone is too big for a man to carry. Did Henry Hudson actually carry a stone ashore?"

"No, Nouriel," said the prophet. "This is a dream. The discovery and founding of this island actually happened. But what you're seeing now is symbolic."

We followed him to a site near the water's edge, where he set the stone on the ground. He then took out a hammer and chisel and began engraving letters into the stone's top side.

"It's the stone," I exclaimed, "the stone in the dream!"

"This *is* the dream," said the prophet. "You're still in it."

"The stone that was exposed at the building's foundation after the collapse."

"Yes. Would you now like to read what it says?"

"Yes."

So he led me over to the stone, and I read the engraving.

"Ezekiel 13:14," I said. "What does it mean?"

"Ezekiel 13:14 is the verse that speaks of the breaking down of the wall and the uncovering of its foundation."

"The fall of the house exposes its foundation."

"Put it together, Nouriel. What happened to Israel in its day of judgment?"

"Its powers were broken," I replied. "Its buildings came down. Everything was stripped away. And the foundation was exposed."

"Yes, on the day of judgment the nation is brought back to its foundation."

"And so on 9/11, America was brought back to its foundation. Through the calamity the nation's foundation was exposed."

"It is not only that America returned to its foundation on 9/11—it's that America's foundation *itself is* 9/11. Long before it became a day of calamity, 9/11 was the day of America's foundation."

"The mystery of 9/11...I never would have imagined that."

"A convergence of times. It happened in the judgment of ancient Israel. When the Temple of Jerusalem was destroyed by the armies of Rome, it happened on the same day that the first Temple of Jerusalem was destroyed by the armies of Babylon, centuries before—the same exact day."

"And those who destroyed it—did they do it because...?"

"No. It just happened. Nor did the terrorists of 9/11 have any idea. They simply came to bring destruction."

"So it wasn't only what happened on 9/11 that was the sign—it was 9/11, the day itself, that was the sign."

"In the Book of Jeremiah, the nation's judgment was prophesied in these words:

> What I have built I will break down, and what I have planted
> I will pluck up.[2]

"Notice what happens when judgment comes: the breaking down is joined to the building up, the uprooting is joined to the planting. Each is joined to its inverse, its opposite...the mystery of inversion."

"So 9/11 was the day that New York City was *planted*. So it became the day of *uprooting*. And on the day that began its *building*...came the day of the *breaking down*."

"And what is the meaning," I asked, "and the message?"

"As it was with ancient Israel, America's blessings came from God, its economic blessings, its financial blessings, its prosperity, the fruit of its baskets, the bread of its kneading bowls, its power to produce wealth, and its reign as the most prosperous of nations—it all came from God. But if America should repeat the error of ancient Israel and turn against the foundation of all its blessings, how long, then, can those blessings endure?"

———◆◆◆———

"Ana, you haven't said a word or even given me a hint of an expression so I might know what you're thinking."

"When it all happened," she said, "when America came to a standstill on 9/11, I can still remember what I was thinking, but I never could have imagined that behind all those things, all that was going on."

The two sat in silence for a time, Nouriel sipping on his glass of water and Ana just sitting there.

"So what happened next?" she asked. "What was the next revelation?"

"The next dream would take me deeper into the mystery and would involve a man, a microphone, and an eagle in a mystery that would change the world."

Chapter 9

The Night Address

I T WAS NIGHT. I was passing over a landscape of houses, towns, villages, then cities, and then more towns and villages."

"Passing over?"

"Passing over, flying, or being shown all these things as if I were. But more striking than what I was seeing was what I was hearing."

"Which was?"

"A voice, the same voice coming from every town and city, from every building and home."

"What kind of voice?"

"The voice of a man, as if delivering a speech. The voice continued as I passed over a city of monuments and buildings of white stone that resembled classical temples. It was then that I began descending, touching the ground in the midst of that city.

"In front of me was a long series of massive white stone steps leading up to a platform. On top of the platform was a desk."

"A desk?"

"A desk of stone or a large rectangular stone that served as a desk and of the same color and appearance as the stone I saw in the other dream at the foundation of the building. Behind the desk sat a man."

"What did he look like?"

"He appeared to have been in his sixties, wearing glasses, a light-colored jacket, a dark tie, and a black armband in between his left shoulder and elbow. In back of the man, a good way back, was a colossal stone building of the same color and appearance as the desk. And even though it was set back, it was tall enough to be visible from the bottom of the stairs. Engraved on its front wall was the image of a colossal eagle with outstretched wings, several stories high."

"How could you make it out at night?"

"There were lights stationed everywhere. And they allowed me to make out another detail: resting on top of the desk was a cluster of microphones, but of stone, the same stone of which the desk was made. It was then I realized what I was seeing. The man was speaking into the microphones. And it was his voice that was filling every home, town, and city, filling the land. And it was then that I heard him."

"The man at the desk."

"No, the prophet."

◆◆◆

"On the day of calamity, the foundations are exposed," he said. "9/11 exposed the foundation of America's fundamental powers. But there were two. What about the other?"

"America's military power?"

"Yes, its military power. The rise of American economic power was gradual and continuous. But the rise of its military power came differently, dramatically and suddenly. It was the Second World War that transformed America into the world's greatest military power. And it was that power that ushered in a new era of world history. How did it happen?"

"I would imagine you'll tell me."

"It was in the late 1800s that America overtook the British Empire to become the world's leading economic and industrial power. But its military power was relatively weak. Its army was a small fraction of the size of the British army.

"In 1917 America was drawn into the First World War and only for the last phase of that war. When the conflict was over, the nation began withdrawing from foreign involvement and toward isolationism. Its isolation would last through the 1920s and 1930s, even with the rise and growing danger of Fascism and Nazism. In the mid- to late 1930s, the American Congress passed several neutrality acts, which barred or severely limited the nation from any involvement in the conflicts of other nations. With the outbreak of the Second World War, the American president, Franklin Roosevelt, sought to lead the nation out of isolationism and into war against the forces of Nazism and Fascism that were then engulfing the European continent. But he was fighting against public opinion and the resistance of the United States Congress.

"The turning point concerning America's entrance into the Second World War and thus its rise to global superpower came in 1941. In

February of that year, *Life* magazine published an editorial calling for the end of American isolation and the beginning of what it called 'the American century.'[1] The next month, Congress passed the Lend-Lease Act, which allowed massive aid to go toward assisting Allied nations in their war efforts. As a protective measure, in April, Roosevelt authorized the stationing of American troops in Greenland, and three months later troops were sent to Iceland. In August, Roosevelt and the British prime minister, Winston Churchill, met secretly off the coast of Newfoundland, where they formulated a statement of eight shared goals for a postwar world in what would be seen as the beginning of the British-American alliance and known as the Atlantic Charter. But to Churchill's disappointment, Roosevelt refused to commit to entering the war. Without the support of Congress and public opinion, his hands were tied.

"But that would soon change. And the change would come in late summer when a US Navy Ship, the *USS Greer*, was fired on by a German submarine it had been following. It fired back in turn with depth charges. It was the first time an American Navy ship had exchanged fire with a German ship. One week after the incident, the president went on the radio to address the nation."

"So that was the voice I heard coming from the houses?"

"Yes, and that's him," he said, pointing to the man sitting at the desk on top of the platform of stairs.

"And what is he saying?"

"Let's go up and find out."

So we began the long ascent up the white stone steps. I could still hear his voice reverberating in the distant buildings and houses, but I couldn't make out the words. It would become clearer as we reached the top of the platform, where we came to a stop about ten feet in front of his desk. There we listened as he spoke into the microphones seemingly unaware of our presence.

> "But let this warning be clear. From now on, if German or Italian vessels of war enter the waters, the protection of which is necessary for American defense, they do so at their own peril."[2]

"With those words," said the prophet, "Roosevelt initiated what would be known as the Shoot on Sight policy. From that moment on any American ship that spotted a German or Italian warship in waters deemed necessary for American defense would open fire. It was a guarantee of America's entrance into the war, the crossing of a Rubicon, from which there could be no return. It was a turning point that would change the course of the war and then of world history."

It was just then that I noticed the beginning of a transformation. The microphones were changing shape, elongating, stretching upward, taking the form of a cluster of arrows, and yet still of stone. The president then gathered the cluster together and placed them across the armrests of his chair. It was then that I realized he was sitting in a wheelchair. He turned himself around so that he was now facing the wall of the great building. He then wheeled himself over to the image of the colossal eagle and placed the arrows in front of its talons. At that, the image began to move and then emerge from the wall, still of stone, but no longer an engraving, now a fully three-dimensional being. It glanced down at the arrows and grasped them with its talons. "Now arise," said the president to the eagle, "and make war." At that, the colossal creature flew up into the night sky, which was now filled with storm clouds, and disappeared into the darkness.

"The president's declaration," said the prophet, "would make America's official entrance into the war and the far-reaching consequences of that entrance inevitable. Three months later, with the Japanese attack on Pearl Harbor, it would become official, but with the president's declaration that night and the commencement of the new policy, it had already begun. The speech was the manifestation of a critical decision already made: America not only would enter the war but would assume the reins of world leadership.

"The meaning of the president's address was made manifest in headlines, commentaries, and editorials appearing throughout the nation in response. The speech was:

> ...an unofficial *DECLARATION OF WAR* against Nazi Germany and Fascist Italy...The duly elected President of the nation *has now committed* 132 million Americans to travel a road *from which there is no turning*. They cannot afford to LOSE *THE WAR*.[3]

> …the American people recognize *that there can be no turning back*…[4]

"Historians would likewise view that address as the effective declaration of war and America's unofficial entrance into the war."

"The desk," I said, "and the wall and the eagle and the arrows—they were all of the same color and substance as the stone that I saw in the other dream at the bottom of the house, the foundation stone. Does that mean…?"

"That what you saw," said the prophet, "was the revelation of a foundation, the other foundation…the foundation of America's emergence as the world's greatest military power. What you saw was all part of the day on which it was all sealed—the day on which the American age was sealed."

"The day on which the American age was sealed…what day was it?"

"The day was September 11."

"September 11!"

"It all began on 9/11."

"So Roosevelt made his speech to the nation…"

"On the night of September 11."

"The same day as America's other foundation."

"It was September 11 that sealed America's entrance into war. It was September 11 that determined the outcome of that war. It was September 11 that began the rise of America to the pinnacle of world power as the strongest military power on earth."

"9/11! It was 9/11 that caused America to become a superpower."

"Yes. It was 9/11 that began the American age, the day the American superpower was born. Long before it became something else, 9/11 was the foundation of all these things."

"And 9/11 was the day that the Pentagon, the symbol of American military power, was struck."

"Yes."

"So the symbol that represented America's military power was struck on the day of its birth."

"And it was even more than that."

"What do you mean?"

"Hitler had hoped to avoid a war with America until first defeating the

Soviet Union. But Roosevelt's speech of September 11 was seen by the leaders of Nazi Germany as marking the beginning of war. They too saw it as the turning point from which there would be no return.

"Two days after that speech, the German foreign minister, Joachim von Ribbentrop, sent word to the Japanese government warning that Roosevelt's actions would lead to open war against the Axis powers, of which Japan was one. He then began pressuring Japan to attack America. Hitler had now come to believe that a war between Japan and America would distract and hinder America's ability to wage war in Europe. Mutual assurances of military alliance between the Axis nations came in early December. Then, on December 7, 1941, Japan attacked America at Pearl Harbor. The undeclared war was now declared."

"So then even Pearl Harbor was linked to 9/11."

"Yes. But Pearl Harbor concerned America and Japan. Without entering a war in Europe against Nazi Germany, America would never have become the world superpower it became at the end of the war. All that would be sealed four days after Pearl Harbor when Nazi Germany issued its declaration of war against America. The German declaration opened the door for America to enter the war in Europe, which it did that same day. The German declaration also contained and centered on one date above all others as the beginning event that ultimately led to war—the date of 9/11."

"So everything goes back to that day."

"9/11 brought America into the war and thus propelled it to become the strongest military power on earth and then the world's greatest superpower, a superpower with soldiers stationed throughout the earth and its navy patrolling the world. 9/11 thus birthed a new era, one in which America would reign as the head of nations, the American age. Everything began on 9/11."

"And as it all began on 9/11," I said, "so on 9/11 it would all return."

"Remember the scripture, Nouriel—in the days of judgment, that which has been built up is broken down, and that which has been planted is uprooted. The planting and building are joined to the uprooting and destroying. So 9/11 was the day on which America's global military power was planted."

"And the day that America's economic power was planted...both powers."

"And so," said the prophet, "the day of the planting, the foundation, must become the day of the breaking down... the 9/11 of the foundation must become the 9/11 of the calamity."

"And the meaning and message..."

"If America does not turn back to the God of its foundation, then the powers that were founded on that day will collapse."

———◆◆◆———

"And the next mystery?"

"Would run parallel to this one but would center on an event unknown to most of the world, an event that would take place in a field in between a river and a cemetery, in a convergence so precise it would leave me stunned."

Chapter 10

The House by the River

IT WAS NIGHT, but unlike the last dream, I knew dawn was near. I was in a boat with four others."

"Others?"

"At the beginning of the dream, I couldn't tell much more than that. Their faces were obscured by the darkness and by the fact that they were all wearing cloaks that covered their heads. And they were looking away from me, to the sides of the boat…except for the one who appeared to be the leader. He sat in the front of the boat and gazed forward into the distance. I was right behind him. So I couldn't see his face either. To the side of each of the four was a large rectangular stone of the same color and appearance as the desk in the last dream and as the foundation stone in the dream before that."

◆◆◆

"Who are you?" I asked. I was addressing my words to all of them but was facing the leader. "And what are we doing here?"

"Builders," said the leader. He said that without turning his gaze to look at me. "Builders, who dwell by the river."

"And today is the day of the crossing," said another of the four.

"That we might lay the foundation," said another.

"Of what?" I asked.

"Of a great house," said still another, "a house by the river."

"Today," said the leader, "it all begins."

The boat then arrived on the river's other side. As we prepared to disembark, the leader turned around and removed his hood. I recognized him immediately.

◆◆◆

"Who was it?"

"It was George Washington. He picked up the stone, rose to his feet, got out of the boat, and stood ashore, waiting for the others. I joined him there. I looked back at the boat. The figure that had been sitting behind me now removed his hood. I recognized him as well. It was Thomas Jefferson. He lifted the stone, rose to his feet, got out of the boat, and joined us ashore. Then the third figure did likewise. It was Abraham Lincoln. And then last, it was Teddy Roosevelt."

"I've got it," said Ana.

"What?"

"I've got the mystery. It's Mount Rushmore. All four of them are on Mount Rushmore."

"That's right. That's what I thought as well. But it has nothing to do with the mystery."

"All right, so what happened next?"

"As we stood on the shore, the sun began to rise. We began walking inland until we came to a large open expanse. In the middle of the expanse sat a man in a wheelchair."

"Roosevelt," said Ana, "Franklin Roosevelt."

"Yes, with something of a dark cape or shawl draped over his shoulders and a stone at his feet, of the same size, shape, and color as the others.

"After greeting the others, he wheeled his chair back from the stone. The four of them then approached the stone and began laying down their stones beside it, one after the other, in the same order in which they had been sitting in the boat. Then they stepped back until they formed something of a loose circle. The stones now also formed something of a loose circle.

"Then Roosevelt leaned forward in his chair and began to speak. 'We will remember this day. It is the day we crossed the river to lay the foundation of a great house and a great power that will mark the turning of history. And though we lay its stones away from the eyes of the world, this day shall be known for generations to come.'

"And then they all froze in place, everything froze, except for me and one other."

"One other?"

"The prophet. I don't know when he came, but at that moment, he was there, behind me."

———◆◆◆———

"What you just saw," he said, "what do you think it means?"

"The stones had the same appearance as that of the desk in the other vision and of the foundation stone in the fallen house. So I would think this is the revelation of a foundation. And since the central figure was Franklin Roosevelt, as in the other vision, I would think it has to do with a foundation that was laid in the days of his presidency. I would think it has to do with the rise of American military power or the rise of the American superpower."

"Very good, Nouriel. And what was the critical year, the year of the turning point?"

"1941."

"Yes, as it was the day of Roosevelt's declaration and America's unde-clared entrance into the war. But 1941 was the turning point for another reason; it was the groundbreaking year of American military power. In 1941, American military spending quadrupled, as did the size of the American military forces. In 1940, American military personnel num-bered under five hundred thousand. But by the end of 1941, the number was approaching two million. 1941 was the watershed year.

"But it wasn't only the military's armed forces that mushroomed. In 1941, the number of War Department personnel had reached twenty-four thousand. They were scattered in seventeen buildings across Wash-ington, DC. With war raging across the world and Hitler's armies now occupying most of the European continent, the need to consolidate the War Department into one central location became critical. But no building inside Washington was large enough for the need.

"So the army's chief of staff, General George C. Marshall, commis-sioned Brigadier General Brehon B. Somervell, head of the army's Con-struction Division, to come up with an answer. Somervell set out to con-struct a single building large enough to house the entire War Depart-ment, tens of thousands of personnel, under one roof. To undertake such a monumental task, Somervell had to look outside the city and to the other side of the Potomac River."

"Across the river. The Potomac—that was the river we crossed to get here."

"Yes."

"But with Washington, Jefferson, Lincoln, and Teddy Roosevelt, I thought that was to direct me to a place, to Mount Rushmore."

"It *was* directing you to a place, but not there."

"Then where?"

"When you asked those in the boat who they were, what did they answer you?"

"Builders, who dwell by the river."

"That was your first clue. The one who told you that was Washington. From Washington came this city. The city of Washington dwells by the Potomac River."

"And what about Jefferson?"

"Look over there," said the prophet, pointing to a domed building on the other side of the river. "That's his memorial, where he stands on a black granite pedestal. And look over there," he said, now pointing to what looked like a Greek temple. "That's Lincoln's memorial, where he sits in white marble."

"And Teddy Roosevelt?"

"Over there," he said, "that's his island, the Theodore Roosevelt Island, in the middle of the river, where he stands in bronze. Even the memorial to Franklin Roosevelt is right there across the river as well. They're all here by the river. They all point to this land."

"And this land is…?"

"Look, Nouriel, at the stones they laid here for a foundation. What shape do they form?"

"I took it that they were trying to make a circle."

"Not a circle," he said. "What shape is it?"

"A pentagon," I replied. "*A pentagon*. This is the ground on which was built 'the great house' for the War Department—the Pentagon."

"And when was it built? It was begun in 1941."

"The turning point year," I said, "of America's military power. So in the year of the foundation, the foundation of the Pentagon was laid."

"Yes. The building that would embody America's global military power was begun in the very year that would inaugurate that power. And the victory that would cause America to become the world's greatest military power would be planned and led from this ground, from this house.

"The Pentagon was intended as a temporary answer to a temporary need. It was assumed that after the war was over, the building would be put to some other use as the American military returned to its prewar state. But that would never happen. The American military would never return to normalcy, and the Pentagon would become the permanent house of a new global power.

"What began in 1941 was the transformation of a nation into the greatest military power in world history. And the building that began at the beginning of that transformation and rise would become the embodiment of that power. The Pentagon would become the most universally recognized symbol of American global military power.

"But what began in 1941 was more than that. The rise of America's military power was an intrinsic part in the rise of the American superpower and the beginning of the American age. And so this same house came to be the symbol not only of the world's strongest military but of a global power that towered over every nation and surpassed every kingdom and empire in history.

"And it all began here on this ground with no great display or fanfare. It all began as workers first gathered on this ground to begin the construction."

"The groundbreaking."

"Yes," said the prophet, "the groundbreaking. The groundbreaking moment of the groundbreaking building of the groundbreaking year of the American superpower—the groundbreaking of the American age."

Then he looked at me but said nothing.

"What?" I asked.

"I don't think you noticed it."

"Noticed what?"

"The stones," he said. "Look at the stones, Nouriel."

So I looked but didn't notice anything.

"The first stone, Nouriel. Go over to it and tell me what you see."

So I did. That's when I noticed an engraving.

———— ◆◆◆ ————

"What did it say?"

"IXXI."

"And what did it mean?"

"That's what I asked the prophet."

———— ◆◆◆ ————

"What is it?" I asked.

"Roman numerals," he replied. "XI is ten plus one, and IX is ten minus one."

"I still don't get it."

"It stands for a date."

"What date?"

"The date on which the ground was broken, the day of the groundbreaking."

"What day?"

"September 11."

"September 11!"

"The ground was broken on September 11."

"September 11...the groundbreaking day!"

"The groundbreaking day of the groundbreaking year. They gathered to this site to begin the construction on September 11, 1941."

"So the Pentagon was born on September 11.

"The *foundation* day," said the prophet.

"And so *everything* comes back to that day."

"What did the scripture say about the foundation?" he asked.

"The wall will be broken down so that its foundation will be exposed."

"So it had to happen on that same day," he said, "the breaking down of the Pentagon that the foundation would be exposed. And it wasn't just the foundation of broken wall that was exposed—it was the day itself that was exposed, the day of the Pentagon's foundation—9/11."

"And what was the Pentagon to America? It was the nation's wall, its defense and protection. So the wall was broken down and its foundation revealed."

"When the terrorists struck the Pentagon on 9/11, did they do it because it was the same day that...?"

"No. They had no idea, no more than did the Romans who destroyed Jerusalem on the same day on which the Babylonians had destroyed it. The terrorists did it to inflict destruction on their enemies. But everything led up to that day. It's the biblical principle of judgment, the exposing of the foundation."

"And that which was built up on 9/11," I said, "the Pentagon, will, on 9/11, be broken down."

"Yes," he replied, "the juxtaposition, the inversion of judgment."

"And the day of the declaration, Roosevelt's address to the nation and to the world, when the line was crossed. The Pentagon was begun on the same day that would change the course of the war."

"Yes, the president addressed the nation on the night of the day of the groundbreaking."

"Did they plan it that way, to go together?"

"No. It just happened to happen that way."

"So on the morning of the night that would seal America's entrance into the war, the Pentagon was begun."

"The groundbreaking night of the groundbreaking day."

"So the Pentagon was begun on the day that began the American age."

"Yes, built to replace the old State, War, and Navy Building, which had housed the War Department and navy from the late 1870s onward. It was in the late 1930s that the War Department began relocating from the now massively overcrowded building to a temporary residence in the Munitions Building on the Washington Mall. The departure from its old headquarters came at a symbolic moment. Within days of the War Department's departure, Germany invaded Poland and the Second World War began. So in the very same days that the American War Department was departing from its old headquarters, the war that would transform the War Department and America itself was being set in motion.

"It was the end of an era. The old building had served as the headquarters of the American military for sixty years. What happens if you count sixty years from the beginning of the building that replaced it, the Pentagon, from 1941—what year does it bring you to?"

"2001!"

"And if you count sixty years from the exact date, the day of the groundbreaking, the day that began the new era, to what day does it bring you?"

"September 11, 2001...the exact day!"

We said nothing after that, for some time. The people around us, the boatmen, the presidents, were still frozen in place. The prophet began walking away from the scene, back to the river.

"Wait!" I said as I caught up with him. "I have a question."

"Ask."

"The Pentagon is a symbol not only of military power but of America as the world's predominant military superpower, and the era in which America has reigned as the head of nations, the American age. And what took place here, on this ground, sixty years before 9/11, on that first September 11, was the foundation of that era..."

"Yes."

"Then the second 9/11, the 9/11 of the breaking down, would mark the beginning of another era. If the groundbreaking of the Pentagon marked the beginning of all these things, then what would its breaking down mark? Would it not mark the ending of all these things, the beginning of the end of the American age?"

"It was a warning," said the prophet. "And as to what will happen, that depends on if the warning is taken."

◆◆◆

"It was all there!" said Ana, "It was all there, and we didn't see it. Everything began on 9/11. And it just happened to happen on that day, not because anyone planned it but because of what was written thousands of years before. It's gigantic."

"And there was still one more piece to the mystery of times," said Nouriel, "something that the world missed, a sign that appeared on 9/11 itself, something I thought was a dream, a vision—but it turned out to be real."

Chapter 11

The Mystery Ship

IT WAS NIGHT. I was standing on a shore at the edge of a city."

"What kind of city?" she asked.

"It was hard to tell in the dark, and I was looking away from it. But it was a modern city. I was overlooking a river. Moving across the sky in accelerated motion was a half-moon. It disappeared, as did the night. It was now morning, a peaceful morning at first. Then I heard the sound of explosions and sirens."

"What was it?"

"I didn't see. It was all coming from behind me. And I never turned around but kept looking out into the harbor. And then I was enveloped by a white cloud, not of fog but dust. Everything became misty. At times I could only see a few feet ahead of me. At other times, I could see across the river, and at other times, somewhere in between."

"I saw people, masses of them, standing along the shoreline, waiting to be taken away from the city, away from the chaos and the mist."

◆◆◆

"What do you see, Nouriel?" said the prophet, who was now standing to my right.

"I see people trying to get away. Something happened."

He didn't say anything. We both stood there watching as ferries, tugboats, and other vessels came into the harbor for the people waiting on the shore.

"What do you see, Nouriel?" he asked again.

And that's when I saw it. Emerging from the mist in the middle of the river was a ship. It was unlike anything else in the water that day. Everything else was of the modern world. But the ship was from another century, wooden, with white trapezoidal sails and three masts topped by three flags. It stood out from everything else that was taking place around it, not just because of its appearance but because it seemed to separate from the chaos surrounding it, as if two different ages were colliding in the water. It disappeared into the mist and reappeared, over and over again. The whole thing appeared almost ghostly."

"I see a ship," I replied, "a ship that doesn't belong in the scene."

"You don't recognize it?"

"Should I?"

"You should. It appeared in your other dream. In fact, you were aboard it."

"The ship of the foundation," I replied. "The ship that discovered Manhattan and marked the beginning of New York City...the ship that laid the foundation of the first power and the rise of America as the strongest economic power on earth."

"It has a name," said the prophet. "It's called the *Half Moon*."

"Yes, I learned about it in school. But why am I seeing it now? It doesn't go with the rest of the scene."

"But it does."

"What am I seeing? The people are fleeing the city because..."

"It's 9/11."

"So what is the *Half Moon* doing in the waters of New York City on 9/11?"

"On what day did the *Half Moon* first sail into these waters to discover this island?"

"On September 11."

"So then it all does go together."

"So it's the juxtaposition of the two events. The vision is showing me the prophetic connection between the day of destruction and the day that New York City was born, the two 9/11s."

"No," said the prophet, "The vision is *not* showing you that."

"Then what?"

"It *is* about the connection. But it's not a vision that's showing you that."

"What do you mean?"

"You're not seeing a vision."

"A dream."

"You're in a dream, but what you're seeing is not a vision."

"Then what am I seeing?"

"Reality. You're seeing reality."

"What do you mean? The *Half Moon* sailed these waters how long ago?"

"Four hundred years ago."

"But I'm seeing the *Half Moon* sailing in the river on September 11, 2001."

He paused before responding to that.

"Because it did."

"But it's impossible."

"The *Half Moon* was there on 9/11."

"I don't understand."

"It sailed again...and you weren't the only one who saw it. On 9/11, the *Half Moon* appeared in the waters of New York City. It appeared to those fleeing the city."

"It makes no sense."

"In the midst of the calamity and through the mist of the destruction, the *Half Moon* appeared in the Hudson River, making the same journey it had made centuries before when it all began on the first 9/11."

"A ghost ship?"

"No," said the prophet, "a sign...a sign manifesting on the day of destruction...a sign given to the city and the nation."

"How?" I asked.

"The same way it always does. No one planned it out. But all events converged that it would happen. It just happened to happen that at the end of the 1980s, the *Half Moon* was rebuilt to match the appearance and scale of the original ship. And on the morning of 9/11, it approached the island of Manhattan, as it had done four centuries earlier on that same day—but this time it did so on the day of calamity.

"As it sailed up the waters, the two great towers collapsed and a massive cloud of dust filled the harbor. Those fleeing the calamity witnessed the image of a centuries-old Dutch ship with masts and sails making its way through the mist of the calamity. The meaning of what they were seeing undoubtedly made no more sense than the calamity itself. But they were witnessing a sign, the origins of which went back centuries and the mystery of which went back to ancient times."

"And the meaning?"

"In the days of judgment, the foundation is exposed; it becomes visible. The *Half Moon* was part of the foundation. So on 9/11, it again became visible; it reappeared in the same waters. The building up is juxtaposed against the breaking down. So the *Half Moon* that sailed past those same waters along the island of trees and hills on the day of planting now sailed past the streets and skyscrapers on the day of the breaking down."

"It's the mystery in imagery. In the city was the imagery of the breaking down, but in the waters was the imagery of the building up. So the *Half Moon* represented the planting of the city, and the destruction represented the uprooting. So the ship of the planting passed by the ruins of the uprooting. The two images were juxtaposed, the image of the one 9/11 against the image of the other."

"Yes," said the prophet. "But what was planted on the day the *Half Moon* first sailed into that harbor was not just a city but a power, the rising of the greatest economic power on earth. So the reappearance of that ship on the day of calamity was a sign not only to a city but a nation."

"So everything returned," I said, "not only to the day but to the place, to New York and Washington, DC. And as New York was the first foundation, so it was the first to be struck."

"Yes," he replied. "And what part of Manhattan specifically marks the foundation, the very beginning? The southern tip. The southern tip of Manhattan was the first part of the island to be seen on the day of its discovery. And where did the World Trade Center stand and fall?"

"On the southern tip of the island."

"And do you know what the city began with at that southern tip, the first thing the Dutch built there?"

"No."

"A trade center."

"A trade center!"

"Yes, the ancient mystery of judgment—everything is brought back to its foundation. So on 9/11, everything returned to the same place and to the same day. 9/11 returned America to the 9/11s of its rising. And in each place, there was an object, a building, that represented the power that had risen there. And on that day, each object was struck down."

It was then that I realized that the *Half Moon* was gone. I turned to the right and looked up the river. And there it was, disappearing into the distance.

"Nobody could have put all that together," I said.

"No," said the prophet. "Long before the 9/11 that shook the nation to its core, 9/11 itself was the foundation of the nation's powers."

"And it's all a warning," I said, "that what was planted will be uprooted, and what was built up will be broken down."

"Yes."

◆◆◆

"The next mystery would be different from the others, and yet all the others were leading up to it."

"And what did it involve?"

"Something I had never heard of and yet that had been in existence for ages. And on the morning of 9/11, it all fell into place."

Chapter 12

The Parasha

I WAS STANDING AT the entrance of an ancient building of white stone with a classical facade and massive white columns. I knew I was supposed to enter it. So I did. Inside the building were more massive columns, marble floors, giant halls, tables and chairs, and a multitude of scrolls. I took it to be some sort of library."

"A library," she repeated.

"Some sort of ancient library."

"As I walked through the hall, an old man in a dark-red robe, a white beard, and flowing white hair approached me."

"I am the keeper of the scrolls," he said. "May I help you?"

"I don't know," I replied. "I'm not exactly sure why I'm here."

"Have you come to inquire into a day?"

"Perhaps," I said.

"A day of importance?"

"Possibly."

"Then you're looking for the Book of Days."

"The Book of Days? I've never heard of it. What is it?"

"The book in which are found the appointed times and the appointed words of the appointed times. Come," he said, "and I'll show it to you."

He led me down the hallway and up a stairway, then down more hallways and up still another stairway, and down another hallway until we came to a pair of giant doors of engraved stone. What the doors revealed as they opened had the appearance of another realm. The chamber or building we had now entered was so big that I couldn't tell where the ceiling was or, for that matter, where the floor was—as there were many floors, many levels, and all lit up with the light of oil lamps. Most striking of all were the scrolls. There had to have been thousands of them, tens of thousands, all resting on shelves, one beside the next, one on top of the next. The scrolls appeared to be thin. But their numbers were so vast that the resulting vision was overwhelming.

"What is this?" I asked.

"This," said the man, "is the Book of Days."

"Which one?"

"All of them. All of them together."

"All this is the Book of Days?"

"Yes."

He then led me down one of the walkways, surrounded to the right and to the left by rows upon rows and stacks upon stacks of scrolls.

"Of course, the book is made up of many sections, many portions, and many moments and times."

"Moments and times?"

"For example, right now we're passing through the section appointed for the fifteenth century. Soon we'll be passing through the sixteenth, and on and on toward the present."

"I'm not understanding."

We continued walking through the hallways of scrolls, around corners, and up still more staircases.

"The twentieth century," he said. "We've reached the twentieth century!"

We continued walking. Finally, he stopped.

"What year did you say you were looking for?"

I didn't say. But the section we were in was the year 2001.

He led me further down.

"And in what month?"

"September," I said.

He led me a little further still.

"The appointed words are timed to every seventh day of each week. Which day of September are you looking for?"

"The eleventh."

"Do you want the word that followed it or the word that led up to it?"

"Whichever is closest to that day."

"The word closest to September 11 was that which led up to it, the one appointed to be read three days before."

"That's the word I want."

At that, the man removed a scroll from the shelf and handed it to me.

"And there you have it," he said. "Open it."

So I began unrolling it as best I could without having a table or surface on which to lay it down. I looked at the words but had no idea what they meant, as it was written in a foreign language.

"Do you know what you're looking at?"

"No."

"It's called *Ki Tavo*."

"Ki Tavo," I repeated. "What does that...?"

I turned around to finish the question. But he was gone. But there in his place was the prophet.

"What is this all about?" I asked. "What do all these scrolls represent?"

"The Word of God."

"But why is it called the Book of Days?"

"Because these particular scrolls are scriptures appointed for the set times."

"Appointed from when?"

"From ages past."

"And appointed for what, exactly?"

"To be read, recited, and chanted on the appointed Sabbath day. They're called the *parashas*."

"And what does that mean?"

"A passage or portion of scriptures."

"Which scriptures?"

"The main portion comes from the Torah, the five books of Moses...the first five books of the Bible."

"All these thousands and thousands of scrolls...come from five books?"

"Each scroll in this chamber represents the word appointed for *each* Sabbath of *every* week of *every* year...for centuries and ages."

"The man in the red robe who led me here, the keeper of the scrolls, is he significant?"

"I would say so. That was Moses."

"Moses wore a red robe?"

"It's not that Moses wore a red robe. It's that Moses is often portrayed as wearing a red robe. He's a symbol of Moses."

"And what was the word that he called the scroll?"

"Ki Tavo."

"But what does it mean?"

"Every parasha has a name. *Ki Tavo* is the name given to one of the appointed words."

"The scripture appointed to be read just before 9/11?"

"Three days before it happened."

"Was it significant?"

"Most significant."

"What exactly is Ki Tavo?"

"It comes from the last of the five books of Moses, from the Book of Deuteronomy, from the last passages of that book. It represents Moses' last words to the nation of Israel."

"What does it say?"

"It speaks of what will happen in the days to come, the blessings of the nation that follows God and the curses of the one that doesn't."

"And the nation that once knew God but then…"

"Yes," he replied, "that is specifically what the passage centers on, a nation that once knew God but then departed from Him and turned against His ways."

"Sounds like a warning."

"It is."

"So the word appointed for the last Sabbath before 9/11 was a *warning*?"

"It was not only a warning but one specifically directed to a nation that once knew God but had turned away."

"And what exactly does it prophesy?"

"That which will befall such a nation."

"And what is it that will befall such a nation?"

"Calamity," he said. "Judgment."

"So the word appointed for the Sabbath before 9/11 was a warning to a nation concerning coming calamity and judgment?"

"Yes."

"What calamity?"

"Come," said the prophet, "and we'll see."

He led me down the hallway, around corners, down staircases, and down more hallways and corners until we passed through the chamber's large stone doors. Then we descended two flights of stairs until we found ourselves in one of the library's main halls full of tables and chairs for studying. It was at one of these tables that the prophet sat down and motioned for me to join him.

"Kind of like the New York Public Library," I said, "except with no electricity."

He didn't respond but motioned for me to hand him the scroll, which I did. He unrolled it.

"Are the words of the appointed scripture a prophecy of America?" I asked.

"The words are a prophecy of Israel and with specific warnings of judgment unique to that nation, its exile, its scattering to the world. But they speak to and warn any nation that has known God and then turned against His ways. The words of the scripture contain the signs of national judgment."

"As in America?"

"As in more than America...but as in touching America."

"As American civilization was, from its beginning, especially connected to ancient Israel."

"Yes, and so that which was given to ancient Israel could be used to speak to America and manifest as signs of warning and judgment. The appointed passage of Scripture contains not one calamity but a multitude, a list of signs concerning a nation under judgment."

"And those signs of national judgment were recited throughout the world just days before 9/11."

"Throughout the world," he replied, "and specifically in New York City."

"So what calamities were recited just before 9/11?"

The prophet began moving his finger across the words of the scroll. Since they were in Hebrew, he first read them to himself, then spoke the translation.

"It begins by speaking of the nation that knows of God and walks in His ways.

> Now it shall come to pass, if you diligently obey the voice of the LORD your God...all these blessings shall come upon you....Blessed shall be...the produce of your ground and the increase of your herds.[1]

"And so, inasmuch as America followed the ways of God, America was blessed, and more so than any nation has ever been blessed. The scripture speaks of fruitfulness and the produce of the land. So America's soil was blessed with fruitfulness to the point that it would be known as the bread basket of the world. The scripture also uses the word *increase*. So America became the nation of productivity and increase in every realm.

> Blessed shall you be in the city, and blessed shall you be in the field.[2]

"So America would be known not only for the blessings of its fields but, as it grew as a nation and a world power, for the greatness of its cities.

> Blessed shall be your basket and your kneading bowl.[3]

"The scripture speaks of prosperity, abundance, the blessings of a nation's economy. And so America was blessed with a level of prosperity no nation had ever known. The appointed scripture goes on:

> The LORD will cause your enemies who rise against you to be defeated before your face; they shall come out against you one way and flee before you seven ways.[4]

"And what blessing is this?" he asked.
"The blessing of military power."
"And thus America would defeat its enemies in war, be kept safe from attack in peace, and become the strongest nation on earth, so strong that many believed it invincible.

> The LORD will command the blessing...in all to which you set your hand.[5]

"Thus America became known for doing what other nations would have deemed impossible, becoming the world's leading technological power and blessed in all it set its hand to do, from overseeing the world order to setting a man on the moon.

> Then all peoples of the earth shall see that you are called by the name of the LORD, and they shall be afraid of you.[6]

"So America would be esteemed and envied throughout the world. Many would seek to emulate it. Few would seek to rise up against it.

> You shall lend to many nations, but you shall not borrow.[7]

"The blessings of God would apply not only to the nation's economic realm but also to its financial realm. By the end of the First World War, the United States had overtaken the British Empire to become the world's greatest financial power, with New York City as the world's new financial center. America would become the world's leading creditor nation and 'lend to many nations.'

> The LORD your God will set you high above all nations of the earth....And the LORD will make you the head and not the tail; you shall be above only, and not be beneath.[8]

"And so, in the twentieth century, America would become the head of nations."

He paused from reading text and turned to me.

"But it doesn't end there, not the scripture and not America. At the height of its power, its blessings, and its predominance over the world, the nation began turning, more and more brazenly, away from the God of its foundations."

"And what about the scripture?"

"Do you see all this?" he asked, pointing to all the lines of words beneath those from which he had just read. "All this is a prophecy and a warning to the nation that had known God and His blessings but had now turned away from Him. All these are the calamities. The blessings it was given are undone, one by one."

"Such as?"

"The heights from which it towered over the nations. And so America's global supremacy relative to the rest of the world would start to fade away. Other nations and powers would begin vying for its crown.

"According to the Scripture, the nation will begin losing its military invincibility. So in the midst of its turning away from God, America would suffer the most traumatic military defeat in its history, a defeat that would haunt it for decades to come."

"Vietnam."

"And as for the nation that lent to many nations, listen to the scripture's warning concerning the nation and its rivals:

He shall lend to you, but you shall not lend to him."[9]

"So that," I said, "would mean that America would cease from being the world's greatest creditor nation?"

"It would."

"Did it happen?"

"Yes, and it happened at the same period when the nation was departing from God's ways. In the late twentieth century, America not only ceased from being the world's greatest creditor nation; it was transformed into the world's greatest *debtor* nation."

"From the head to the tail."

"But the mystery goes deeper. This is the word that was appointed to be read on the last Sabbath before 9/11, chanted in synagogues throughout New York City three days before the calamity fell. And it spoke of the signs of national judgment."

"Like what?"

"The nation's hedge of protection will be lifted up. Its enemy will be allowed to enter its borders. The enemy will come…

…against you *from afar, from the end of the earth.*[10]

"So on 9/11, America's enemies came against it from afar, from the Middle East, as from the ends of the earth. With the nation's protection removed, the attacks from which it had, in the past, been protected now come to its shores.

And they shall besiege you at all *your gates.*"[11]

"The enemy will attack the gate. That's the scripture you quoted from!"

"Yes."

"And it was also the appointed word leading up to 9/11?"

"Yes. So on 9/11, the enemy attacked the gate of America, New York City."

"And those in New York City were reciting the prophecy that said that the enemy would attack the nation at its gate. And three days later, the enemy would attack the nation at its gate."

"And the appointed word went on:

> Cursed shall you be *in the city*, and cursed shall you be *in the field.*[12]

"The two sites epitomize the nation's judgment: the city and the field. So the attacks of 9/11 took place in the cities of New York and Washington and in a field by Shanksville, Pennsylvania. In the appointed Scripture, the city is mentioned first, and then the field. So on 9/11, the destruction began in the cities and ended in the field.

> Cursed shall be your basket and your kneading bowl."[13]

"The nation's sustenance," I said, "its economy."

"And so on 9/11, the terrorists attacked the nation's financial center and the Twin Towers of the World Trade Center, the symbols of its global economic power.

> And your heavens which are over your head shall be bronze,
> and the earth which is under you shall be iron.[14]

"To an ancient hearer, these words could be taken figuratively to describe the signs of drought on the land. And yet on 9/11, they had a literal fulfillment. The essence of the World Trade Center was steel. On 9/11, it all collapsed into the ruins of Ground Zero. Steel is an alloy of iron. The base metal of the steel ruins of Ground Zero was iron. In other words, after 9/11, *the earth that was under* those who came to the ruins of Ground Zero *was iron.*"

"What about the bronze?"

"Bronze is an alloy of copper. In fact, the Hebrew word used in the passage, *nechoshet*, also means copper. And the passage can also be translated as "The sky above you shall be copper...""

"And on 9/11?"

"On 9/11 a cloud hovered in the sky over Ground Zero and lower Manhattan. The particles of that cloud remained in the sky above the city for days. It was found that in the cloud and the air of Ground Zero were particles of copper. And thus *the earth under them was iron and the sky above them, copper.*

> The LORD will change the rain of your land to powder and dust.[15]

"Again, to an ancient hearer, these words could be taken as describing the barren dryness of a drought. But on 9/11, there was again a literal fulfillment. From the fall of the two towers came massive clouds of white powder and dust that descended on Ground Zero and lower Manhattan.

> You will grope about in broad daylight like someone blind, and you will not be able to find your way.[16]

"On 9/11, as the clouds of dust descended on the streets, those caught in the midst lost all visibility. Even though it was a sunny morning, they groped in broad daylight as one would grope in the dark.

> The LORD will cause you to be defeated before your enemies; you shall go out one way against them and flee seven ways before them.[17]

"And so on 9/11, America's enemies were victorious. Those who should not have prevailed did prevail and brought a great nation to a standstill. America suffered a traumatic defeat at the hands of its enemies. And with each strike, the nation's enemies came in one direction and those on the ground of destruction fled in many directions. Tell me, Nouriel, what realm does this judgment involve?"

"War," I replied, "the military realm."

"So this is a strike against the nation's military power. And so what was struck on 9/11?"

"The Pentagon," I replied, "the striking of the nation's military power."

"Notice something," said the prophet, "the numbers. '*You shall go out one way against your enemies and flee in seven.*' When it speaks of the nation dealing with its enemies, the ratio is one to seven. How did 9/11 begin?"

"With the attack on the towers," I replied.

"The first plane—what flight was it?"

"I don't know."

"It was flight 11. The number 11 is made up of 1 and 1. And what flight was it that struck the Pentagon?"

"I don't know."

"Flight 77. The number 77 is made up of 7 and 7. So we have the same numbers as in the appointed word and the template of judgment, the number 1 and the number 7. What is the ratio of 11 to 77?"

"1 to 7."

"And the ratio is linked to the attack of the enemy. And the prophecy *begins* with the number 1 and *ends* with the number 7. And so the striking of the first building was marked by the number 1, and the striking of the last house, by the number 7."

"The nation's enemies will come from far away. Does it say anything else about them?"

"The passage describes them as:

> ...a people whose language you will not understand, a people of fierce countenance, who will show no reverence for the elderly nor grace to the young.[18]

"So the terrorists of 9/11 spoke a language that most Americans could not understand. So too they were of fierce countenance. And so too they showed no respect to the old or favor to the young. They were brutal and merciless.

"The passage speaks not once but four times of the enemy attacking or causing distress at the gate. But one of the references mentions something else:

> They shall besiege you at all your *gates* until your high and *fortified walls, in which you trust, come down.*"[19]

"You quoted that Scripture as well, when you spoke about the wall."

"And what did it mean?" he asked.

"America's gate is New York City, and its wall, its defense, is the Pentagon. And the Pentagon is built after the pattern of a fortress with fortified walls. So on 9/11, the enemy attacked first the gate and then the wall, the towers of New York City and then the Pentagon of Washington, DC. And all that was in the appointed word that was recited just before 9/11!"

"Yes. Did you notice a pattern in the prophecy?"

"No."

"In the first part of the scripture, the nation is blessed in the city and the field. In the second part, it's cursed in the city and field. In the first part, it's blessed in its basket and kneading bowl; in the second part, it's cursed in its basket and kneading bowl. In the beginning, they lend to many nations. In the end, they borrow from other nations. In the beginning, their enemy flees from before them. In the end, it is they who flee from before their enemies. In the beginning, rain falls on the land as a blessing; in the end, there falls a rain of powder and dust, the sign of a curse.

"The second part of the prophecy is the *inverse* of the first. The judgments at the end are the opposites, the inversions of the blessings at the beginning."

"The mystery of inversion."

"And juxtaposition," he said. "The two things are joined together. And so the mystery of why it happened on 9/11 goes all the way back to the words of Moses, to this passage."

"The day of building up becomes the day of the breaking down—9/11."

"And so," said the prophet, "on the last Sabbath before 9/11, three days before the calamity, the appointed passage was being chanted all over the world and all over New York City. It would speak of enemies who would come from a faraway land, who would speak a foreign language and be of a fierce countenance. They would show no respect for the old and no compassion for the young. They would attack the nation's gate and bring destruction. In the midst of the attack, people would flee in every direction. A curse would come upon the city and then upon the field. It would affect the nation's economic power and military power. There would be iron on the earth and copper in the sky. And powder and dust would rain down from above. In broad daylight people would be groping as in darkness, unable to find their way, as if blind. The attack would begin with the striking of the nation's gate but would conclude with the bringing down of the nation's wall. It would be a day that joined together the nation's building up with the breaking down and the planting with the uprooting."

"So the ancient words that were chanted that day," I said, "they would *become* 9/11."

"And all from the appointed passage that identifies the nation that had known God and His blessings but had turned away from blessing...to judgment."

The prophet rolled up the scroll, got up from his chair, and motioned for me to do likewise. With the scroll in hand, he led me over to a small, high table, around which were no chairs. The table was illuminated by a shaft of sunlight coming down from a high window on the library's opposite wall. He laid the scroll down on the table and unrolled it. It was now bathed in light.

———————◆◆◆———————

"Why did he take you there?"

"He told me that the table was made for deeper study, for the illumination of a single word or verse."

"So he was going to open up a different revelation."

"It would be a revelation within a revelation."

Chapter 13

The Birds of Prey

"THREE TIMES," HE said, "the judgment foretold by the prophets came to Israel, three days of utter destruction."

"How can a nation be destroyed three times?"

"Because it came to three different Israels. In the days after King Solomon, the nation divided into two: the northern kingdom, known as Israel or Samaria, and the southern kingdom, known as Judah. The northern kingdom was the first to descend into the depravity that was so great that it involved the offering up of their own children as sacrifices. Though the Lord sent prophets to warn them and to call them back, they rejected the warnings and defied the call to return. Finally, in 722 BC, the destruction of which they had been warned came upon the land.

"It came through a brutal and merciless kingdom—the Assyrian Empire. The Assyrian army laid siege to the nation's capital, broke through its walls, took the people captive into the nations, and wiped the kingdom off the face of the earth. And it had all been foretold by the prophet Hosea:

> He shall come like an eagle against the house of the LORD.... Israel has rejected the good; the enemy will pursue him."[1]

"And the second destruction?"

"Would come to the southern kingdom of Judah. In the case of that nation, the apostasy would take longer, but in little over a century after the fall of Samaria, it too had descended to the same depths of immorality and had passed the point of no return. The people of Judah had, likewise, been warned by the prophets of the coming calamity. And, likewise, they had rejected it. The destruction would come in 586 BC. This time it came through the armies of the Babylonian Empire in a siege against the capital city, Jerusalem. They would breach the walls, raze the city to the ground, and take the people captive to Babylon.

"The prophet Ezekiel had foretold the approach of that calamity as he spoke of Nebuchadnezzar, Babylon, coming to the land as...

> A great eagle with large wings and long pinions, full of feathers of various colors...[2]

"The prophet Jeremiah would describe the coming of Nebuchadnezzar and the armies of Babylon upon other lands this way:

> Behold, He shall come up and fly like the eagle, and spread His wings over Bozrah.[3]

"What do you notice about the words of the prophets?" he asked.

"Each prophecy speaks of an eagle."

"And who is the eagle?"

"The enemy, the attacker, the one who brings destruction."

"Yes."

"Why an eagle?"

"The invasion of the enemy would come like the strike of an eagle. The eagle strikes its prey with power, suddenness, and ferocity. Power, suddenness, and ferocity describe the way the enemy came upon Israel on the day of destruction. Both Assyria and Babylon were known not only for their military power but for their rapidity and ferocity of conquest. So the image of an eagle flying through the sky was a fitting representation of their attacks. Beyond this, Assyria filled its carved reliefs with images of eagle-headed beings, seen as protective spirits. And as the eagle spreads its wings and overshadows, overwhelms, and comes down upon its prey, so on the day of destruction, the Assyrians and Babylonians would each overshadow, descend upon, and overwhelm their prey...in this case, the people of Israel."

"And what about the third destruction?"

"Years after the Jewish people were taken captive to Babylon, God restored them. They returned to their homeland, rebuilt the Temple, the city of Jerusalem, and the Jewish nation. But in time, they again turned away, hardened their hearts, and deafened their ears to His call. Likewise, they were warned."

"By the prophets?"

"By the Messiah," he replied, "the man called Yeshua, or Jesus. He warned the people of Israel of the coming calamity:

> But when you see Jerusalem surrounded by armies, then know
> that its desolation is near....And they will fall by the edge of
> the sword, and be led away captive into all nations.[4]

"The prophecy would be fulfilled in AD 70, when the armies of Rome destroyed Jerusalem, left the land in devastation, and led the Jewish people captive into the nations. When the Roman army came upon the land, they did so with overwhelming power and ferocity."

"As the eagle."

"Yes. In fact, the eagle was the symbol of Roman power. To the Romans the eagle represented the reigning god of their pantheon, Zeus, Jupiter. And thus it became the foremost symbol of Roman military power. Thus the eagle was the symbol of Rome at war and thus of its attack and destruction of the Jewish nation."

"So each enemy, the Assyrians, the Babylonians, and the Romans, the destroyers of Israel, each was connected to the same symbol...each came upon the nation as an eagle."

"So the day of destruction is linked to the eagle."

I don't know why it didn't dawn on me before that moment—maybe because it was a dream—but when it hit me, the revelation left me shaking.

"On 9/11, the enemy came upon the land as an eagle—the sign of judgment."

"Yes," said the prophet, "as it is written...

> *He shall come up and fly like the eagle...*[5]

"So on 9/11, the enemy came from the skies. The enemy came up and flew like the eagle over the land...all nineteen terrorists taking flight as eagles over the skies of America. And so it is written:

> *He shall...spread His wings.*[6]

"On 9/11, the enemy took up wings of metal and came upon the land as did Assyria, Babylon, and Rome, as an eagle comes upon its prey for one purpose—to bring destruction. And how does the eagle strike its prey?"

"With power, ferocity, and suddenness."

"And so 9/11 was marked by all three of these things. The attack was so fast and so sudden that America was caught entirely off guard and, for some time, had no idea what was happening.

"And on the day of destruction, the enemies of ancient Israel came as an eagle not only on the land but specifically on the city. So the terrorists of 9/11 came specifically upon the city...New York City. And in the case of ancient Israel, the enemy came as an eagle specifically upon the *capital city*. So on 9/11, the terrorists came as eagles upon Washington, DC.

"And when Assyria, Babylon, and Rome came as eagles to the city, they came to destroy its wall, its gates, and towers. So on 9/11, the enemy came in like an eagle to bring destruction to America's wall, gate, and towers."

"A question: The prophecies that you mentioned of the enemy coming to the land as an eagle come from the prophets Hosea, Jeremiah, and Ezekiel—not Moses. But aren't we here to read the prophecy of Moses?"

"Yes. The first one to prophesy of the enemy coming to the land as an eagle wasn't any of these—it was Moses."

At that, he began unrolling the scroll. "The word appointed to be read three days before 9/11 foretold the day of calamity, the attack of the enemy, the siege at the gate, the breaking down of the wall, a rain of powder and dust, and more. But it contains yet another sign of judgment. It tells how the enemy will come upon the land:

> A people against you from far away, from the end of the earth, as *the eagle flies*, a people whose language you will not understand, a people of fierce countenance..."[7]

"*That* was also in the word appointed to be read just before 9/11?"

"Yes. It was all proclaimed just before it happened. It would be the day of the eagle, the day of wings, the day when destruction would come to America from the sky. And the word was recited all over New York City...Boston...and Washington, DC."

I had no words.

"But there's more," said the prophet. He placed his finger on the text of the unrolled scroll. "In the original language," he said, "it reads this way:

ka'asher yid'eh nesher.

"*Ka'Asher* means as or like. *Nesher* means eagle. But the key word here is *Yid'eh*. *Yid'eh* speaks of the eagle in flight. It can be taken to mean fast or swiftly. But it speaks of a more specific kind of flying, especially in regard to the context in which it appears."

"Which is what?"

"It means to swoop down," he replied. "And so the words are also translated as:

...like an eagle swooping down...[8]

And it will swoop down on you.[9]

"On 9/11," said the prophet, "exactly how did the enemy come? Not only as an eagle flying—but as an eagle *swooping down*. The attack began as the first plane swooped down from the sky to strike the North Tower. The second plane followed, swooping down from the sky to strike the South Tower. The third plane swooped down so low that it was nearly at ground level as it struck the Pentagon. And the fourth plane was forced to swoop down so dramatically that it crashed into the earth.

"So on September 11, 2001, the enemy came upon America as he had come upon the land in ancient times, in accordance with the appointed word recited three days earlier: *ka'asher yid'eh nesher...* like an eagle swooping down."

He paused. I thought it was the end of the revelation. But there was one more thing to be revealed.

"When the armies of Rome came upon Israel to destroy it, the image of the eagle played a part in the destruction beyond what was written in the prophecies."

"What do you mean?"

"It was there in concrete form."

"How?"

"When the armies of Rome invaded the land, they did so marching behind the preeminent standard of Roman military power, the aquila. *Aquila* means eagle. The aquila was typically a golden eagle crowning the top of a staff or pole with outstretched wings."

"He shall spread his wings," I said, repeating the words of the prophecy he had shared with me earlier.

"So the eagle would lead the Roman legions into battle, remain lifted up for the duration of the battle, and crown the victory or the ruins left by the victory at the battle's end. So the image given in the ancient prophecies of Israel's judgment actually appeared on the day of its ful-fillment.... It would happen again."

"What would happen?"

"The image would manifest once more on the day of destruction."

"When?"

"On September 11, 2001."

"How? The terrorists didn't use military standards in their attacks."

"No," he replied. "They used planes. And it was the plane, the first to take off from Boston on 9/11, the first to hit its target, the North Tower of the World Trade Center, and the one that would inaugurate the calamity—it was *that* plane that carried not only the terrorists but the ancient symbol of judgment.

"As 9/11 began, on the back of the plane carrying the terrorists was the same symbol carried by the Roman legions on the day of Israel's judgment."

"The image of an eagle?"

"Yes, there on the rudder of the plane...the eagle."

"So then 9/11 began with the image used in the prophecies to represent the day of judgment."

"And it wasn't the only one. The first plane to head for Washington, DC—that plane as well carried the ancient sign of judgment, the eagle."

"And, of course, nobody planned it. It had to be the emblem of the airline."

"Yes," he replied. "It just happened to happen. And the ancient prophecy speaks not only of an eagle but of an eagle swooping down."

"And?"

"The planes that bore that emblem were of American Airlines. And the image that was borne on the plane that struck the tower and that which struck the Pentagon was that of an eagle with its wings raised high above its head, its talons extended, and its head turned downward...in other words..."

"An eagle swooping down."

"And do you know the number of the two flights that bore the image of the eagle?"

"No."

"The same two of which I told you earlier, flight 11 and flight 77, the two that bear the ratio spoken of in the appointed passage, one to seven. And that ratio specifically marks the attack of the enemy..."

"And the attack of the enemy is described in that passage as that of an eagle swooping down."

At that, he rolled up the scroll.

"And so, in the early days of September 2001, the prophecy of the enemy coming to the land, as an eagle swooping down, was recited and chanted all over New York City, Boston, and Washington, DC. And three days later it all happened...the enemy came from a faraway land, struck the nation's gate, broke down its wall, brought a rain of dust on the city so that people groped in broad daylight, caused the ground to become iron and the sky, bronze, and then the image spoken of in that scripture appeared in the skies above America as the enemy came upon the land as an eagle swooping down."

◆◆◆

"The next mystery would be the final one."

"The final one?"

"Of the unrevealed."

"And what was it about?"

"A sign from the time of the prophets that manifested in New York City to signal the coming of the calamity *before* anyone realized it was coming."

"What kind of sign?" she asked.

"The sign of the watchmen."

Chapter 14

The Watchmen

WAS STANDING ON the wall of an ancient city, on the rampart. It was just around daybreak. To my left, standing inside one of the towers built into the wall, stood a man in ancient garments and gazing out intently into the distance. Strapped to his side was a shofar, the ram's horn."

"As in the seal," said Ana, "the seal you were given by the girl in the blue coat."

"Yes, as in the seal."

"The watchman."

"One of several watchmen. He never turned in my direction but stayed fixed on the distance ahead of him. I looked but didn't see anything there. And then the sun began rising and lighting up the landscape. The watchman's focus and gaze grew all the more intense.

"It was then that I saw what he was seeing. In the distant hills was an army. The early sunlight glistened on the metal of their shields and chariots. The city was going to be attacked.

"The watchman grabbed his horn, set it to his mouth, and began sounding it in every direction but primarily toward the city within the walls. Then I heard the sound of a second ram's horn coming from another section of the wall, from another tower, from another watchman, and then a third, and a fourth, and another, and another. The watchmen were now all sounding their alarms.

"But within the walls there was no reaction. It seemed as if most of its inhabitants were asleep. And the few I saw on the streets seemed oblivious to the sound of the horns. They just went about their business, their tasks and errands, without any sign of having heard the alarm.

"The army drew nearer…soldiers, horsemen, chariots, and siege works. The watchmen continued to sound their horns from every tower. But still there was no reaction from the people inside. It was then that I noticed the prophet standing beside me on the rampart. The sounds of war that had surrounded us now grew softer. It wasn't that the attack had stopped, but it was as if it was all being muffled so I could hear the words of the prophet."

◆◆◆

"Why aren't they responding?" I asked.

"Many are still sleeping," he replied.

"But those who are awake aren't hearing it either."

"They *are* hearing it," he replied, "but they aren't listening; they're not heeding it."

It was then I noticed an object in his hand. It wasn't there when I first saw him, but being that I was in a dream, anything was possible. It was a ram's horn.

"The shofar," he said, "the watchman's trumpet, his most important possession. In his hands it could save a kingdom. It meant the difference between life and death. To ignore its sound was to put one's life in peril. Thus the sound of the shofar became associated with the day of calamity and judgment. So the prophet wrote:

> I cannot hold my peace, because you have heard, O my soul, *the sound of the trumpet, the alarm of war.* Destruction upon destruction is cried....*Blow the trumpet in the land*; cry, 'Gather together.'...Take refuge! Do not delay!...The destroyer of nations is on his way....Your cities will be laid waste."[1]

"So the shofar," I said, "was sort of the early warning system of the ancient world."

"Not sort of," said the prophet. "It *was* their early warning system."

"And today we have radar and intelligence systems, alarms."

"Modern versions of the shofar."

Just then, everything began to change. The ancient city transformed into a modern one. The rampart transformed into the roof of a skyscraper in the middle of a modern cityscape. The prophet was still beside me, and so, by the edge of the roof and turned away from us, was the watchman, sounding the ram's horn into the distance. Then, as in the first part of the dream, I heard the sound of a second shofar. It was coming from the roof of another skyscraper, on top of which stood another watchman. And then I heard another and another and another. There were watchmen stationed all over the city, each one on top of a building, each sounding the shofar into the distance.

"'What does it mean?" I asked.

"There is a month," he said, "in the biblical calendar called Elul. It was ordained from ages past that during Elul the shofar is to be sounded."

"Why?"

"To prepare for the days linked to judgment, the high holy days."

"Elul," I said. "Isn't that the same month in which the prayers of judgment are spoken?"

"Yes," he answered, "the selichote."

"And when exactly are the trumpets sounded?"

"In the morning, at the end of the traditional morning prayers said by the Jewish people and known as the *shacharit. Shacharit* means the dawn, as these particular prayers may be spoken as early as the first breaking of daylight. So at the end of Elul, all three elements converge, the selichote, the prayers concerning judgment and mercy, which end at dawn; the shacharit prayers, which begin at dawn; and the sounding of the trumpets."

"And the reason why this relates is..."

"It was on one of those mornings in the month of Elul that it all began. As the darkness of night faded into the first light of dawn, the prayers of judgment were completed, the prayers of dawn began, and then the trumpets, the alarm that warns of a coming attack, were sounded. All these things were taking place on the morning of 9/11 when a band of men from the Middle East were setting in motion their plan to bring terror on America. So the ancient rite marked the timing of 9/11—but also the place."

"How could it mark the place?"

"The break of dawn and the sunrise are not just matters of time, but of space. On September 11, dawn broke on Asia, Europe, and Africa hours before it broke on America."

"And why is that significant?"

"Because the ancient rites are timed by the dawn. They follow the dawn. The dawn of 9/11 came upon one specific place in America before it came anywhere else."

"Where?"

"Maine."

"And?"

"The attack began in Boston, in Logan Airport, with the taking off of the first planes that would bring destruction. But it had a pre-beginning, a flight before the flight. For reasons still unknown, Mohamed Atta, the leader of the attack, chose to begin the operation in Portland, Maine. September 11, 2001, dawned on America in Portland at 5:47 a.m. And thus the reciting of the prayers of judgment had to be completed there by 5:47."

"And?"

"Because the mystery pinpoints a time and place, 5:47 in Maine. At 5:47, the leaders of 9/11 were in Maine, at the airport. At 5:45 a.m., two minutes from the moment of dawn, they were passing through the security check to begin their mission. It was then that they were caught on the airport's security cameras. As they made their way to the gate to bring devastation upon New York City, the prayers of judgment, the ancient words that speak of the enemy coming in the form of violent men to bring devastation on the city, were officially completed.

"And then, the breaking of dawn moved westward from Portland, Maine, to Boston, Massachusetts. And so, Mohamed Atta and his accomplices flew from Portland, Maine, to Boston, Massachusetts. The dawn and sunrise continued to move from Boston to New York City and then from New York City to Washington, DC. So the calamity of 9/11 would likewise move from Portland, Maine, to Boston, from Boston to New York City, and from New York City to Washington, DC.

"And as the dawn and sunrise moved from Maine to Boston to New York City and Washington, DC, so did the ancient rite, the utterances of judgment and the sounding of the trumpets."

"As the Jewish people in each place spoke the words and sounded the trumpets."

"Yes. And in ancient times, it was the sounding of the trumpets that warned of the enemy's approach. And so on September 11, 2001, as the enemy approached the city, the trumpets began to sound."

"But those who sounded them didn't know the attack was coming."

"No," said the prophet. "But again, the signs manifest regardless of whether those manifesting them have any idea. The sounding of the trumpets was an ancient biblical sign now manifesting to a modern nation."

"And that modern nation," I said, "had the most advanced and sophisticated early warning systems in the world. And yet on 9/11, it all failed. The government was caught unaware. The Defense Department was caught unaware. Everyone was caught unaware. And yet the biblical alarm began to sound."

"Yes," he replied. "The same sound that was heard in ancient Israel on the day of destruction was now heard in America on 9/11. When the terrorists passed through the gates to board their planes at Logan airport, the trumpets were sounding in Boston and throughout New England. When the first plane took off from Boston at 7:59 a.m., the first plane to strike New York City, the trumpets were sounding in Boston and New York City. When the second plane took off from the same airport at 8:14, the trumpets were sounding. When each of those flights was taken over by the terrorists, the trumpets were sounding. When the plane that would be flown into the Pentagon took off from Dulles airport in Washington, DC, the trumpets were sounding in Washington, DC. And when the last plane took off from Newark airport in New Jersey, the trumpets were sounding in New Jersey.

"On the morning of 9/11, the trumpets were sounding in all the boroughs of New York City and across the water in New Jersey. And one could almost hear the words of the prophet Amos echoing to New York City:

If a trumpet is blown in a city, will not the people be afraid?[2]

"The trumpets were sounding as the two planes that came from Boston changed course and headed to the towers of New York City. And the voice of the prophet Zephaniah echoed to lower Manhattan:

A day of trumpet and alarm against the fortified cities and against the high towers.[3]

"The trumpets were sounding as the first plane swooped down from the sky as an eagle to inflict destruction. And one could hear the words of Hosea's prophecy to Israel:

Set the trumpet to your mouth! He shall come like an eagle."[4]

"How long," I asked, "did the trumpets sound on 9/11?"

"The trumpets sealed the shacharit morning prayers. Those prayers were to be completed within a four-hour window beginning with sunrise."

"So when did the sun rise on New York City on 9/11?"

"Just after 6:30."

"So the four-hour window would come to an end just after 10:30."

"Yes, so the time for the trumpets to sound would end just after 10:30."

"And when did the last of the two towers fall?"

"The last tower fell just before 10:29."

"Just before the last trumpet."

"Yes, the destruction ended, and the trumpets stopped sounding. The window closed. For the sound of the trumpets is the alarm of the watchmen—to warn of destruction. Thus when the destruction was over, the trumpets ceased to sound."

"Except that these trumpets were appointed to sound on that day and until that particular minute...from ages past."

"And so we have a mystery."

◆◆◆

"It's overwhelming," said Ana, "overwhelming and amazing and scary at the same time. So if no one took the sounding as a warning, why the trumpets? What does it mean?"

"Before judgment falls on a nation, God sends warning that those who will take the warning will be saved. The trumpets were a symbol of that warning. They sounded, but no one heard. They were a sign to a nation that has deafened itself to the voice of God...and to His warnings. And that, in itself, is another sign and warning. What happens to a city that doesn't listen to the sound of the trumpet, that doesn't hear the sound of its own alarm?"

"It's destroyed."

"So then what happens to a nation?"

Chapter 15

The Land of Two Towers

"THE DREAMS CAME to an end."

"So where did that leave you?"

"It left me with no idea. I didn't know if there was more to be revealed or if that was it...or what I was supposed to do with what I was shown."

"But it wasn't the end," she said.

"No. It was the end of the first revelations, the unrevealed, the revelations that had not been revealed to me in my first encounters with the prophet."

"The first part ended as it began."

"How?"

"With the watchman," she replied, "just as it began with the seal of the watchman."

"You're right."

"So then what happened?"

"The absence of revelation went on for some time. Every time I went to bed, I wondered if that would be the night when it would happen. But it never did. And then something else happened.

"I had just finished doing a television interview. There was to be a book signing for the studio audience at the end of the taping. They arranged for me to be sitting in the lobby behind a counter with a line of people coming from my left to have their books signed. I was about halfway through the signing when it happened.

"I didn't see her at first. She was standing in line behind a large man, who obscured her."

"The little girl?"

"The girl with wavy blonde hair and blue eyes and in the same light blue coat. I was tempted to get out from behind the counter and question her as to what was going on. But of course, I didn't. I knew that she had come to tell me something. And I would wait until she did."

◆◆◆

She approached the counter without a book for me to sign.

"He returned," she said.

"He did," I replied, "in a sense."

"And you were given revelation."

"I was."

"And he showed you that which could not have been shown you at the beginning."

"He did."

"And now what?" she asked.

"You're asking *me*? I was hoping you could tell me that."

"There's more for you to see, Nouriel, more for you to be shown. So now begins the next revelation."

"And the next revelation is what?"

"A revelation different from the first," she replied. "The first concerned that which was but had not yet been revealed. But the mystery hasn't stopped. No. It has progressed."

"So the next revelation concerns..."

"That which came after."

"After 9/11?"

"After 9/11 and after those things the prophet revealed to you in your first encounters."

"After the harbingers?"

"Yes and no," she replied. "The mystery never stopped, and neither did the harbingers. They've continued."

"Up to when?"

"Up to the present time."

"And all this will be revealed to me?"

"It will."

"How?"

"Do you have the seal I gave you?"

In my first encounters with the prophet, I had learned to keep the seal with me at all times. And in the absence of dreams, it was the only thing I had to go on.

"May I have it back?" she asked.

So I handed it back to her, and she placed it inside her coat pocket.

"Here," she said as she placed another seal in my hand. I didn't look to see what was on it but immediately secured it in my pocket.

"So this will lead me to the next revelation?"

"It will help lead you," she replied. "But you'll need more than that."

"Like what?"

"The next revelation will begin in the land of the two towers, around which flow the waters of the pure."

"And what exactly does that mean?"

"I believe that is for you to find out."

"Can you give me something more, something to go on?"

"There's nothing more for me to tell. I've done what I was sent to do."

At that, she turned and began to walk away. I knew there was no point in trying to follow her. I would not be told anything more than I was meant to know. But then she turned back to me.

"The prophet," she said with a smile.

"What about the prophet?"

"The prophet will tell you more."

"I haven't seen him lately."

"But you will. He will appear as he did before."

"In the same way?"

"As he appeared then…in a way you don't expect."

At that, she turned around and disappeared into the crowd.

◆◆◆

"And so what happened?"

"A veil was about to be removed."

"How so?"

"I was about to see what was right before my eyes and that which I had been mostly blind to. I was about to be shown the mystery that never stopped, that which manifested or was revealed *after* I wrote the first book…the signs and harbingers."

"The signs and harbingers…Tell me."

"Ah," said Nouriel, "that would be an entirely other revelation. We couldn't possibly open it up now."

"Then when?"

"Another time."

Part III

THE

MANIFESTATIONS

Chapter 16

The Man on the Hill

So is this the 'another time'?" asked Ana.

"I believe it is," he replied.

It had been just over a month since his last visit to her office. She greeted him wearing a light outdoor jacket.

"It's a beautiful day," she said. "I thought we could go for a walk...to the park."

He agreed. So they made their way to the elevator, down to the first floor, across the lobby, and out to the sidewalk. They would spend the rest of that day in Central Park, walking along its paths and sitting down to rest on its benches and grass. But Ana wasn't about to wait to reach the park before asking her first question.

"So tell me what happened," she said. "How did it begin?"

"It began, as before, with a dream. I saw a man with flowing black hair and a black beard. He was dressed in dark clothes with a large round collar of ruffled white fabric."

"A ruff."

"What?"

"A ruff," said Ana. "That's what they called it, a decorative collar they used to wear centuries ago."

"That would be it," he replied. "He was carrying a large white rectangular rock...not just white, but radiant white. In front of him was what appeared to be a small mountain. He ascended it. Upon reaching its summit, he laid down the stone. On the side of the stone were engraved words, but I had no idea what it said—it was in a foreign script.

"He then backed away from it. Around the stone there began to rise a structure, as if it was meant to house it, a chapel or shrine. Then around the chapel arose other structures, buildings, homes, churches...until resting on top of the mountain was an entire city. After the last building had risen, the man turned around and began descending the mountain. When he reached the bottom, he turned back to gaze up at the city,

101

which was now not only radiant but bathed in brilliant sunlight. He turned around once more and departed.

"Then everything changed. Clouds began filling the sky, obscuring the sun, darkening the city. Its radiance was gone. Its white stone was fading and now filled with stains. I could now hear the sound of revelry, conflict, and chaos.

"The man with the black beard reappeared and once more ascended the mountain. I saw him walking its streets. He appeared startled at the transformation that had taken place in his absence. The city's walls were now chipped and in disrepair and decay. Its buildings were covered with graffiti. I saw the man trying to read the writing on one of the walls, but he had stopped and turned away. He gazed up at the high buildings that towered above him. Along their walls were moving images, carnal and vulgar.

"I saw him searching for the chapel or shrine that housed the stone he had laid. But when he found it, he became especially grieved. Its roof was gone, about half of its walls were broken down, and the half that remained was covered with graffiti. He went 'inside' to see the stone. But it wasn't there. It had been taken away.

"He exited the structure and sat down by one of its remaining walls, staring out into the city and weeping. Finally, he looked up toward the sky and said, 'It is this of which I warned. But they've turned away. They've removed the stone. And now what will become of them?' And with that question, the dream came to an end."

"And there was no prophet," said Ana, "to tell you what it meant?"

"The dream had no prophet. He never showed up."

"But I thought the little girl told you that he would."

"She did."

"But he never showed up."

"It troubled me. What was the point of being given a dream if there was no one to help me understand it?"

"So what did you do?"

"I waited. I thought maybe the meaning would be given in another dream. But nothing came. I looked at the seal the little girl had given me."

"The seal," she said. "You never told me what was on it."

"It was the image of a city, the same city I saw in the dream, with the same exact shapes and outlines. But that didn't help me. It pointed to the dream, or the dream pointed to the seal, but I still had no idea what it all meant."

"And?"

"And then I remembered the words of the little girl. The next revelation, she said, would begin in a land of two towers, around which flow the waters of the pure. Perhaps that was the missing piece. If I could figure out what she was referring to, I would have the answer."

"It's New York!" Ana exclaimed. "Manhattan! The land of the two towers, the Twin Towers. And water flows around it."

"Yes," said Nouriel, "that's what I thought at first. But one thing didn't fit: 'the waters of the pure.' New York City isn't usually associated with purity in any form."

"Maybe the city has a water purification plant with two towers?"

"No. So I tried to figure out where there would be pure waters. What places would be known for that...and have two towers? I went over what she said again and again. And then it hit me.

"She didn't say 'pure waters' or even 'waters of purity.' She said 'waters of the pure.' It wasn't about pure waters but the waters of the pure."

"I'm not getting it."

"*The pure* can refer to people—a pure people or people associated with purity."

"I still don't get it."

"The Puritans! That's how they got their name...because they were associated with purity."

"And the water?"

"The Puritans were linked to the Massachusetts Bay Colony. The waters of the pure are the waters of the Massachusetts Bay."

"And where did that lead you?"

"Nowhere. I couldn't connect it to the other clue, *the land of the two towers.*"

"So what did you do?"

"I decided to make a journey. I would drive to the coast of New England, to Massachusetts Bay, and see if I could find anything that would answer to the land of the two towers. And if I could, then perhaps I could begin to unlock the mystery. So I drove to the southern end of the bay near Cape Cod. Then I headed north to Plymouth and Boston, then up to Cape Ann. I was now at the northern end of the bay and had found nothing.

"I decided to pull over to the side of the road, get out, and make my way to the shore. I sat down on the sand and just stared out into the ocean, discouraged. At that point, I wasn't looking to find anything, and I was lost in a barrage of thoughts. That's probably why it took several minutes to see it."

"See what?"

"An island…an island on which stood two towers."

"An island," said Ana, "around which flow the waters of the pure. An island. Of course."

"It was called Thacher Island. Its history went back to the time of the Puritans."

"And what were the two towers?"

"Lighthouses, two old stone lighthouses."

"So what did you do?"

"Somehow I had to go there. I booked a room for the night in a nearby hotel, and the next day, rented a kayak."

"A kayak?"

"Yes, that's how you go there, three miles of kayaking. By the time I reached the island, I was exhausted."

"And what did you find?"

"Walking trails…one of which I took. When I came to its end, I saw a lighthouse. And just beyond the lighthouse, over a ridge of rocks toward the ocean, stood a man. I couldn't see his face because he was turned away, facing the water. He had on a long dark coat. I slowly approached him. I was about fifteen feet away from him when he turned around."

"Don't tell me it was the…"

"If I don't tell you the story, I can't give you the revelation."

"Don't tell me it was him."

"It was him."

"The prophet!"

"Yes."

"It wasn't a dream?"

"It was as real as my sitting here with you right now."

"But the little girl," said Ana, "she told you he would come as he did before. He came to you before in a dream."

"She told me he would come as he did before, which was to be *in a way I didn't expect.* The first time she said that, I didn't expect him to come in a dream. So that's how he came. But this time, I expected he *would* come in a dream. But instead he came in flesh-and-blood reality. And so he came to me as before, in a way I didn't expect."

"But at the end of your first encounters, didn't he say you would never see him again."

"He told me I wouldn't see him again unless the Lord should deem it otherwise."

"Then..."

"The Lord deemed it otherwise."

"So what happened?"

"He looked much the same as I remembered him and as I saw him in my dreams."

"Nouriel!" he said, "how good to see you again!"

I didn't know what to say. It was jarring. I hadn't seen him for years, and yet now I was getting used to seeing him in my dreams. But there he was, standing in front of me, in flesh-and-blood reality. It was disorienting. For a moment I wondered if it was a dream.

"Well," I replied, "I happened to be in the neighborhood."

"There's no neighborhood," he replied. "And, of course, you didn't happen to be here. This is where you had to be."

"You knew I was coming," I said, "and so you were here in the exact place at the exact time—just like old times. You were here because I was coming."

"No," said the prophet. "You were coming because I was here."

"I never understood how he did it, how he was always there in the exact place at the exact time. Our encounters were always like that."

"He's a prophet," said Ana. "What do you expect?"

"So you've fulfilled the charge given you?"

"Through a book."

"And they haven't returned?"

"No," I replied. "You asked me the same thing in my dream. Was it you? Were you actually there in my dream?"

"Does it make a difference?" he replied.

"And that's what you said in the dream."

"There was a little girl," he said. "She told you I would return. What did she say?"

"That there would be another revelation."

"And so it begins."

"And you've returned because..."

"The mystery hasn't stopped...and the harbingers haven't stopped manifesting."

"That's what she told me. But why here? Why on this island?"

"It is here," he said, "that you'll find the mystery behind the things you've seen and what is yet to be shown you. It's not the island, Nouriel. It's *where* the island is.

"Come," he said, motioning me to follow him. He led me over to the lighthouse. We walked through its entranceway and ascended its spiral staircase. We then stepped outside onto a lookout porch that encircled the tower just under the lantern room. Before us was a vast panorama in every direction. The prophet directed me to one specific direction—south.

"Do you know what you're looking at?" he asked.

"The Massachusetts Bay."

"You're looking at the beginning. It was here that much of American civilization began. It was into these waters that the Mayflower sailed."

"To Plymouth."

"Yes. And it was on these shores that they laid the foundation stone."

When he said that, it triggered my remembrance of the dream.

"The foundation stone...that's what I saw in my dream, a man carrying a foundation stone up a mountain."

"Tell me your dream," he said. So I did.

"So what does it mean?" I asked.

"The man in your dream was John Winthrop."

"The name is familiar."

"It's been said that if George Washington could be called the father of his country, John Winthrop could be called the grandfather. Winthrop was a Puritan who led the first massive wave of immigrants from England to America. He sailed through these waters on a ship called the *Arbella*. Soon after arriving here, he was made governor of the Massachusetts Bay Colony. He would be central in building the colony into a major settlement. And what he built would become central in the establishment of what we now know as America."

"So in my dream, he was laying the foundation stone of America."

"Yes, but it was more than what he did on these shores. It was what he began before he ever set foot here."

"Which was what?"

"He wrote down a message and shared it with the passengers of the *Arbella*, those who would pioneer the new commonwealth. It was his vision of what that commonwealth was to be and become. It was the vision for what would become America."

"Did he realize what it would become?"

"Not that it would become the United States, but what it was to become as a civilization. Do you have the seal that was given to you by the little girl?"

"Yes." I reached into my pocket and gave it to him.

"Winthrop's vision spoke of a new commonwealth coming into the world for the will and purposes of God…a unique civilization, to which all the nations of the world would look. It was from this vision that the most enduring symbol of American civilization was given. He said this:

> For we must consider that we shall *be as a city upon a hill*. The eyes of all people are upon us.[1]

"The new civilization was to be a *city on a hill*."

"That was my dream—it was a city on a hill."

"And on the seal," he said, "the city was America. The foundation stone was its planting, the vision. From that foundation stone rose the city. From that vision, from Winthrop's planting, came America."

"Why a city on a hill?"

"The image comes from the Bible.[2] It speaks of that which is lifted up as an example. So America was to be lifted up among the nations and was to become an exemplary civilization, a model, a nation that others would seek to emulate, a civilization called to give light to the world."

"The city in my dream was filled with light, radiant."

"There was another civilization called to give light to the world: Israel. And so Winthrop's vision overflowed with references to the Scriptures and to ancient Israel. American civilization was founded and patterned after ancient Israel. One would be hard-pressed to find any other civilization so strongly bound to ancient Israel from its foundation."

"The writing on the stone that I couldn't decipher...it had to be Hebrew."

"Yes," said the prophet, "as the foundation stone of American civilization...is Hebrew. And the connection goes further. Israel had entered into a covenant with God. Thus it is the *covenant nation*. So at the founding of America, Winthrop would write,

> Thus stands the cause between God and us. We are entered
> into covenant with Him for this work."[3]

"What does that mean?"

"The Bible records that God made a covenant with Israel. The case of America is different. But we do know that America's founders made a covenant with God, based on Israel's covenant with God."

"Which means...?"

"That inasmuch as they followed in the paths of righteousness and kept the ways of God, the blessings of heaven would fill their land. So Winthrop's vision prophesied what would happen to the new civilization if it followed in those paths:

> The Lord will be our God, and delight to dwell among us, as
> His own people, and will command a blessing upon us in
> all our ways, so that we shall see much more of His wisdom,
> power, goodness and truth.[4]

"His vision followed the promises and prophecies of blessing given to ancient Israel. And it would become even more specific:

> We shall find that the God of Israel is among us, when ten of
> us shall be able to resist a thousand of our enemies."[5]

"It sounds like the words of Moses."

"Yes. In fact, it comes from the words that Moses gave just before Israel entered the Promised Land. So now Winthrop gave the same prophecies to the pioneers of the new commonwealth just before they entered the New World."

"So embedded in America's foundation was a prophecy of its future...and its course was joined to ancient Israel from the beginning."

"Yes, and the prophecy given to America at its beginning would come true. It would be lifted up among the nations. It would be blessed *in all its ways* until it became the most prosperous, powerful, exalted, and emulated nation on earth."

"But that wasn't the end of my dream."

"No," said the prophet. "Nor was it the end of Winthrop's prophecy. There are many who have spoken of his vision of America as a city on a hill...but almost no one mentions that which came after."

"Which was what?"

"A warning... a prophetic warning...beginning with the words

If we shall deal falsely with our God..."[6]

"What does that mean, to deal falsely with God?"

"The prophecy goes on to explain it:

But if our hearts shall turn away...[7]

"The warning is for an America that turns its heart away from God and rejects His ways:

...so that we will not obey...[8]

"The prophecy goes on:

...but shall be seduced, and worship other Gods...and serve them."[9]

"What other gods?" I asked.

"Gods of its own making," said the prophet. "American gods and American idols. The prophecy identifies them as

...our pleasure...[10]

"It warns an America that turns away from God to the gods of pleasure, sensualities, carnalities, self-gratifications, lusts...and to another kind of god:

...and profits...[11]

"An America that has turned from God to serve the gods of profit, increase, gain, and material possessions."

"It sounds as if that part of the prophecy has also come true."

"And that too was based on ancient Israel. As America was founded after the pattern of ancient Israel and blessed after the pattern of Israel's blessings, so too if it fell away from God, it would do so after the pattern of Israel's fall...and so it did. As Israel fell away from God, it embraced a culture of carnality and sexual immorality."

"And so too did America."

"And as Israel, in its fall, it began to offer up its own children as sacrifices."

"So too America has offered up the lives of its unborn children."

"And as Israel then began to war against the ways of God and those who remained faithful to them..."

"So too has America."

"And it was all foretold in Winthrop's warning and prophecy."

"And the city in my dream was darkened and lost its radiance, and its walls were covered with graffiti, vulgarities, profanities, and obscenities. And then when the man returned, he grieved over what the city had become. And they removed the foundation stone."

"So too," said the prophet, "America, the city on the hill, has removed the stone on which it was founded."

"At the end of my dream, the man asked, 'What will become of them?' Did Winthrop speak of what would happen?"

"He did. He wrote this:

> So that if we shall deal falsely with our God in this work we
> have undertaken, and so cause Him to withdraw His present
> help from us, we shall be made a story and a by-word through
> the world.[12]

"And again,

We shall surely perish.[13]

"The words came, again, from the prophecy given to Israel of the judgments that would come with the nation's departure from God. Do you understand what this means, Nouriel?"

"Tell me."

"To the civilization that was founded after the pattern of ancient Israel, blessed after the pattern of Israel's blessings, and fallen after the pattern of Israel's fall...will come judgment after the pattern of the judgment that came to ancient Israel. That's the mystery behind it."

"Behind what?"

"What happened to America, the lifting up of the hedge, the shaking, the coming of the enemy to the gate, the striking of the towers, and the breaching of the wall. All those things were the judgments of Israel. That's why everything came together the way it did, so that the day of the breaking down would be the day of the building up. That's why the word appointed for the days of America's calamity was the same word that prophesied the days of Israel's calamity. That's why the enemy came in like an eagle swooping down...and that's why the trumpets of Israel were sounding. It all came as it had come in ancient times."

◆◆◆

He gave me time to stand there on the porch of the lighthouse to take in what he had told me. Then he led me back inside, down the spiral staircase, out the door, and over to the rocks where he was standing when I first saw him. And there, overlooking the ocean, we sat down.

"It was all there," he said, "from the very beginning, in the prophecy given at the birth of American civilization, the mystery that joined it to ancient Israel, in its blessings, in its falling, and in that which would come upon it. It lies behind everything you've been shown..."

"Even the harbingers," I said.

"Yes," said the prophet, "especially the harbingers. And it is to that that we must now go in order to open up the mystery."

"The mystery of what?"

"Of that which came after 9/11," he replied, "that which has manifested up to this moment...the mystery of that which came after."

Chapter 17

The Harbingers

"THAT'S THE SAME thing the little girl used when she told me I would be given another revelation."

"What?" he asked.

"That which came after."

"What else did she tell you?"

"That the mystery never stopped…that it's continued."

"Yes," he replied. "It has continued to manifest."

"How?"

"In order for that to be revealed," he replied, "we must first lay the foundation. We must return to the mystery of the harbingers. Do you remember what they were?"

"I should," I replied, "since I wrote about them."

"Then you'll be the one to lay the foundation," he said. "So tell me, Nouriel, the mystery of the harbingers."

"Tell you what you revealed to me?"

"Yes."

"All of it?"

"In the time we have," he replied, "that wouldn't be possible. But in a nutshell, lay the foundation. Tell me of the nine harbingers."

So I began telling him the revelation he had, years earlier, given to me.

"In the last days of ancient Israel, nine harbingers appeared in the land, warning of national calamity and coming destruction….The same harbingers of warning, the same nine signs of a nation under judgment, have now manifested on American soil. Some have appeared in New York City and Washington, DC, and some have involved American leaders. They've all reappeared, all nine of them, and in precise and eerie detail. And those involved in their reappearing had no idea of the mystery or their part in fulfilling it. And yet it all replayed on American soil, warning of national calamity and judgment."

"And what was the first harbinger of the nine harbingers to manifest in ancient Israel?"

"The breach," I replied. "It happened in the year 732 BC, when Israel's hedge of protection was lifted. An enemy was allowed to strike the land. The strike brought destruction, a destruction that was limited in its scope and duration. But it was enough to shake the nation. It was the wake-up call to a civilization that had grown so hardened and deafened to the call of God that nothing else would get through to it. It was a warning and a call to return."

"And with America?"

"The first harbinger, the breach, manifested on American soil on September 11, 2001, when America's hedge of protection was lifted.

"The enemy was allowed to strike the land in the form of nineteen hijackers. The strike brought destruction in New York and Washington, DC. And yet it was limited in its scope and duration. But it shook the nation. 9/11 was a wake-up call to an America that had grown so hardened and deafened to God's voice that only such an event would get through. And 9/11 was a warning to America and the call to return."

"The second harbinger..."

"The terrorist. The strike on ancient Israel was carried out by the soldiers of the Assyrian Empire. The Assyrians were the world's first terrorists, the first to employ terror as a means to a political end. They were fierce, brutal, and merciless. They would bring terror to the people of any land they chose to invade. So it was when they invaded Israel. The second harbinger was the sign of the terrorist. The destruction is masterminded and carried out not only by the nation's enemies—but by terrorists."

"And with America?"

"The sign of the terrorist appeared on American soil on 9/11. The attack was masterminded and carried out not only by America's enemies but specifically by terrorists. The Assyrians were the fathers of terrorism, and those who carried out the attacks of 9/11 were their spiritual children. Beyond that, the terrorists originated in the same region of the world from which the Assyrians came, the Middle East. And when the Assyrians carried out their strike against Israel, they did so by communicating with each other in Akkadian, a long extinct Middle Eastern language. The closest language in the modern world to ancient Akkadian is

Arabic, the same language spoken by the terrorists of 9/11 and by which they carried out their attack against America."

"And what comes next in the template of judgment?"

"After the attack, things returned to normal, or they appeared to."

"And why do you say they appeared to?" he asked.

"Because things didn't really return to normal. The warning had come. The nation was now given a reprieve, a window of time, a chance to change its course and return to the Lord."

"And if they didn't return?"

"Then, at the end of the window would come greater shakings and calamities."

"And how did Israel respond to the warning?" he asked. "And what did they do in the window of time given them?"

"They refused to listen. They refused to take warning. Instead, they hardened themselves and responded in defiance. They made a vow. The vow was recorded in Isaiah 9:10. And from that vow and verse come the seven other harbingers. They said this:

> The bricks have fallen down, but we will rebuild with hewn stones; the sycamores are cut down, but we will replace them with cedars."

"And what does it mean?"

"They wouldn't repent. They wouldn't be humbled. They wouldn't change their course or relent from their apostasy. Instead, they would come back stronger and greater than before. It was a vow of defiance."

"And what happened to America in the wake of 9/11?"

"America followed the same path of ancient Israel. It responded to the calamity not with humility, not with any return to God, but with defiance."

"And the third harbinger…"

"'The bricks have fallen down.' When the Assyrians invaded the land, they caused bricks to fall. The sign of fallen bricks speaks of destruction, the breaking down of walls, the fall of buildings, and the heaps of ruins that were left in the wake of the Assyrian destruction."

"And with America?"

"The attack of 9/11 specifically involved the fall of walls and buildings.

And the most iconic image in the wake of the calamity was of the heaps of ruins at Ground Zero. And within those ruins were fallen bricks."

"And the fourth harbinger…"

"'But we will rebuild.' They vowed to replace the bricks of clay with hewn stone. Hewn stone would allow them to build stronger buildings than before, bigger, higher, greater. Their buildings would embody the nation's pride. When Isaiah recorded their words, he wrote that they were being spoken in pride and arrogance.[1] In Hebrew, the word he used for *arrogance* is linked to the word for *tower*. The fourth harbinger is the rebuilding of what had fallen, the rise of the tower."

"And how did the fourth harbinger manifest in America?"

"After 9/11, American leaders vowed to rebuild the fallen towers, and not just rebuild them, but rebuild them bigger, better, stronger, and higher than before. The rebuilding of Ground Zero would focus on a single object—*a tower*. The plan was to build the tower of Ground Zero bigger, stronger, and higher than the towers that had fallen.

"It was to reach a height of 1,776 feet, the number that marked the nation's birth. As in ancient Israel, their rebuilding was to become the focal point of the nation's pride and defiance and the embodiment of the nation itself."

"And the fifth harbinger…"

"'But we will rebuild with hewn stone.' The project of rebuilding began with the laying down of hewn stone. The Hebrew word behind hewn stone is *gazit*. The word *gazit* refers to a stone quarried from mountain rock and used for constructing buildings of strength and magnitude. The gazit stone was most often a massive rectangular block of quarried rock. So the people of Israel went to the mountains and quarries and brought back the gazit stone to the ground of the fallen buildings. The gazit, or quarried, stone became the start of the nation's rebuilding, the embodiment of its vow, and the symbol of its defiance."

"And how did the fifth harbinger manifest in America?"

"Nearly three years after 9/11, a massive object descended onto the floor of Ground Zero. It was a gazit stone. It had been quarried out of the mountains of upstate New York, twenty tons of hewn stone. As in ancient times, it was brought to the ground of destruction where the buildings had fallen. On July 4, 2004, American leaders and spectators gathered around the stone in a ceremony that was to mark the beginning of the tower. The leaders pronounced vows over it. One of them, the governor of New York, proclaimed that they were performing the act in the 'spirit of defiance.'[2] As in ancient times, the gazit stone became the embodiment of the nation's vow and the symbol of its defiance."

"And the sixth harbinger..."

"'The sycamores are cut down.' When the Assyrians invaded Israel, they brought destruction not only to the nation's buildings but to its land. The fallen building spoke of the destruction in the cities. But the fallen sycamore epitomized the destruction of the land."

"And in America?"

"On 9/11, in the last moments of destruction, the North Tower of the World Trade Center began to collapse. As it plummeted to the ground, it sent forth a metal beam into the air. The beam struck an object, a tree growing in the soil at the corner of Ground Zero. The tree was a sycamore as in the prophecy. It would be put on display and memorialized and known as the Sycamore of Ground Zero, the sixth harbinger of the vow."

"And the seventh harbinger..."

"'But we will replace them with cedars.' The word *cedar* in the translation stands for the Hebrew word *erez*. The seventh harbinger is the erez tree. The word *erez* speaks of a strong tree, particularly a conifer and, more specifically, a tree of the Pinaceae family. The people of Israel would plant the erez in place of the fallen sycamore. As the erez tree was stronger than the sycamore, it was another symbolic act of defiance; the nation would rise up stronger than before."

"And how did it manifest in America?"

"In 2003, at the end of November, a tree appeared in the sky at the corner of Ground Zero. It was being lowered into place where the Sycamore of Ground Zero had once stood and was struck down. People gathered around the tree and held a ceremony. They noted the symbolic meaning behind the planting of the new tree where the old had once stood. They gave the tree a name. They called it the Tree of Hope and heralded it as a sign of the indomitable nature of human hope. The tree wasn't a sycamore. It was a conifer tree. It was of the Pinaceae family. As in the prophecy, it was an erez tree. So they replaced the fallen sycamore with an erez tree. The ancient sign of defiance and judgment, the sign of the erez tree, that had manifested in ancient Israel now had manifested in New York City at the corner of Ground Zero."

"And the eighth harbinger..."

"The eighth harbinger is the vow itself, the utterance of the vow. In order for the vow to have meaning, it had to represent the nation's course. And so its leaders had to give it voice. And since Israel's leaders ruled from the city of Samaria, it would have been declared in the nation's capital. The leaders utter the words of the vow."

"And its manifestation in America?"

"On September 11, 2004, the third anniversary of the calamity, the Democratic candidate for the vice presidency, Senator John Edwards, gave a speech in the capital city. He opened the speech with the words

> The bricks have fallen, but we will build with dressed stones;
> the sycamores have been cut down, but we will put cedars in
> their place.[3]

"The ancient vow was uttered by an American leader in the nation's capital city. And it wasn't only those words; *the entire speech* was an exposition on that one verse, Isaiah 9:10. It was the utterance of the ancient vow. He had no idea what the words actually meant, or he never would have uttered them. He spoke of the striking down of the sycamore without realizing an actual sycamore had been struck down on 9/11. He spoke of the gazit stone without realizing an actual gazit stone had been laid on Ground Zero to begin the rebuilding. He spoke of the planting of the erez tree where the sycamore had been struck down without realizing that this had actually taken place. And he connected it all to 9/11. He proclaimed a verse that spoke of the warning strike of a nation in the form of a terrorist attack and connected it to 9/11—the verse that identified a nation undergoing the first stage of judgment."

"And the ninth harbinger..."

"The prophecy," I replied. "The vow was not only a declaration but a prophecy of things yet to come. And by appearing in Isaiah 9, it became part of a prophecy of national judgment as well as a matter of national record. So the vow was spoken not only by a national leader and in the capital city but as a prophecy of what was still to come and as a matter of national record."

"And to America?"

"On September 12, 2001," I answered, "the very day after the calamity, the American Congress gathered on Capitol Hill to issue its response to

9/11. The man charged to present that response was the Senate majority leader, Tom Daschle. As he reached the conclusion of his address, he said,

> There is a passage in the Bible from Isaiah, that I think speaks to all of us at times like this.... 'The bricks have fallen down, but we will rebuild with dressed stone; the fig trees have been felled, but we will replace them with cedars.'[4]

"So on the day after 9/11, the nation's response was *exactly* the same as the response of ancient Israel in the wake of the ancient calamity, the first strike of judgment. Daschle spoke of the fallen tree without knowing that there actually existed a tree struck down at the corner of Ground Zero that answered to the tree in the vow. He spoke of the rebuilding with the gazit stone, which would be fulfilled three years after he spoke it. And he spoke of the planting of the erez tree, an act that would manifest two years after he proclaimed it.

"From Capitol Hill and before the United States Congress, the nation, and the world, the Senate majority leader uttered the same words on the day after 9/11 that the leaders of ancient Israel had uttered in the days after their calamity—word for word. And without having any idea what he was doing, he connected the calamity of 9/11 with the calamity of ancient Israel, the opening moment in the judgment of a fallen nation. And so on the day after 9/11 and from Capitol Hill, the leader of the United States Senate unwittingly pronounced judgment on America."

"Well done, Nouriel," said the prophet. "You've laid the foundation. Now we can move to the next revelation. The signs of a nation under judgment...the same signs that appeared in the last days of ancient Israel now manifested in America. And to where do they lead?"

"To the window," I replied, "to the time given for the nation to return."

"And in the case of ancient Israel, what happened?"

"Instead of turning back, they turned away all the more. They went further and further away from God."

"Yes," said the prophet. "When a nation is given the chance to turn back and rejects that chance, it will become all the more brazen, and its fall will deepen and accelerate. The purpose of the shaking is to wake the nation, to turn it back, and to avert the greater calamity."

"Then it begs the question," I said, "it's been years since we last spoke of these things. Since that time, has there been any turning back?"

"No," said the prophet. "America's overall descent from God has only progressed. And it was all set forth on the day after 9/11 on Capitol Hill. After the Senate majority leader finished proclaiming the ancient vow of defiance, he said, 'That is what we will do.'[5] He was proclaiming that America would follow in the path of ancient Israel, the path of defiance, apostasy, and destruction. It would respond to the calamity of 9/11 as had Israel in its last days as a nation. It was all there the very day after 9/11."

"But did America have to follow in the ancient course?"

"No. But it did. That was its choice. And so the mystery continues."

"So in the time since we last saw each other, America's fall from God has continued."

"Not only continued," he said, "but accelerated and deepened and in virtually every way and realm...from abandoning the ways of God to increasingly warring against them, from tolerating immorality to brazenly championing it, by indoctrinating its children away from the ways of God, by vilifying those who refuse to join in its apostasy but hold true to the ways of God, by seeking to silence and punish them, by shedding innocent blood, by not only calling evil good and good evil but establishing it, legislating it, and executing it, by sanctifying the profane and profaning the sacred..."

"So where does this all leave us with regard to the harbingers?"

"As the nation's fall has continued, so have the manifestations of the harbingers."

At that, he reached into his coat pocket; took out a seal of the same size, shape, and color as the others; and placed it in my hand. Then he rose to his feet.

"Until we meet again," he said as he turned away from the ocean and began walking away.

"Do you need a ride?" I asked. "I have a boat, you know."

He turned around and smiled and, within a minute, was gone.

◆◆◆

"How do you suppose he left the island?" she asked.

"I don't know. I learned not to ask or try to figure it out."

"And the next mystery..."

"A hidden mystery," said Nouriel, "an ancient mystery hidden before the eyes of an entire nation."

Chapter 18

The Babylonian Word

S O WHAT WAS on the seal?"

"It was hard to figure it out. The overall image seemed amorphous. But within it was a second shape, slightly less undefined, something of a rectangle, but irregular, with no absolutely straight lines. Within the rectangular-like shape were two symbols, two letter *I*'s or two number 1s."

"So what was it?"

"I had no idea. But it wasn't the only clue. I had a dream."

"As with the city on the hill," she said, "you were given a seal and a dream."

"Yes," said Nouriel, "that was the pattern now. Every revelation would be linked to a seal and a dream. The difference was that now the prophet wasn't appearing in my dreams—but in reality. Maybe that's why I was given a seal as well, because I needed more to go on. I had to try to figure out the meaning of the mystery on my own—at least until the next time I encountered him."

"So what was the dream?"

"It came soon after I returned from Massachusetts Bay. It wasn't long or complex, but it was puzzling. I was overlooking a landscape of ruins. I saw what seemed to be a sheet of parchment covered with writing rise up from the ruins and stand upright on its edge. Then another parchment rose up from the ruins and stood edge to edge with the first...then a third and a fourth until they formed a square, and then a fifth that covered the top to form a box—but all of parchments. Then I noticed a stirring in the ruins under the box, more parchments, larger than the first, rising to their edges to form another square and box that lifted up the first box. The process repeated itself over and over again until it formed a tower, a tall, stepped tower of parchments."

"A ziggurat," said Ana, "a ziggurat of parchments. So what did you make of it?"

"The dream began in the ruins. The image on the seal was amorphous, like ruins. The rectangular shape, I believe, represented the parchment. So I figured it had something to do with the tower at Ground Zero."

"The ruins and the tower, yes."

"But beyond that, I didn't know where to go with it."

"But you went somewhere with it."

"I went to New Jersey. I had just finished attending a meeting there and had about two hours of free time. I decided to go outside to go for a walk. I made my way to the waterfront, where I found a park. It was technically a park, but it looked more like a wooden pier or dock. Across the river were the steel and glass buildings of lower Manhattan now beaming with the orange light of the late afternoon sun. Most striking was the tower."

"The tower of the World Trade Center."

"Yes, the harbinger. I stood by the railing at the edge of the park and gazed across the Hudson. And then he appeared."

"The prophet."

"Yes, in his long, dark coat, standing to my left and gazing with me across the waters."

"Another appointed moment."

◆◆◆

"So what have you been able to make of the mystery?" he asked.

"It has something to do with the tower and parchments or *a* parchment."

"When Jerusalem was destroyed by the armies of Babylon, the prophetic word came forth from the ruins. It became the Book of Lamentations. After the calamity of 9/11, the eyes of America were drawn to the ruins of Ground Zero. Could there have been a prophetic word waiting there, hidden in the ruins?"

"In the ruins of Ground Zero?" I replied. "If there was, I never heard of it."

"There was," he said. "There was a word in the ruins."

"A word on what?"

"On paper."

"The parchments in my dream and on the seal."

"It was unlikely that such a fragile object would survive the destruction of 9/11 intact and the days of burning at Ground Zero. There were some other papers around it but mostly burned, charred, obscured, or pulverized. But one remained intact, visible, with charring, but legible. It was hidden there for many days, waiting in the ruins to be uncovered."

"By whom?"

"A photographer who was chronicling the mission of the rescue workers there. It was night. He was standing in the ruins by a steep incline and a cement barrier. He noticed some charred papers at the barrier's edge. He asked the one overseeing the operations for permission to find out what was there and to record it. Permission was granted, but he was told to make it as fast as possible since the area was dangerous.... And then he saw it."[1]

"What was it?"

"It was a page from the Scriptures. The Bible was gone, but the page remained. As he readied to record it, he was called to come out. He quickly recorded a few images, then exited the site, leaving the scripture behind."

"Did he see what it said?"

"No, he didn't have time. But later that night, with the aid of a magnifying glass, he began examining the proof shots of what he recorded that day. When he read the words of the scripture, he was left in shock. He broke down and wept."[2]

"What was it?" I asked.

"It was a scripture that spoke of a tower."

"What tower?"

"A tower that was built for the pride of man."

"The Tower of Babel?"

"Yes."

"So in the ruins of the fallen towers was a word about the Tower of Babel?"

"Yes."

"The ziggurat in my dream."

"The tower that embodied the coming together of the world."

"As did the World Trade Center."

"The word in the ruins spoke of those who set out to build it and the reason why:

They said, 'Now let's build a city with a tower that reaches the sky, so that we can make a name for ourselves.'[3]

"So too those who set out to build the Twin Towers did so to erect the tallest buildings on earth, *towers that would reach the sky*, or, as other versions render it, whose tops would be '*in the heavens*.' The word from Ground Zero also spoke of the materials by which the tower would be built:

They said to one another, 'Come on! Let's make bricks and bake them hard.' So they had bricks to build with.[4]

"They used bricks. Does that sound familiar?"

"'The bricks have fallen,' the words of Isaiah 9:10, the words of the vow."

"And behind the English, the same Hebrew word used for the building of the Tower of Babel is used of the fallen buildings in the vow of Isaiah 9:10—'the bricks have fallen.'"

"And that word," I said, "was found in the actual ruins of the fallen buildings...and in those ruins were actual fallen bricks."

"So in the ruins of the World Trade Center was a scripture that spoke of a tower built to reach the heavens, a tower that embodied the coming together of the world, and a tower that embodied the pride and arrogance of man."

"And all those things could be said of the Twin Towers."

"And the words on that page spoke of something else."

"What do you mean?"

"They spoke of judgment," said the prophet, "the judgment that came against the tower."

"Something I don't understand: the parchment on the seal didn't have any writing on it, just two symbols. What did they represent?"

"What did you think they were?"

"Two I's or two 1s."

"Not exactly."

"The two towers?"

"The two towers were built in the same shape, but no. It was the number 11."

"An 11 as in September 11?"

"Yes."

"And flight 11, the plane that struck the first tower."

"Yes," he replied, "it was a day of elevens. But the reason it appeared on the parchment of the seal was because of Babel."

"What do you mean?"

"The Tower of Babel appears in the Book of Genesis. Do you know where?"

"No."

"In the *eleventh* chapter. It appears in the eleventh chapter of that book and the eleventh chapter of Scripture itself."

"So September 11, the day of elevens, was linked to the eleventh chapter of the Bible...and lying in its ruins was the eleventh chapter of the Bible—the account of a tower that embodied the pride of man and led to judgment."

"Yes, but the scripture wasn't only about that which had been," said the prophet, "but that which was yet to come."

"How?"

"The scripture of Ground Zero spoke in the future tense: 'Now let's build a city with a tower.'[5] It was a call to embark on a construction project, the call to build a tower. So the words were prophetic. America would again set out to build itself a tower. And unlike the fallen World Trade Center, that which would rise up in its place would take the form of just one tower, as in the scripture of the ruins.

"And as in the ancient scripture, the tower that rose up from Ground Zero was begun with the intention of constructing the tallest building in the world. The account begins with these words:

> The people of the whole world had only one language and used
> the same words.[6]

"What did we say was the connection between the tower and the world?"

"The tower embodied the world coming together as one."

"Notice the words that appear in that opening verse—the word *world* appears once, and the word *one* appears twice, just as it does in the original Hebrew. So the scripture in the ruins of Ground Zero spoke of a tower linked to the words *one* and *world*. And thus the name of the tower would be...*One World* Trade Center."

"Why did they name it that?"

"The name was formed from its address. But the result was a tower intended to be the tallest building in the world and marked with the words *one* and *world*…as in the Tower of Babel."

"And both towers," I said, "were built in the spirit of defiance."

"And there was another mystery in the word of the ruins."

"Tell me."

"The call of defiance that led to the Tower of Babel and was preserved on that piece of paper was this:

> Now let's build a city with a tower."[7]

"And?"

"When, in ancient times, the Hebrew Bible was translated into Greek, in a translation called the Septuagint, when the translators came to Isaiah 9:10, to the vow of defiance, they did a strange thing. They rendered it:

> The bricks are fallen down, but *come…let us build for ourselves a tower*."[8]

"You had told me of that translation in our first encounters."

"The ancient translation connects the words of Israel's vow of defiance in Isaiah 9:10 with the words spoken in Genesis to build the Tower of Babel. And those same words were hidden there in the wreckage of the fallen tower."

"How many times do those words appear in the Bible?" I asked.

"Only twice," he answered, "in the call to build the Tower of Babel in Genesis and in the vow to rebuild the ruins of Israel in Isaiah 9:10."

"So, 'Come let us build for ourselves…a tower' is a translation of Genesis 11 and of Isaiah 9:10. And the words all there in the ruins of Ground Zero…the words of Babel and the words used to translate Isaiah 9:10, the vow from which the harbingers come. It was all there."

"Yes," said the prophet, "from the very beginning, from the moment the towers fell, from the moment the bricks were fallen, it was all there. As it was written in ancient times, the 'bricks are fallen down, but come…let us build for ourselves a tower.'[9]

"And the words were prophetic. They would build for themselves a tower at Ground Zero. And they would do so in the spirit of Babel. For the same spirit that possessed the people of Babel and, then, the people of Israel now possessed America.

◆◆◆

"And what happened to the page?" asked Ana.

"No one knows. The photographer regretted that he didn't attempt to take it with him as he rushed off the site. Undoubtedly it was lost in the ruins. But it was preserved in the photograph."

"How did those who heard of the picture react?"

"Some took the fact that it had to do with the building of a tower as a good sign, an encouragement to rebuild, not realizing how far removed this was from its actual meaning. But others realized right away that for a scripture to appear in those ruins, telling of the Tower of Babel, was nothing other than ominous."

"And what happened next?"

"The prophet asked me for the seal, which, of course, I gave him. He slipped it into his coat pocket, took out another, and placed it in my hand."

"What was it?"

"Something so simple that I didn't know how to interpret it or if there was anything to interpret at all. And yet it would lead me to a sign, a transformation taking place in the midst of New York City overlooked by the thousands who passed it by...and yet a warning of judgment from the time of the prophets."

Chapter 19

The Withered

A ND SO WHAT was it?"

"A branch," he replied. "I didn't know what to make of it. I tried searching the internet to see if I could identify the tree it was from. But there were too many branches too similar in appearance to the branch on the seal. And then I had a dream.

"I was walking inside a very large covered garden."

"Covered with..."

"With vines and branches. But not just covered...surrounded. The vines and branches were all around me, forming the garden's walls and curving into the roof. Nothing was straight. Everything was curved. And everything was withered, the leaves, the plants, the fruits, the vines—everything.

"As I continued walking, I spotted a little girl at the other end. She was holding a pitcher of water and crying. I approached her and asked why she was crying. She replied, 'Because my garden won't grow. I did everything right. I planted it in good soil. I watered it every day. I cared for it. But no matter what I did, it withered away. No matter what I do, still it withers away.'

"I tried to comfort her, but she wouldn't be consoled. So I continued walking through the garden until I saw an opening, an exit in its walls, which I took. I then found myself in the middle of the city, standing on a sidewalk, with multitudes passing by. I turned back to look at the covered garden. It was only then that I saw what it was. It was all shaped into the form of an eagle—a colossal eagle of vines and branches. And the dream ended."

"So what did you do?"

"Both the dream and the seal had to do with plants or trees. So I decided to make a trip to a place that might give me something to go on—the New York Botanical Garden."

"You had been there before in your first encounters with the prophet, when you were trying to figure out the meaning behind one of the seals he had given you."

"Yes."

"And from what I remember, it was a dead end."

"Yes. But now it was the only thing I could think of. So I went there and inquired if there was anyone there who could help identify the branch on the seal. They referred me to one of their experts. He examined the image. But there wasn't enough detail for him to make any identification."

"Another dead end," said Ana.

"Not exactly. The other reason I went there was because it was filled with covered gardens, glass-covered gardens, but still covered, and many of them curved, as in the dream."

"So what did you find?"

"A lot of beautiful plants and flowers and trees."

"No little girl with a watering pitcher?"

"No, and nothing to go on. Finally, I decided to go outside and walk the grounds. I found myself in a forest, a unique forest...fifty acres of forest, streams, pools, Indian trails, and trees, many of which went back centuries. I was on one of the walking trails deep into the woods when I saw him, standing there waiting for me."

"The prophet...in the woods?"

"Yes."

———— ◆◆◆ ————

"A nice place for a walk," he said.

"I didn't know you went for walks."

"I came to walk with you, Nouriel. Come," he said. So I walked with him down the trail, deeper into the heart of the forest.

"This," he said, "is what New York City looked like before there was a New York City."

"It's a bit different," I said, "certainly more peaceful."

"Tell me what you've found."

So I told him of the dream and my failed attempt to find a match for the branch on the seal.

"You came here the last time seeking the meaning of the fallen sycamore."

"Of Isaiah 9:10, yes."

"And so the mystery has brought us again to a place of trees. In the Scriptures, trees are of great significance. They represent life and blessings, but also people, nations, and kingdoms. And they can signify more than that. They can also stand as warnings and signs of judgment."

"How?"

"Show me the seal."

So I pulled it out of my coat pocket and gave it to him. He held it up as we walked, so I was able to look at it as he spoke.

"You were seeking to find out what kind of branch it was. But that wasn't the key. It wasn't so much the type of branch that mattered, but its state. Look at it. Did you notice it had no fruit…or leaves? And your dream, it wasn't so much about what was in the garden, but the state of a garden itself."

"It was withered," I replied. "And the branch on the seal was a withered branch?"

"And do you know what withering represents in the Bible?"

"No."

"A sign of judgment. The withering of trees and plants stands for the withering of people or nations, the judgment of kingdoms. So it is written in the psalms of those who commit evil:

> For they shall soon be cut down like the grass, and *wither as the green herb.*[1]

"So the withering of the green plant stands for the judgment that comes on those who commit evil. So, in Isaiah, the Lord warns of the judgment to come on an evil culture:

> *For you will be like a tree whose leaves wither,* like an orchard that is unwatered.[2]

"And so in the Book of Jeremiah, God warns the entire nation of the coming calamity:

> At the time of their punishment they shall be brought down…There will be no grapes on the vine and no figs on the fig tree, *and the leaf will wither.*[3]

"The same prophetic symbolism appears in the New Testament with the withering away of the fig tree, an event taken to signify coming judgment."

"And what does it have to do with now?"

"In Isaiah 9:10, in the wake of the attack on the land, the people of Israel vowed to replace the fallen sycamores with a stronger tree."

"The Hebrew erez tree."

"And in America, in the wake of 9/11, the people of New York City replaced the fallen sycamore with a stronger tree, the erez tree. And the erez tree was made into a symbol of resurgence, just as it was in the ancient vow."

"And they planted it in the exact spot in which the fallen sycamore had been struck down."

"They did exactly as Israel did in its last days before judgment. And as in ancient times, it was an act of defiance. The erez tree was a symbol that the nation would rise up stronger and greater than before. Do you remember when the erez tree was planted at Ground Zero?"

"It was in November of 2003."

"And since then, Nouriel, the mystery hasn't stopped and the harbingers have not ceased to speak."

"What do you mean?"

"The erez tree was planted on ground where other trees had prospered and in the exact spot where another had blossomed. It should have prospered.

"But something else happened instead, something as biblically significant as the tree itself. The ancient phenomenon began to manifest."

"The withering?"

"Yes, the ancient sign of judgment began manifesting at the corner of Ground Zero. The erez tree, the symbol of America's resurgence, began to wither away."

"Why?"

"No one knew why. It was a mystery. The keepers of the grounds tried everything they could to make it prosper. But no matter what they did, no matter what solution or treatment they applied, it just kept withering away. It took on an increasingly sickly appearance, and yet no sickness could be identified.

"Every year, it became that much more barren. And what green was left on its branches began transforming to a deathly brown.

"The keepers of the grounds planted shrubs in a line starting near the fence that enclosed the property and ending by the tree, just a few feet from its roots. The shrubs farthest away from the tree were strong, green, and healthy. The shrubs closest to the tree began to likewise wither away, turning brown, dry, sickly, and deathly. It was as if there was a curse on that tree and on whatever came near it."

"That's what my dream was about. The garden was withering away, and the little girl couldn't stop it. Even though she planted it in good soil, it still withered away. No matter what she did, it kept withering."

"Yes, and the same imagery was used two and a half thousand years ago, in the Book of Ezekiel, when the Lord gave a prophecy concerning the days of judgment that would come upon the king and his kingdom:

> It was planted in good soil by many waters, to bring forth branches, bear fruit....All of its spring leaves will wither....Behold, it is planted, will it thrive? Will it not utterly wither...? It will wither in the garden terrace where it grew."[4]

"So it could have almost been written about the tree at Ground Zero."

"The tree in the prophecy," he said, "was a symbol. So too the tree at Ground Zero was a symbol. It was the seventh of the nine harbingers. And in the ancient vow, the erez tree was the symbol of the nation's defiance of God and the embodiment of its intention to come back stronger and greater than before."

"So it was the withering of a sign," I said.

"And a sign," said the prophet, "of withering."

"The withering of what?"

"Of that which the sign represents. So what was it that the erez tree represented?"

"The nation's coming back stronger and greater than before, but without God."

"And so its withering is a sign that all these things will be undone, and more than that. The erez tree ultimately represented the nation itself. The nation would become as strong as an erez tree and stronger than its former state, as an erez tree is stronger than a sycamore. The tree stood for the nation."

"In my dream...the garden was shaped into the form of an eagle...because it represented America."

"What was the name they gave to that erez tree at Ground Zero?"

"The Tree of Hope."

"They were transforming it into a symbol, a symbol of hope, an embodiment of a people, a nation, rising up from calamity and the ground of destruction."

"So then the withering of that tree, that symbol..."

"Signifies the withering of a nation," he replied.

"The withering of America?"

"Yes."

"How?"

"Morally," he said, "and spiritually, America was withering away. A diseased tree, on the surface and for a time, may appear strong and alive as in past days, but below the surface is decay. So it was with America. It was a nation withering, its core decaying, its center deteriorating, a civilization in spiritual and moral decay."

"No matter what the little girl did to save it, it kept withering."

"As so it was with the Tree of Hope."

"So then is there hope for the tree?" I asked. "Can it be saved?"

"Do you mean for the Tree of Hope, or America?"

"For America. Is there hope?"

"A disease that lies in the spirit cannot be cured by that which doesn't."

"Meaning?"

"A spiritual disease cannot be answered by cures rooted in other realms, political cures, economic cures, ideological cures. No such cure can stop the withering. A spiritual disease can only be answered by a spiritual cure. Apart from that there is no hope."

"And so for America..."

"America was planted as a tree of hope. But if such a tree should cut itself off from its roots, then what hope is left. Then it has no choice but to wither away."

◆◆◆

"It must have been disturbing," said Ana, "for those who planted the tree at Ground Zero to watch it wither away like that."

"It was," he replied, "but there was nothing they could do about it."

"So the prophet gave you another seal?"

"Yes, as we came out of the forest."

"And what would it lead to?"

"Something very different," said Nouriel. "It would take me to a place I had never been to before, and to an ancient day I had never heard of, and to ramifications that were, to say the least, ominous."

Chapter 20

The Ninth of Tammuz

So what was on the seal?"

"An ancient-looking building with columns, capitols, a frieze, a triangular-shaped roof, and wide steps leading up to its entrance. I imagined it was some sort of Greek or Roman Temple. To the right and left of the steps were two figures, a man and a woman, each seated on some sort of throne. But the strange thing about the temple was its columns. There were eight of them. Two began at the same base, then spread out upward to end at two separate capitols. Two others crisscrossed each other, forming a giant *X*."

"And what did you think it meant?" she asked.

"I came up with several different ideas, but none of them led me anywhere."

"And then?"

"And then I had a dream. I was inside some sort of ancient temple."

"As on the seal?"

"I couldn't say. I didn't know what it looked like from the outside. But inside the temple were priests."

"What kind of priests?"

"I would imagine, pagan priests."

"How would you know what pagan priests look like?"

"I wouldn't. But they looked as I would have expected pagan priests to look like, had I known what they looked like. Their heads were shaved, and they were wearing long, dark robes. I counted five of them. They were holding a parchment."

"All of them?"

"Yes. It was a large piece of parchment, the size of a small table. Together they carried it up a stone staircase. They reached the top and were overlooking a stone altar by a blazing fire. They raised up the parchment, then dropped it into the flames.

"And then everything changed. I was now standing outside the colossal walls of what I presumed to be an ancient city. Surrounding me was an ancient army with shields and spears and siege works. But they were just standing there, waiting. I'm not any kind of expert on such things, but for some reason I knew it was the army of Babylon.

"Suddenly, there was a commotion. The soldiers began pointing upward to pillars of smoke that were ascending to the sky from inside the walls. I knew that the smoke was coming from the altar inside the temple. It was the parchment that had been cast into the flames.

"'It is the sign,' said one of them, the one who appeared to be their commander, 'a sign that today is the day that their walls come down and their hedges will be broken.' At that, the army began attacking the colossal wall, pounding it with their siege works over and over again until a breach opened up. And then it all collapsed.

"I had expected to see the inside of an ancient city. Instead, the breaking of the wall opened up to me a vast landscape of many cities, fields, towns, and houses. It was as if I were looking at an entire nation, a civilization. The soldiers began pouring through the opening. And the dream came to an end."

"And what did you make of it?" she asked.

"As far as the priests and the parchment, I had no idea. But the scene at the wall seemed clear enough. It was the siege of a walled city, and yet it had to do with more than a walled city."

"So where did you go from there?"

"And apart from the possibility that the temple on the seal could have been the same as in the dream, I didn't see any connections. I looked for images of ancient priests, but I didn't find anything that quite matched what I saw in my dream or anything that had to do with the burning of parchment."

"So what did you do?"

"Nothing, until one day as I was reexamining the seal, it hit me. What if the image wasn't that of an ancient temple...but a modern one?"

"What do you mean?"

"There are modern buildings that look like ancient temples."

"Where?"

"In the nation's capital. I began searching the internet for images of buildings from Washington, DC."

"And?"

"It wasn't long before I found it. It had eight columns, as did the building on the seal. Leading up to its entrance were wide steps framed with two statues, a seated man on one side, and a seated woman on the other. It could easily have passed for a classical temple."

"Which building?"

"The Supreme Court."

"But what would the Supreme Court have to do with ancient Babylonians?"

"That's what I set out to find."

"Set out?"

"For Washington, DC. I booked a hotel there for three nights. I figured it would be enough time to find whatever I was meant to find. But it turned out that I wouldn't need it. My train arrived in Union Station in midafternoon. I took a taxi to my hotel and then, from my hotel, to the Supreme Court. I arrived there in the early evening. The building was lit up, giving the wall behind the columns a warm glow of incandescent yellow and orange.

"I had, of course, taken the seal with me. I removed it from my coat pocket and compared it with what was before me. Everything matched, the shape, the steps, the roof, the two statues, everything but the strange anomalies in the columns of the image."

◆◆◆

"The highest court in the land," said the voice.

I turned around, and there he was. His gaze wasn't directed at me but upward to the building's facade.

"The *Supreme* Court," he said. "Here the judges preside, and from here they hand down their judgments. But it is not the highest court. There is one of much higher authority…and a Judge far more supreme."

"Why are we here?" I asked.

"Tell me your dream," he said, "and I'll tell you why we're here."

So I told him.

"What you saw in your dream was the beginning of the end of Jerusalem and the kingdom of Judah. The army outside the city walls was, as you believed, that of Babylon. The end began in the fourth month of the Hebrew year."

"How?"

"The Book of Jeremiah records how it happened:

> Nebuchadnezzar king of Babylon and all his army came against Jerusalem, and besieged it....In the fourth month, on the ninth day of the month, the city was penetrated.[1]

"It was on that day that the first of Jerusalem's defensive walls was broken through. The city's defenses were breached. The account continues:

> So it was, when Zedekiah the king of Judah and all the men of war saw them, that they fled and went out of the city by night, by way of the king's garden, by the gate between the two walls.[2]

"With the breaking down of the city's wall of defense, the end was sealed. Those charged with the city's protection abandoned it and fled. The way was now opened for destruction and judgment. Just four verses after the words that record the breach in the wall comes this:

> And the Chaldeans burned the king's house and the houses of the people with fire, and broke down the walls of Jerusalem. Then Nebuzaradan the captain of the guard carried away captive to Babylon the remnant of the people who remained in the city.[3]

"The breaching of the city's wall of defense led directly to the destruction of the Temple, the city of Jerusalem, and the nation itself. Thus the day it happened was most significant and critical. The account reveals the day:

> In the fourth month, on the ninth day of the month...[4]

"It was the ninth day of the fourth month."
"And the fourth month of the Hebrew year is called what?" I asked.
"*Tammuz*," he replied, "the month of Tammuz."
"So the ninth of Tammuz was the day that the end began."
"Yes," said the prophet, "and so it became a day of sorrow, fasting, and mourning."

"OK, so the ninth of Tammuz was the day that sealed the destruction of Israel. But I'm not seeing what it has to do with the Supreme Court."

"Come," he said.

At that, he led me up the steps and over to the right by the platform on which rested the statue of a seated man. He held a sword in his left hand and a tablet of stone against his shoulder.

"The Guardian of Law," he said. "His charge is to guard the law. But what happens if the nation itself turns away from the law of God?"

"I don't know."

"When a nation turns away from God and the foundation on which it was established, the turning of spirit will inevitably lead to a turning of values, the changing of standards, laws, and precepts. It will rewrite the tablets. It will alter the underpinnings on which it stands. That which it had long upheld as right, it will now judge as evil, and what it had long opposed as wrong, it now champions.

"So it was for ancient Israel. What they once knew as immoral they now celebrated, and what they once revered they now despised. Those who opposed the ways of God, they now lifted up, and those who upheld His ways, the righteous and the prophets, they now persecuted. So the prophet Isaiah wrote of his nation's metamorphosis:

> Woe to those who call evil good, and good evil; who put darkness for light, and light for darkness; who put bitter for sweet, and sweet for bitter![5]

"In the last days of ancient Israel, this metamorphosis entered the realm of sexuality. The nation's culture had once upheld the sanctity of sexuality and of marriage as its sacred vessel. But now it turned away from both and embraced sexual immorality. Marriage was defiled and desecrated. The sacred was profaned; the profane was sanctified.

"And what of America?" asked the prophet. "If America has likewise turned away from God, then we will witness the same metamorphosis, the same transformation of values. And what the nation once knew to be right, it will now war against, and what it once knew to be wrong, it will now celebrate. It will turn away from the sanctity of marriage and sexuality and will embrace that which wars against the ways of God."

"And it has," I said.

"Who was it," asked the prophet, "in ancient Israel that sanctioned this transformation, who authorized the metamorphosis of its values?"

"Its kings?"

"Yes, its kings and its priests, the keepers of its values."

"And the priests of America would be its clergy?"

"America has no single clergy," he said, "but it does have priests of another kind, a secular priesthood that has sanctioned the altering of its values."

"The priests I saw in my dream officiated in the temple, and the temple represented the Supreme Court. So its priests would be the judges, the justices of the court...in their dark robes."

"Come," he said as he led me up the remainder of the steps. We were now standing in front of the great bronze doors that formed the building's entrance.

"Beyond these doors," said the prophet, "reside the high priests of American culture, those who sit as the keepers of the nation's standards, the sanctifiers of its values. The priests play a central role in the apostasy of a civilization and the fall of a nation. They will either uphold its spiritual and moral foundations and resist the nation's apostasy...or they will sanctify, sanction, and seal the nation's apostasy. In the fall of ancient Israel, they sanctified it...and so too in the fall of America. So the sealing of the metamorphosis will be manifest in this house, in this temple."

"There are nine Supreme Court justices," I said. "But in my dream, I only saw five. Why?"

"Because your dream concerned a specific event. And there were five who took part in it."

"The parchment," I said, "what was it? What did it represent?"

"It represented a sacred foundation on which civilization has stood for ages."

"Which was?"

"Marriage," he said. "And upon that foundation has rested the family, and upon the family, society, and upon society...civilization. And yet, it was even more than that. Marriage is intrinsically bound to the foundation of human life and human nature, the distinction and bond of male and female."

"And the destruction of that parchment represented a specific act or sin against that foundation?"

"More than a specific sin and beyond any specific act, person, or people. All have sinned, and thus all are in the same place, and to all He extends His mercy and love, and so must His children. But what you saw represented the turning away of an entire civilization."

"What I saw was the priests letting the parchment fall into the flames of the altar."

"Yes, and so this Supreme Court took the covenant of marriage as it had been known and upheld for ages and brought it to an end."

"To an end?"

"The end of what it had been for ages. Its essence, its core, the covenantal bond of male and female, was, with one act, struck down, the reason for its existence nullified, the sacred vessel annulled."

"Annulled," I repeated.

"Divorced from its purpose," he replied.

"But I still don't see the connection between what happened here and what happened in my dream...at the wall."

"But in your dream," he said, "it was connected. It was the smoke from the burning parchment that alerted the soldiers at the wall that the day had come."

"Yes, but what would the Supreme Court ruling have to do with a wall?"

"The fall of ancient Israel began with a breach in the wall, the breaking of the hedge that protected the city. What took place in this house, this court, was the breaching of the wall, the breaking down of a hedge by which a civilization was preserved."

"So that's the connection?"

"More than that," he said, "in the case of ancient Israel, it was the breach in the wall that protected a civilization that had fallen from God and was heading toward judgment. Once the wall was breached, there was nothing to stop its descent to judgment.

"America is now a civilization fallen from God and heading toward judgment—yet it was even more than that."

"What do you mean?"

"That ruling, the ending of marriage as it had always been known, came on June 26, 2015."

"And?"

"But on the Hebrew calendar, the biblical calendar, the day had a different name."

"What day was it on the Hebrew calendar?"

"The ninth of Tammuz."

"The ninth of Tammuz!"

"The day of the falling walls. The day of the breach. The day of the breaking down of the hedge...the ninth of Tammuz, the same day that the soldiers of Babylon penetrated the walls of the holy city, the day of victory and celebration for Babylon but of sorrow and mourning for the people of God, as it would remain for ages."

"And the day, you said, that the nation's defenses were abandoned."

"Yes," said the prophet, "when its princes and leaders, those entrusted with the protection of that civilization, ceased from protecting it."

"And so with America..."

"Yes," said the prophet, "as it was for Israel, so too it was for the nation founded after its pattern. On the ninth of Tammuz, the wall that formed a protective hedge surrounding American civilization was broken."

"And for ancient Israel," I said, "the ninth of Tammuz was the beginning of the end. And with America?"

"The breaching of the wall by the Babylonians opened up a floodgate that would usher in the nation's destruction....So too with America."

"The ninth of Tammuz," I said, "was the day that the walls holding back judgment fell down. So that which takes place on the ninth of Tammuz unleashes events and forces that lead to destruction. What happens on that day constitutes the beginning of the end."

"After which," he replied, "it is only a matter of time."

It was then that it hit me. I don't know why I didn't see it before. I pulled the seal out of my pocket and looked at the temple, at the irregular columns of its facade.

"Those are Roman numerals," I said.

"Yes. The two columns at each end are framing the number."

"And this is a *V*," I said of the two columns that spread upward and outward, "the Roman numeral five. And this is an *X*," I said of the intersecting columns, "the Roman numeral ten. And the rest of the columns represent the Roman numeral one."

"Put it together, Nouriel."

"The *I* and the *V* to its right would form the number four. And the *I* with the *X* to its right would form the number nine.... The fourth month, the ninth day...the ninth of Tammuz!"

"Yes."

"A nation on the brink of judgment. Is this what *could* happen...or that which *must* happen...and *will* happen?"

"If the course is unchanged, Nouriel, then so too will be its end."

He was silent after that. I didn't know if he was waiting for me to say something or letting me take it in. But there was nothing I could say.

"Come," he said, turning away from the building and toward the street. "Let's leave this place."

He began walking down the steps. I followed. When we reached the bottom, he turned around one last time, looking up at the building.

"This is not the *supreme* court," he said. "There is one higher."

And then it was as if he was no longer speaking *of* the court but *to* the court.

"If a nation," he said, "should uphold the ways of the Almighty, then it shall be upheld. But if it should pass judgment upon the ways of the Almighty, then upon that nation shall the judgment of the Almighty be passed."

He turned around and began walking away. But I just stood there. There was something about what he had just done that left me shaken.

He turned around once more.

"Are you coming?"

He waited until I caught up with him, then asked me for the seal. I gave it to him, and he handed me another.

◆◆◆

"And what was the next mystery?" she asked.

"It concerned a word that determines the destiny of nations...the fate of America...a hidden word."

"Hidden?"

"Hidden somewhere in New York City...a word I was to search for and find."

Chapter 21

The Hidden

WHAT WAS THE image on the seal?"

"Letters," replied Nouriel. "I took it to be a word inscribed in an ancient script. In back of the letters was a cloud. I recognized the script. I had seen it before. It was Paleo-Hebrew, the oldest form of written Hebrew. But of course, I had no idea what it meant."

"And you had a dream?"

"Yes. I saw an ancient king sitting on a throne. The throne was metallic red. On the armrest to the king's left was a red chisel. And on the armrest to his right was a red hammer. Taking one in each hand, he rose from his throne and walked into the distance ahead of him. He came to a massive structure of scaffolding, as at a construction site, maybe fifty feet high. He ascended a series of wooden steps within the scaffolding until he reached the platform that formed its top.

"In front of him was a cloud, hovering low to the earth, half of it below the king and half of it above him. He set the chisel toward the cloud, lifted up his hammer, and drove it into the chisel as if to sculpt or engrave it."

"How do you engrave a cloud?" asked Ana.

"I don't know, but the moment the chisel struck the cloud, there came flashes of red sparks. He struck the chisel again and again and again. He was engraving letters, glowing red letters, onto the white of the cloud. The letters were of the same script as on the seal, Paleo-Hebrew. When he finished engraving what I took to be a word, the cloud and the word moved to his left, and another cloud came from the right to take its place. Again, the king chiseled out a word in red letters, and again, the cloud moved to his left. This happened several times.

"The clouds, with their red letters, formed a ring. When the king finished his engraving, the ring began to rise slowly into the sky until it was hovering over the buildings of an ancient city. When it completed its ascent, it turned black. The letters, though, remained glowing red.

The sky darkened. The clouds began to flash from within, as if they were filled with red lightning. The letters also began to flash. Then bolts of red lightning began shooting out of the clouds upward to the heavens and downward to the city. And the dream ended."

"It matched what was on the seal," she said, "the letters against the cloud. So what did you make of it?"

"A king engraving letters on a cloud...not much. The dream provided me with context, but it was the seal that contained the most definite clue—the actual ancient letters. I searched online for anything that could help me unlock the meaning of the word. I was able to match each symbol on the seal with a letter from the Paleo-Hebrew alphabet, but I had no idea what it meant. I decided to go to the New York Public Library, to the reading room, to research it further and see if I could find anything that would unlock the meaning."

"And what did you find?"

"Not what...but *who*. I was ascending the library's front steps when I heard a voice.

◆◆◆

"You won't find the answer to this one here," he said.

It was, of course, the prophet. He was standing near the top of the steps, near the library's entrance and over to the left. He descended a few steps, then sat down in front of a base, on which stood two pillars, and motioned for me to join him there. So I sat down beside him.

"Then how *will* I find it?" I asked.

"Tell me your dream."

So I did.

"The words," he said, "were those of a king. That's the critical fact."

"Why?"

"Because a nation's king or priest or leader represents the nation and is most critical in determining its course. The words of kings determine the fate of nations. The principle appears throughout the Scriptures. The words of Pharaoh determined the fate of Egypt. The words of the kings of Assyria and Babylon determined the fate of their empires. And in the case of Isaiah 9:10, the vow of defiance would only have consequence if spoken by the nation's leaders. Only they could set the nation's course in defiance and, thus, seal their kingdom for judgment."

"And so the mystery," I said, "has to do with the word of a king that determines the fate of a nation."

"Yes."

"What king?"

"A king you know of."

"What kind of word?"

"A hidden word," he said.

"But if it's the word of a king, why would it be hidden?"

"It was not hidden...but now it is."

"And what does that mean?"

"It's where the word is hidden."

"I don't understand."

"It's hidden in this city."

"The word of a king hidden somewhere in New York City?"

"Yes."

"Where?"

"That, Nouriel, is what you'll have to find out."

And with that, he rose to his feet and began descending the steps.

"It's a big city!" I shouted after him. "Where do I even begin?"

"Not here," he said without turning to look back or pausing his descent. "That should help."

◆◆◆

"So you had to find the word of a king hidden somewhere in New York City."

"Yes, the needle of a mystery in the haystack of a metropolis."

"So what did you do?"

"I thought, 'Where would the word of a king be in New York City?' I went to the Metropolitan Museum and searched through ancient artifacts, medieval artifacts, more recent artifacts...but nothing. Then I searched through the Jewish Museum. But again...nothing. It was then that I questioned my strategy. How could I find something *hidden* in a museum?

"I thought more about the dream and the seal. Both placed the word on a cloud. And since no one writes or engraves words on clouds, the cloud had to represent something else, something on which words *could* be written or engraved. I took the cloud to represent the heights, the highest place on which a word could be written. And the word was somewhere in New York City. What's the highest place a word could be written in the city? A skyscraper. And the tallest skyscraper, the highest possible place, was precisely that which I had always avoided."

"The tower at Ground Zero," she said.

"The harbinger," he replied, "of defiance."

"You avoided it because..."

"Because of everything it represented. I had never set foot inside. But there was a chance that it now held the mystery I was searching for. So I went down to Ground Zero. It was late afternoon when I got there. I couldn't bring myself to go in or even to approach it. I just looked at it from a distance. So many things were running through my mind, so many things connected to it.

"And then I heard the voice."

◆◆◆

"Well done," said the prophet. He was standing beside me.

"So the word of a king is hidden there."

"Yes. Shall we go in?"

"We'd be going inside a harbinger."

"That's where the mystery is. Come."

So we approached the tower and entered one of its ground-floor entrances. He led me to the elevator. He had already arranged for whatever tickets and reservations were needed. And of course, it was all based on the certainty that I would be there at that exact time, which, of course, I was. The elevator was crowded with tourists excited about the prospect of ascending the tower. But I was more apprehensive than anything else.

"We're in an elevator inside a harbinger," I said.

He didn't answer. The ascent was rapid, taking less than a minute to reach the destination. We arrived at the tower's observatory. We were surrounded by glass windows that allowed us to see for miles in every direction. He led me first to the window facing westward to the Hudson River and the New Jersey shoreline.

"Remember the connection," he said, "between the tower and the word. The Tower of Babel was birthed with a word. So too in Isaiah 9:10, that which they rebuilt was begun with a word, the vow of defiance. So too this tower was begun with the utterance of a word. It was birthed the day after 9/11...on Capitol Hill."

"With the speech," I said, "of the Senate majority leader to Congress and the nation."

"With a word," he replied. "'The bricks have fallen, *but we will rebuild*'—not just a word but the ancient vow. So this tower was brought into being by the ancient vow. It's a manifestation of that vow...and that scripture. This soaring American skyscraper was born of an ancient mystery."

"So the tower," I said, "is the manifestation of the word. And the word was given first by the leaders of ancient Israel. So is that the mystery?"

"It's not *this* mystery," he replied.

"Then what?"

"The mystery replays itself in the modern world. So it would be the word of a modern king."

"A modern king?"

"If America is replaying the mystery of ancient Israel, then who would be the modern equivalent of the ancient king?"

"Its leader?"

"Yes."

"So the word of the king is the word of the president."

"Yes."

"Hidden in this tower?"

"Yes."

"The president of the United States hid a word in this tower."

"Yes."

"How?"

"He came to this place."

"To the observatory?"

"No, the tower wasn't finished when he came. But it was rising. It was nearing its completion. So he came to Ground Zero."

"When?"

"Soon after you wrote your first book, the president came to the harbinger."

"And what happened?"

"Before I tell you what happened, we must open up the vow."

"What do you mean?"

"What is the vow?" he asked. "What is its essence?

> The bricks have fallen down, but we will rebuild with hewn
> stones.[1]

"It contains, in essence, three declarations," he said. "The first speaks of what has been, the remembrance of the destruction, the attack: 'The bricks have fallen down.' The second speaks of the nation's undoing of what took place, the calamity, the destruction. It's the nation's defiance in the face of the attack: 'But we will rebuild.' And the third speaks not only of undoing the destruction and rebuilding what had fallen, but of rebuilding something stronger and greater, not with clay bricks but 'with hewn stones.' The nation is declaring that it will come back stronger than before.

"And the next line:

> The sycamores are cut down, but we will replace them with
> cedars.[2]

"It's known as Hebrew parallelism. The vow is repeated in a different form. But note, its essence stays the same. It is, again, made up of three declarations. The first speaks of what has been, the remembrance of the destruction: 'The sycamores are cut down.' The second speaks of the nation's undoing of the destruction: 'But we will replace them.' And the third, the replacing of sycamores with cedars, speaks of coming back stronger than before."

"I understand. But what does it have to do with..."

We walked to the next window. We were now facing southward, toward the New York Bay and the Atlantic Ocean.

"When the president came to Ground Zero, it was for a ceremony. They presented him with a beam. It was a most important beam. It was to be placed on top of the World Trade Center, to seal and embody the tower's completion. He had come to inscribe words on that beam.

"They gave him a pen with which to write the words, a red marker."

"Red," I said, "as in my dream, the king's hammer and chisel were red. What color was the beam?"

"White."

"As with the cloud."

"So the ceremony," he said, "centered on the word of the king. And the word would be inscribed on the beam, and the beam would complete the building of the tower. He could have written anything on that beam."

"So what did he write?"

"How many declarations or aspects did the ancient vow have?"

"Three."

"So the president inscribed three declarations on the beam. How did the ancient vow begin? What was its essence?"

"The first part speaks of the destruction...the remembrance of the calamity."

"The first declaration of the president's inscription was this:

> We remember.[3]

"It was speaking of what had taken place, the destruction. And what was the second declaration of the ancient vow?"

"The nation would undo the destruction: we will rebuild."

"The second declaration of the president's inscription was this:

> We rebuild."[4]

"The same declaration—the same word."

"And the third—what was it?"

"The nation would not only come back—it would come back stronger than before."

"The third declaration of the president's inscription on the beam was this:

> We come back stronger!"[5]

"It's the vow!" I said. "He wrote the vow on the tower."

"Let's put it together, the essence of the vow and the words on the beam. First is the remembrance of the destruction. And the first line on the beam was what?"

"We remember."

"Second is the vow to rebuild. And the second line on the beam was what?"

"We rebuild."

"Third is the vow to come back stronger. And the third line on the beam…"

"We come back stronger."

"The leaders of ancient Israel spoke the vow in the language of their land and day. The leader of America spoke it in the language of his land and day. But the vow remains the same. Listen to the words of a commentary written on Isaiah 9:10, speaking of the words Israel spoke in its last days as a nation:

> *They boasted that they would rebuild* their devastated country and *make it stronger* and more glorious than ever before."[6]

"It speaks of the ancient declaration. Yet it describes as well what the president inscribed on the last beam of the tower. We rebuild. We come back stronger."

We walked to the window facing eastward to the East River, Queens, and Long Island.

"So the tower," he said, "was brought into existence by a word, and, by a word, was sealed."

"Finished with the same word by which it began."

"Because the tower was the manifestation of that word."

"When the word was spoken on Capitol Hill, it was the actual vow, Isaiah 9:10, word for word. The Senate majority leader even said that it was from Isaiah. But when the president wrote those words on the beam, did he realize that?"

"No. And yet he still wrote what he wrote."

"He summed up the vow."

"And more than that," said the prophet.

"What do you mean?"

"I'm going to speak the vow in its original language, as it was spoken and written down two and a half thousand years ago. When I do so, I want you to count the words.

"*L'venim.*"

"One."

"*Nafaloo.*"

"Two."

"*V'Gazit.*"

"Three."

"*Nivneh.*"

"Four."

"*Shikmim.*"

"Five."

"*Gooda'oo.*"

"Six."

"*V'Arazim.*"

"Seven."

"*NaKhalif.*"

"Eight."

"Eight words. The entire vow in the original language consisted of only eight words. By eight words, a nation's fate was decided. By eight words, its judgment was sealed. And by eight words, its entire existence was brought to an end."

"Eight words," I said. "In my dream, the king wrote a word on each cloud. There had to be eight of them. But on the seal, there was only one word. Why?"

"A word of how many letters?" asked the prophet. "Could there have been eight?"

"Yes."

"It wasn't a word, Nouriel. It was eight letters, the eight letters that began the eight words of the vow."

"What about in English? How many words does the vow come out to?"

"Translated into English, the vow comes out to over twenty words. Now I'm going to speak the words that the president inscribed on the tower. I want you to count again as I speak."

"We."

"One."

"Remember."

"Two."

"We."

"Three."

"Rebuild."

"Four."

"We."

"Five."

"Come."

"Six."

"Back."

"Seven."

"Stronger."

"Eight."

"Eight words. Not only does the president's inscription match the ancient vow in its meaning, but it matches the number of words in the ancient vow."

"A vow of eight English words to match a vow of eight Hebrew words."

"By eight Hebrew words, a Hebrew kingdom was destroyed. And now the same vow becomes eight English words."

"And inscribed on the harbinger."

"In the center of the president's inscription, the fourth word, what was it?"

"We remember. We rebuild. The fourth word is *rebuild*."

"The fourth word at the center of the ancient vow is the Hebrew word *nivneh*."

"And what does it mean?"

"Rebuild."

"The same word!"

"It means rebuild, specifically as in 'we will rebuild.'"

"And the word appears on top of the object that represents the very rebuilding spoken of in the vow."

"Eight words on ancient parchments, eight words on the beam of an American skyscraper."

"And by eight words an ancient nation was sealed for judgment and destroyed. And now by eight words…"

"Remember what I told you, Nouriel—the words of kings determine the fate of nations."

"Then it's even more ominous."

"So the tower of defiance, the embodiment of a nation's defiance of God, was crowned with the words of defiance. The harbinger was sealed with the same vow that brought it into existence—a tower of judgment brought to its completion with the words of judgment."

He then led me to the window facing the north. We could now see the rest of the city, the Empire State Building and the skyscrapers of Midtown Manhattan. The sun had set, and everything was lit up.

"Where is it?" I asked.

"Where is what?"

"The words, the inscription. Can I see it?"

"No," he replied. "But you're as close to it now as you'll ever be. The words are hidden inside the walls on the beam that crowns the tower."

"Everything comes together without anyone planning it…all according to the mystery."

"And so it did six months later."

"What happened six months later?"

"Six months after the president inscribed the words on the beam, he was inaugurated for the second time. He chose a man to seal the inauguration with the reciting of a poem. The man called the nation to give thanks not to God but to 'the work of our hands.'[7] Then he gave praise to the work of the nation's hand, to an object, the tower of Ground Zero."

"He called America to give thanks for the harbinger!"

"As he sealed the president's inauguration, he directed the nation to

> …*the last floor* on the Freedom *Tower jutting into a sky* that *yields to our resilience.*[8]

"What does that remind you of, Nouriel?"

"Babel. The last floor of a tower, the top of a tower 'jutting into a sky'…'a tower whose top is in the heavens.'"[9]

"He directed the nation to the top of the tower, to the last floor. What was it that was specifically there on that last floor of that tower?"

"The inscription," I said, "the vow of defiance."

"Defiance," said the prophet, "a tower 'jutting into a sky that yields to our resilience.' The president's inauguration was sealed with words that spoke of the harbinger and called forth the imagery of Babel."

"And the words of Babel," I said, "were there from the beginning in the ruins of Ground Zero, from which the tower would rise."

"And so the highest words in New York City, the highest words in America, the words that its king lifted up to the heavens…were the words of a nation in defiance of God, in defiance of heaven, and under the shadow of judgment."

◆◆◆

"It all goes back to the beginning," said Ana, "to the tower and that vow…a nation in defiance of God.…amazing…and ominous."

"We headed to the elevator and down the tower. I was silent the entire time, not because we were inside the harbinger but because of the ramifications of what he had revealed to me there. It was after we left the building that he asked me for the seal and handed me another.

"This revelation would involve a dream, from which I would awaken in a cold sweat. And it was the reality behind the dream that was even more ominous than the image I was about to see. It belonged to the realm of nightmares. But it was real."

Chapter 22

The Image

THE IMAGE YOU were about to see," she said, "do you mean the image on the seal?"

"No," said Nouriel. "The image on the seal was just the beginning."

"What was the image?"

"I saw a man in robes on his face, bowed down before a pedestal, on which sat a man...or, rather, on which was a seated figure. The figure wasn't human. It was too large in relation to the one bowing before it."

"Then what?"

"I took it to be a statue, an idol, a god."

"And what did you make of it?"

"I had no idea. I decided to search the web for images of ancient gods and idols."

"And what did you find?"

"A lot of ancient gods and idols. It didn't lead me anywhere. And then I had a dream. I saw a steep and colossal mountain towering over an ancient city. Ascending the mountain were men with hammers and chisels. They began pounding their hammers and chisels into the rock face. They were carving out an image. It wasn't long before the image became apparent.

"It was a face, a colossal, stone face, the face of a man, bearded, with curly hair, and wearing a crown. But then it began changing into the face of a man, clean-shaven and bald, and then the face of a woman with long wavy hair adorned with jewels. Then it changed again. It kept changing and changing into one face and then another. And while all this was happening, the people at the bottom of the mountain began to worship and sing praises to the image on the mountain. The face again became that of a woman. That's when it stopped changing. The face smiled.

"And then the mountain rock began cracking apart and breaking off until it revealed the stone body of a colossal creature. It was the rest of her, the body of the face. She had, at first, been seated on the ground, but now she rose to her feet. She was colossal. As she rose, the people began bowing down before her in homage.

"In her right hand was a sword. She lifted it to the sky. Then she raised another arm…and then another…and another."

"How many arms did she have?"

"Eight arms. Then she began to walk as if oblivious to the people under her. They began screaming and running from her path. She made her way to the city and stood in its midst, in between its tall buildings and towers. It was only then that a strange headdress appeared on her head, a mix of square ridges and a spike protruding from its center. She opened her mouth to speak. 'I am death,' she said, 'the destroyer of worlds.' And then she began to laugh maniacally as she raised her sword over the city.

"And that's when it ended. I woke up with her maniacal laughter ringing in my mind."

"Wow!" said Ana. "I understand why you woke up in a cold sweat. So what did you make of it?"

"I decided to draw a picture of what I had seen while it was still fresh in my mind. I put it in my coat pocket where I kept the seal. It was that same day that the mystery began to unfold.

"I was in Lower Manhattan. It was midday, lunchtime. I had stopped near a street corner where there was a food vendor and bought a falafel. It was then, standing there eating that falafel, that I saw it."

"Saw what?"

"The headdress," said Nouriel, "the headdress that the woman or thing was wearing. I pulled out my drawing and held it up to what I was seeing. The creature's headdress was much more compressed than what I saw in the distance, but it was the same, the same shape, the same structure."

"What was it?"

"It was the Empire State Building."

"The Empire State Building! A headdress?"

"The top of the building…I don't know, maybe the top fifteen stories and the spire that crowned it…the square ridges, the spikes—that's what she was wearing."

"She was wearing the top of a building? What did it mean?"

"I had no idea," Nouriel replied, "but I had to find out. So I jumped in a taxi and took it up to 34th Street, to the Empire State Building, went inside, and took the elevator up to the Observation Deck."

"You were there before."

"Yes. With the prophet. I was hoping he would be there again. Without that I wouldn't have known what to look for. When I got up to the Observation Deck, I immediately began searching for him through the crowd. The first time I saw him there, he was looking through one of the telescopes they have there at the edge of the deck. So I paid special attention to those using the telescope as I scanned the crowd. But there was no sign of him.

"I didn't know what to do. I decided to go around one more time. So I did. And there he was, looking through one of the telescopes into the cityscape."

◆◆◆

"How did you get here?" I asked.

"I assume the same way you did," he replied. "I used the elevator."

"I just checked a minute ago, and you weren't here."

"The last time I checked, I was."

I realized it was useless to argue the point.

"I have no idea how you're going to make sense of this one."

"Why don't you start at the beginning?" he said. "I assume you had a dream?"

"Yes."

So I told him what I saw and showed him the drawing and how it matched the top of the building.

"The image on the seal," he said, "is exactly what you believe it to be, the temple of a god, the shrine of an idol. And your dream had to do with the same thing, an idol, a god."

"What does it have to do with..."

"When Israel turned away from God, they didn't turn to nothing; they turned to something else. They turned to other gods, foreign gods, the gods of the nations, idols. It's always that way. You see, we're each made to worship God. So if we turn away from God or if we never know Him in the first place, we'll end up worshipping something else, other gods, idols, the works of our hands."

"Why idols? Why does man turn to idols?"

"Because to create your own god is to become the creator...and thus your own god. And if you can create your own god, you can create your own truth, and alter it.

"So when the people of Israel drove God out of their lives and culture, the gods came rushing in to fill the void. And since, unlike the God of Israel, the gods that came in from the nations to replace Him could be seen and touched, their appearance triggered a metamorphosis away from the worship of the unseen to the worship of the visible, the physical, the material, the carnal, the sensory, and the sensual. That too is what follows."

"So if America is following the course of Israel's fall, then would it also..."

"Turn to idols?" asked the prophet.

"Yes."

"Do you remember what the warning was at America's founding...the warning of John Winthrop?"

"Remind me."

> "But if our hearts shall turn away, so that we will not obey, but shall be seduced, and worship other gods, our pleasure and profits..., and serve them...[1]

"So it was for ancient Israel. As their hearts turned away from God, they were seduced to worship and serve other gods. And thus the warning of ancient Israel became the warning given to America at its inception. The warning is this: if America should turn away from the God of its foundation, it will end up worshipping and serving other gods."

"So would you say it did?"

"It was in the mid-twentieth century that America's removal of God from its public squares and culture became overt and overtly progressive. It's no accident that in that same period of time, another transformation took place, the metamorphosis of American culture away from the unseen and toward the carnal, the material, the sensory, and the sensual. And as God was driven out, the gods came in to fill the void."

"But the worship of gods and idols?"

"In modern America and much of the modern world, they don't call them gods or idols, but nevertheless, it is the same thing.... American gods and American idols, the god of success and prosperity, of money, comfort, sexuality, pleasure, the self, and a host of other deities and masters. And when the gods take over, the culture becomes fractured, truth becomes subjective, appearance becomes reality, and man becomes God. When God is abolished, everything becomes God."

"And does this have to do with judgment?"

"In the Book of Second Kings there's a prophetic autopsy concerning the judgment and end of ancient Israel. It says this:

> And they rejected His statutes and His covenant that He had made with their fathers...they followed idols, became idolaters, and went after the nations who were all around them....So they left all the commandments of the LORD their God, made for themselves a molded image...and worshiped all the host of heaven.[2]

"The appearance of gods and idols in the land is, in itself, a sign of coming judgment. And in the last days of Israel, the signs of the gods proliferated.

"It happened not only in the northern kingdom of Israel but in the southern kingdom as well. Before judgment came on the kingdom of Judah, the images of the gods began manifesting everywhere—even in the most holy places. The prophet Ezekiel was taken, in a vision, to the Temple of Jerusalem and given a glimpse of what was taking place in the sacred chambers. He was brought to the gate of the inner court, where he saw an idol he simply described as the 'image.'[3] Then he was taken inside a chamber:

> So I went in and saw, and there—every sort of creeping thing, abominable beasts, and all the idols of the house of Israel, portrayed all around on the walls.[4]

"Note, again, it is the same sign, the sign of images, the signs of the gods. And right after that, he heard a voice:

> Then I heard him call out in a loud voice, 'Bring near those who are appointed to execute judgment on the city, each with a weapon in his hand.'[5]

"It was the pronouncement of the city's judgment and the nation's end. First the images of the gods and then the judgment—the one follows the other. So the pattern is this: In the nation's last days, the people give themselves wholly over to the gods and idols; they proliferate in the land, and their images become manifest. Then comes judgment."

"But how could the images of the gods manifest now? I understand about modern gods and modern idol worship, but if we don't call them gods, or recognize them as gods, or display them as gods, then how could the sign of the gods or an image of a god appear in America?"

"Signs have a way of manifesting regardless."

"What do you mean?"

"It appeared. It manifested. The image of the god appeared."

"What god?"

"The images that appeared in Israel's last days were of foreign gods. So the image that appeared in America was likewise that of a foreign god."

"Where?"

"It appeared in New York City."

"How?"

"When the prophet was brought to the Temple and saw 'all the idols of the house of Israel,' in what form did they appear?"

"In the form of images on the walls."

"So too did the sign of the gods manifest in America, as an image on the wall."

"On what wall?"

"On the outer wall of a building in this city."

"A pagan temple."

"Not exactly."

"I don't understand."

"It was projected onto the building at night, the image of a god, the definition of an idol."

"Of what god?"

"The goddess Kali."

"From India?"

"Yes, India. The images that appeared in the last days of ancient Israel were of gods worshipped in other nations. So too was the god who appeared in New York City."

"Does Kali have more than one set of arms?"

"Yes."

"Then she was the one I saw in my dream. And in her hand, in one of her many hands, was a sword."

"That would be her."

"So the image of Kali appeared in New York City on the wall of one of its buildings."

"Yes," said the prophet, "the face of Kali. The representation was so colossal that her face alone was hundreds of feet high. It had to have been the most colossal image of a god on earth."

"So, in a sense, the entire building became an idol. Which building?"

"You're standing on it," said the prophet. "You're standing on the most colossal of idols."

"The Empire State Building."

"Yes."

"The Empire State Building was lit up with the image of a god?"

"It was," he replied. "The building that for so many years represented the height and glory of American civilization was converted into an idol, into a false god."

"I'm trying to picture it."

"You already did. The idol's headdress...it matched the top of this building not just so you would be led to come here but because that's how it looked when the image appeared. The top of the building formed her headdress, or crown. In fact, we're standing on the crown right now."

"The Empire State Building...an idol," I said, "a strange combination."

"Not really," he replied. "Both are symbols, embodiments of spirits. Now what was it that you saw on the seal?"

"An idol in a temple on a mountaintop."

"It was a high place. The high places were especially dedicated to the gods, to their temples and shrines, to their rites and worship, and to the displaying of their idols. Thus the gods would loom over their surroundings. The Empire State Building is a high place of modern America. And that's where the god was displayed."

"So it loomed over New York City."

"Yes, the face of Kali towered over the cityscape."

"I imagine it was ominous."

"Do you want to see it?"

"What do you mean?"

"Take out your cell phone."

So I did.

"Now go to the web and type in the words *Kali* and *Empire State Building*."

"You use a cell phone?" I asked.

"Would it surprise you if I did?"

"I guess I just never pictured it."

I pressed the search button. And then I saw it. It was chilling, demonic, something from a nightmare. The face had three eyes, one of which was in the center of its forehead, turned vertically. Above her head was the top of the Empire State Building lit up golden-red to form her crown, or headdress. Her face was pitch-black, and her tongue was sticking out and downward, blood red.

"It's monstrous," I said. "Why would anyone put that up?"

"The reason they did it or the reason it was done?"

"What was *their* reason for doing it?"

"It was supposed to be a display of endangered animals. And for some reason they crowned it all with the image of the dark goddess."

"And the reason that it was done?"

"The mystery ordained it," he replied. "As with ancient Israel, the nation that turns from God will always turn to the gods, to idols. The images of the gods will appear in the land. It was not that they were worshipping the image. It was that the image was a manifestation, the sign of a nation that had turned away from God and was now serving the gods, the names of which it would never utter. Do you know what day the image appeared?"

"No."

"It was a Saturday."

"And?"

"The biblical Sabbath."

"So there was an appointed word."

"Yes, a word appointed for the day of the image."

"And was it significant?"

"I would say so."

"What was it?"

"It was a warning," he said, "a warning given to the nation of Israel:

> Take careful heed to yourselves…so you do not corrupt
> yourselves and make an idol in the image of any figure, the
> representation of male or female, the representation of any
> animal on the earth.[6]

"It was the warning of God against idols, against the worship of false
gods, and the making of their images."

"And it was appointed for that very day of the image."

"Yes. And it goes on to warn of the judgment that would come upon
the nation because of its idols and images. The appointed portion even
contained the reiteration of the Ten Commandments:

> You shall have no other gods before Me. You shall not make for
> yourself any idols, or any image of anything in heaven above
> or in the earth below.…You shall not reverence them or serve
> them."[7]

"The Ten Commandments," I said, "prohibit the images of the gods. A
strange thing—the Ten Commandments were taken down from America's walls…and now the image of a god appears on its walls instead."

"Not so strange," said the prophet. "The one follows the other. The
same thing happened in ancient Israel. The Word of God was removed
from the culture, and the gods were brought in."

"So the scripture prohibiting the worship of false gods and the making
of their images was appointed for the same day that the image of the
colossal god went up over New York City."

"And that appointed scripture just happened to be the Bible's central
warning against making idols and the images of gods."

"So then all over New York City…"

"Yes, all over New York City, in all its synagogues from Brooklyn to
Manhattan, they opened up the scrolls and began chanting the ancient
words of warning against the gods and their images…as the image of
the god was being readied to manifest over the city."

"In my dream, the idol walked over to the city and stood by its towers.
It was all about what happened here."

"Yes."

"Why was her face pitch-black?"

"Kali is called the Dark One. She's the goddess of darkness."

"So they used all those lights on the Empire State Building to create the god of darkness."

"Yes," said the prophet, "they put light for darkness and darkness for light. Remember the scripture of a fallen nation:

> Woe to those who call evil good, and good evil; *who put darkness for light, and light for darkness.*"[8]

"In my dream, the idol lifted a sword over the city."

"So Kali wields a sword...and her tongue drips with blood."

"Why?"

"Because she's the goddess of destruction...she's the destroyer."

I turned away from the prophet and gazed out at the immense panorama beneath us.

"So looming over this city was the goddess of destruction?"

"Yes, the goddess of death."

"The goddess of death over New York City."

"The goddess of darkness, destruction, and death."

"A dark harbinger."

"Yes, and so too were the gods whose images appeared in the land of Israel in that nation's last days....So too were they dark harbingers of coming judgment...of death and destruction."

I didn't say anything but just stared into the vast cityscape. I couldn't stop thinking about the image and its ramifications. Finally, I spoke. The words came out almost without my intending them to.

"But if our hearts shall turn away," I said, "so that we will not obey but shall be seduced and worship other gods..."

"Yes, if our hearts shall turn away," he repeated.

We were both silent then, staring out over the city as the wind gusted over the deck.

◆◆◆

"Amazing," said Ana. "And I had no idea that anything like that had ever happened."

"Neither did I," said Nouriel. "But it was the same way when he first revealed the nine harbingers. I had no idea. And most of these things manifested without the world knowing they ever did or what they meant.

But I imagine it's that way with many things, many of the most critical things."

"It must have been a bit chilling to be on top of the Empire State Building when he told you what happened there."

"It was."

"So what happened next?"

"I gave him the seal, and he handed me another."

"And the next mystery was…"

"You've heard the expression 'the handwriting on the wall'?"

"I have."

"It's not just an expression. In the next mystery, I would be shown the handwriting on the wall…with regard to America."

Chapter 23

The Handwriting on the Wall

S O WHAT WAS on the seal?"

"What appeared to be an ancient building with columns and capitals."

"Like the Supreme Court."

"But unlike the Supreme Court, in the center of its front wall was a triangular-shaped roof, under which were four columns. On the building's walls to the right and left of the four columns were what appeared to be words of a foreign script, four words, two on the right side and two on the left."

"Were you able to make any sense of it?"

"No."

"But then you had a dream?"

"Yes. It was night. I was walking up a set of white marble steps to the top, a large white marble platform. Upon reaching the top, I saw what looked like a giant white marble goblet or bowl on a pedestal. It was covered with engravings, designs, symbols, and words. I sensed it was some sort of ceremonial vessel. Beyond the giant vessel was a colossal wall, also of white marble. I couldn't tell if the wall was part of the building or a freestanding wall.

"Then cracks began appearing in the vessel. Through the cracks emanated light, colored light. And then the light began pouring out through the cracks as if liquid, a cascade of liquid light of every color. Soon the white marble floor of the platform was covered with colored light, which then began spreading to the wall and then up the wall. It wasn't long before the wall was saturated with colored light. Then letters began forming on the wall as if an invisible hand was inscribing them."

"How could you see the letters in the midst of all the colors?"

"They were written in an almost blinding white light. I approached the wall to see if I could read what was written. But I couldn't. The words were of a foreign script. I turned back to look at the vessel from which the colored light had poured out, but there was now nothing left of it but broken pieces. And the dream ended."

"So what were you able to make of it?"

"At first, not a lot. But the handwriting on the wall—I knew that it came from the Bible. So I found the account and read it."

"From where in the Bible?"

"From the Book of Daniel. It came from an event that took place in the palace of the Babylonian king Belshazzar. The king threw a great feast for his noblemen. During the feast, he commanded that the sacred vessels plundered from the Temple of God in Jerusalem be brought out to the celebration. So they brought them out, filled them with wine, and began drinking from them as they offered up praises to the gods of Babylon.

"It was then that the fingers of a man's hand appeared and began writing words on the palace wall. No one knew what the words meant. They called in the prophet Daniel, who revealed to them the meaning of the words. It was an omen, a sign, a warning of things to come.[1] It was from this that we get the expression 'the handwriting on the wall.'"

"And how did that help you?"

"The ancient account began with vessels or goblets. So did my dream—the giant vessel. It ended with handwriting on a wall. So did my dream. The two were connected. I began searching for any rendering I could find of what the handwriting on the palace wall would have looked like. I compared what I found to the letters on the seal. They matched. But I still couldn't tell what this had to do with anything else. And then I went to the supermarket. And that's where the breakthrough came."

"In the supermarket…"

"I was at the checkout. The cashier handed me my change. And that's when it came to me, on a twenty-dollar bill."

"The revelation came to you on a twenty-dollar bill…"

"On the back side of the bill was the building on the seal. The building with the triangular roof and the four columns.…It was the White House."

"The White House…But what would that have to do with your dream and the Book of Daniel?"

"I had no idea. But now I had something to go on. So that's where I went."

"To the White House?"

"To the front of the White House, to a park across from the north lawn called Lafayette Square. I arrived there at midday. In the center of the park was a statue of Andrew Jackson in battle on horseback. I went over to it."

"For any reason?"

"The twenty-dollar bill," he said, "on the back of it was the White House, but on the front was Andrew Jackson. It was just a hunch. But I had nothing to lose. And as I made my way to the other side of the pedestal, the side facing the White House, there he was."

"The prophet."

"He asked me to tell him what I had found so far. So I told of the connections I had made between the dream, the seal, and the Book of Daniel."

◆◆◆

"Very good, Nouriel," he said. "Now tell me, in the Book of Daniel, what was it that caused the handwriting to appear on the wall?"

"The vessels," I replied, "the taking of the Temple vessels and using them in the king's celebration."

"And what principle does that represent?"

"I don't know."

"The principle of desacralization."

"Desacralization? I've never heard of it."

"To take something sacred and use it for non-sacred purposes. The vessels of the Temple were sacred. They were made and consecrated for the purposes of God. But now the Babylonians were using them against the purpose for which they had been made and consecrated, as instruments of revelry and pagan worship."

"Could that also be called desecration?"

"It was an act of desecration as well," he said. "And because of the desecration, the handwriting appeared. The handwriting on the wall follows the act of desecration.

"The principle isn't limited to Babylon; it happened in Israel as well. When the people of Israel turned away from God, they began performing acts of desacralization and desecration. They took what had been consecrated to God and used it against His purposes. They took the Temple and used it to perform pagan rites to foreign gods and idols. And then judgment came."

"But what does this have to do with America?"

"When a nation that has known the ways of God falls away, it will take the things of God and use them against His purposes. It will take that which is holy and consecrated to the purposes of God and use it for what is not of God or holy. And as it nears the days of its judgment, its acts of desecration will increase in number and frequency."

"But America…"

"In America's fall from God, it has, as well, performed the ancient act."

"Taking the sacred and using it for what is not?"

"Yes. We've already spoken of such an act and the mystery of its timing. Now we must open the mystery of its nature.

"The account of Daniel begins with the taking out of the sacred vessels of God's Temple. But the most important and sacred of God's vessels are not made of silver or gold or fashioned by craftsmen. The most sacred of God's vessels were fashioned by God's hand in the act of creation. One of those sacred vessels is marriage. Marriage was created and consecrated for the purposes of God, a sacred vessel. It has been a foundation stone of civilization since the beginning of recorded history. On June 26, 2015, America broke the sacred vessel."

"The breaking of the vessel in my dream…"

"It was the ancient act, the taking of that which was consecrated to God's purposes and turning it away from the purposes for which it was created…as with the vessels of God at the feast of Babylon."

"So the vessel in my dream was a representation of marriage."

"And more than that. The ultimate issue is beyond that of any law, person, people, or act."

"Then what?"

"Existence," said the prophet. "To take the sacred vessels of God, as did the Babylonians, and use them for drinking in a celebration of the gods is to proclaim that those vessels have had no real or intrinsic meaning, purpose, value, or sanctity. If you can take a vessel and use it however you please, if you can do with it whatever you want, then what you're saying is that the vessel has no true value or absolute purpose. And this is the issue that manifests in a fallen civilization. It is the same issue, whether it applies to marriage, human life, or existence itself. To fall away from God is to fall away from purpose and, ultimately, from life itself. So the end of such things is destruction. What happened on that day in June concerned far more than marriage. It was a civilization divorcing the sacred vessels from their ordained purposes...the sacred vessels of man and woman...the divorce of man from manhood and woman from womanhood, the turning of each away from the other. The ramifications of that act would not manifest all at once but would begin pouring into every fabric of the nation's culture."

"Like the colored light spilling out from the broken vessel?"

"Yes."

"And what was the colored light?"

"The breaking of the vessel on that day in June caused celebrations throughout the nation and around the world. The celebrations were marked by a sign...a sign of many colors."

"The rainbow."

"It appeared on flags and banners, on signs, on people."

"The colored light represented the rainbow."

"And what is the rainbow?"

"The sign of a movement."

"No," said the prophet, "the rainbow doesn't belong to man—the rainbow belongs to God. It is the sign that He Himself gave and consecrated. Like marriage and like existence, the rainbow is a sacred vessel. And so on that day in June, the sign given by God, the rainbow, was likewise taken from its sacred purpose and became a vessel lifted against the sacred and against the purposes of heaven."

"That would make it another act of desecration," I said. "The first desecration celebrated by a second...a day of desecrations."

"The breaking of the sacred vessel," he said.

"All these things centered on the Supreme Court," I said, "but we're standing here at the White House. This is where the mystery led me and where you chose to meet me. Why here?"

"When a nation falls away from God and seeks to change its values and standards, who is it that we said sanctions that metamorphosis?"

"Its priests," I said.

"Yes," said the prophet, "and also its king. And so it was not only the Supreme Court that sanctioned the change; it was the king...the president. The day belonged to the priests of the high court, but the night belonged to the king. It was the night of that day that the king joined in the celebration and issued his own sanction and blessing on what had been done.

"On the day when God's vessels were desecrated in Babylon, a sign appeared on the walls of the king's palace. And on the day that the vessel of God was desecrated in America, a sign would appear on the wall of the king's palace."

"The king's palace being the White House."

"Yes."

"So a sign appeared on the wall of the White House?"

"Yes, with the president's blessing."

"And the sign was?"

"The walls of the White House were illuminated with the colors of the rainbow."

"The wall in my dream stood for the wall of the White House."

"The highest house of the land, a representation of America itself, now covered in the colors of desecration. And so the White House itself became a vessel of desecration...and defiance against the ways of God. And the whole nation saw it. The whole world saw it."

"The symbol of America...a sign of desecration."

"And do you know what else the rainbow is connected to?"

"No."

"The throne of God. The Book of Ezekiel speaks of the glory of God appearing in the likeness of the rainbow. The Book of Revelation speaks of a rainbow surrounding God's throne.[2] And now, the same sign, the sign of God's throne, His sovereignty, and authority, was used against the authority of God...and on the walls of the king's palace...the throne of man at war with the throne of God."

"The same king who inscribed the words of defiance on the top of the tower now sanctioned the colors of defiance on the walls of the White House."

"And do you know what else the rainbow is connected to, Nouriel?"

"What?"

"Judgment. The rainbow was born in judgment. It was a sign from the days of Noah of God's mercy in the wake of judgment."

"Then it's a good sign."

"Yes," said the prophet, "but what happens if you take the sign of

God's mercy, the sign of His desire to hold back the coming of judgment…and use it against Him? What happens if you turn the sign of His mercy against its purpose, if you break it? Then what is left? Only judgment. When the handwriting on the wall appeared in Babylon, it was a sign that the judgment had been sealed. The enemy would enter the gates of Babylon, and the kingdom would be brought to an end. The act of desecration brings judgment."

"And the day that the sign appeared in America was also the ninth of Tammuz, the day that marked the sealing of Israel's judgment."

"And do you know what happened after that day?"

"No."

"Less than forty days after the White House was illuminated with the colors of the rainbow, another building was illuminated with the colors of a different light. It was right after the illumination of the White House that the Empire State Building was illuminated and the image of the god of death and destruction appeared over the skyline of New York City."

"So the sign on the wall of the White House was a harbinger."

"Before the entire nation."

"The harbinger was the White House itself."

"Yes. The White House itself became the harbinger, and the handwriting appeared on its wall in the colors of the rainbow."

He gave me some time, as he often did, to contemplate what I had been shown, which I did as I gazed at the White House.

Finally, he spoke. "I think we better go now," he said. "The security is beginning to wonder who we are."

So we turned around and began walking away from the White House through Lafayette Square and to the sidewalk at its end. It was there that I gave him the seal and he handed me another.

"And what was the next mystery?"

"An ancient holy day, a leader who changed the Word of God, the return of a harbinger, a sign in the heavens, and a fall on the earth."

Chapter 24

The Judgment Tree

S o what was on the seal?"

"A tree," said Nouriel. "A circle, inside of which was a tree. The tree had no leaves, and its branches were indistinguishable from its roots. So you couldn't tell which part of the seal was the top and which was the bottom."

"And what did you make of it?"

"It seemed pretty plain to me…a tree inside of a circle. But its significance eluded me."

"And you had a dream…"

"Yes. I was sitting in a boat, a small, thin boat. It was nighttime. In front of me was the boatman. I assumed he was guiding it, but I didn't notice any oars. 'Look,' he said, pointing upward. 'It's a new moon. That means it's the first day of the month.' As we continued moving across the water, which I believed was a river, I noticed the night was brightening, the moonlight was growing more intense.

"The boat came ashore. I followed the boatman inland until we came upon a massive object, the bottom of a colossal tree. The moonlight now became noticeably brighter. I looked upward. The colossal object was the Statue of Liberty, but in the form of a tree, or a tree in the form of the Statue of Liberty. Its robe, its tablet, the base of its torch, its arms, fingers, and face were all made of bark. But its hair and the flame of its torch were green, as if made of leaves, but not leaves; they were needles, as in the needles of a pine tree.

"As the moonlight continued to brighten, I began noticing abnormalities in the bark. It was peeling off, and there was fungus and mildew and deep holes and cracks. It was diseased. The boatman now pointed again to the sky. The moon was now full. 'It's time,' he said. At that, a strong wind began blowing against the statue or tree. Then I heard a creaking sound, and the statue began to sway back and forth, a little at first, then more and more and more until its massive roots began tearing up from the soil. And then it came crashing down to the earth with what sounded like a loud explosion.

"Soon after that, the sun rose. I walked among the ruins. The statue had broken in half, the torch was devoid of its flame, and the crown had been removed from its head. 'And now,' said the boatman, 'where will its hope be found?' And the dream ended."

"So where did that lead you?" asked Ana.

"In two directions, and I wasn't sure which one to go in. But I had already gone looking for trees with the other seal, so I decided to take a boat ride to the Statue of Liberty."

"Had you ever gone there before?"

"Never," he said. "It's one of the things you do when you live in the metropolitan area."

"Which is what?"

"Never go to any of the sites. So I headed down to Battery Park to take the ferry to Liberty Island. As I made my way to the harbor, I passed a man sitting on a park bench to my left. I was hardly aware of him as I walked. But then I heard a voice."

———— ◆◆◆ ————

"You won't find it there."

I turned around. And there he was, the prophet, sitting on a bench with a bag of peanuts in his hand.

"So how do I find it?" I asked, not even fully knowing what the *it* was that I was supposed to find.

"Perhaps I can help you," he said.

I sat down beside him and told him the dream, though I was sure he already knew it. Otherwise he wouldn't have been waiting there on that bench.

"The ancient vow leads to two objects, the building that rises in place of the fallen bricks and the erez tree planted in place of the fallen sycamore. Each is a sign of the nation's defiance in the face of God's call. And so after 9/11, America began building its tower on the ground where the bricks had fallen...and planted the erez tree on the soil where the sycamore had fallen."

"The Tree of Hope."

"We've already seen what happened with the tower. But what about the other, the erez tree?"

"It began to wither," I replied.

At that, the prophet rose from the bench. "Come," he said as he began to walk. I got up and joined him. We walked away from the harbor and toward the streets of Lower Manhattan.

"There is a symbol," he said, "given in Scripture that represents the judgment of nations. It's used over and over again."

"What symbol?"

"An image, a metaphor, an event. The prophet Isaiah used it to prophesy the destruction of Ethiopia:

> He will…take away and cut down the branches.[1]

"The prophet Ezekiel foretold the fall of Egypt this way:

> Its branches have fallen…its boughs lie broken.[2]

"And the prophet Jeremiah foretold the judgment and fall of his own nation with the words

> He has kindled fire on it, and its branches are broken.[3]

"What image are they all using?"

"The breaking of a branch."

"Yes, the breaking of the branch is a sign of national judgment."

"And this has to do with the image on the seal?"

"This has to do with the harbinger, the erez tree, the tree that was planted in place of the fallen sycamore, the symbol of a nation's hope. The scripture says that when the 'boughs are withered, they will be broken off.'[4] And so the boughs of the Tree of Hope, the harbinger, withered away… and then they were cut off. The Tree of Hope was dismembered. It stood there at the corner of Ground Zero with its branches cut off, a shadow of what it had been when it was dedicated and given its name. The tree planted to symbolize national resurgence turned instead into a different sign, that of a nation's fall.

"But it wasn't only the transformation of the tree that was significant—it was also the one who came to visit."

"Who?"

"The president."

"Obama?"

"Yes. On the anniversary of the calamity, he came to visit Ground Zero. And there he read from a scripture, Psalm 46. The psalm speaks of the Lord bringing peace on earth and destroying the weapons of war. It says this:

He breaks the bow and cuts the spear in two.[5]

"The bow is the weapon used by archers in warfare, as in the bow and arrow. So the verse spoke of blessing, the ending of war, peace. But the president altered the scripture. He, no doubt, had no idea what he was doing, but nevertheless, he did it. Instead of saying, 'He breaks the bow,' the president changed the word to say,

He breaks the *bough*.[6]

"In English, the sound of the two words is similar, but their meaning, in the context of the scripture, could not be more different. The breaking of the *bow* is a blessing. But the breaking of the *bough* is a biblical sign of a nation's judgment. So the president changed the word of national blessing into a word of national judgment. And when the White House posted the psalm on its website, it likewise altered the words in accordance with what the president had done. It changed, in writing, the word *bow* into the word *bough*. It changed the scripture.

"And as the president spoke of the Lord breaking the bough, a stone's throw away from the ground on which he spoke it stood a tree, withering away and from which the boughs would be broken off."

"Were the boughs broken off when he said it?"

"No. He said it, and then it happened. And yet there is another sign of national judgment even greater than the first. It concerns not only the tree's branches but the tree—its fall and destruction."

"Like the fall of the sycamore?"

"Yes, and even stronger than that. A sign specifically connected to another tree—the erez tree. The prophet Ezekiel spoke of the judgment and destruction of Assyria in this way:

Assyria was an *erez tree*...of high stature...the most terrible
of the nations...have cut it down.[7]

"So the prophet Jeremiah spoke of the judgment that would destroy
his nation with these words:

I will ordain destroyers against you, each with his weapon, and
they will cut down your best *erez trees* and throw them into
the fire.[8]

"And the prophet Zechariah foretold the destruction of Jerusalem this
way:

Open, O Lebanon, your doors that fire may consume your *erez
trees*."[9]

"And why is it so significant that it's talking about the erez tree?" I
asked.
"The answer is in the name. Do you remember what *erez* means?"
"Strong."
"Because the tree was known for its strength. That's the reason it was
invoked in the ancient vow:

The sycamores have been cut down, but we will plant *erez trees*
in their place.

"That's why it's so significant. They were vowing to come back as
strong as the erez tree. That's why the erez tree became the symbol of
their defiance. It was much stronger than the sycamore. So while the
sycamore could be easily struck down, the erez tree, they believed, could
not. Thus they believed themselves immune to any future judgment. As
one commentary put it, they would...

...exchange its feeble sycamores that are cut down for strong
cedars [erez trees] which the wildest gales will spare."[10]

"And so when America performed the same act," I said, "when it
replaced the sycamore with the erez tree and called it the Tree of Hope,
it not only spoke of defiance in the face of judgment but of immunity."

"Not that this was the intent of those who performed the act," he said, "but this was its biblical meaning. Would you like to see it?" he asked.

"The erez tree?"

"Yes."

With the exception of the prophet taking me to the top of the tower, I had avoided going to Ground Zero. But we were now heading in that direction, and there was something he wanted me to see. So he led me to Ground Zero and to the dark wrought iron fence that surrounded the soil on which the sycamore had fallen and the erez tree planted in its place.

"Look, Nouriel," said the prophet. "Tell me what you see."

I gazed through the fence looking for the Tree of Hope.

"I'm not seeing it. Am I looking in the right place?"

"The place is right," he said. "The reason you're not seeing it is because it's not there, it's gone."

"Gone?"

"You're not seeing it because the ancient sign was manifested on this ground."

"The sign of?"

"National judgment."

"What are you saying?"

"The words of the prophets—'The erez tree has fallen'[11]—the sign of national judgment."

"How?"

"It was struck down."

"By what?"

"By those in charge of keeping it alive."

"Why?"

"Because it withered away and no matter what they did, they couldn't save it....So they destroyed it."

"They destroyed the sign of their resurgence."

"They destroyed the harbinger—and by so doing, created another, the fall of the erez tree."

"I had no idea."

"Really?" said the prophet, "Do you not read your own books, Nouriel?"

"I barely have time to write them. Why?"

"You should read them. It was all there in your first book. You wrote it before it happened."

"You've read my books?"

"This is what you wrote concerning the cedar or erez tree, the Tree of Hope at Ground Zero:

> But when a nation such as this places its hope in its own powers to save itself, then its hope is false. Its true hope is found only in returning to God. Without that, its Tree of Hope is a harbinger of the day when its strong cedars *come crashing down to the earth*.[12]

"You wrote that years before it happened."

"It sounds more like your words than mine."

"I may have said it, but you wrote it down for others to see."

"When did it fall? When did they cut it down?"

"They destroyed the Tree of Hope on a Hebrew holy day."

"Which holy day?"

"The one that commemorates the judgment of a nation—Passover, the day that the plague came on a nation that warred against God."[13]

"Two signs of national judgment," I said, "in a single day."

"And there are other signs of judgment that appear not on earth but in the heavens."

"Like what?"

"It is written of the day of judgment, 'the moon shall not give her light' and will become 'as blood.'[14] The darkening of the moon and the turning of the moon blood red are two signs connected to and reserved for the day of judgment. They are yet to manifest in their fullness on that day, but in part they appear already."

"When?"

"During a lunar eclipse. It is then that the moon is darkened and turns to blood red to become that which is known as a blood moon."

"But that would take place whenever the moon and earth are in their set positions, at the set time. We can predict it."

"Yes, but even such set times are of Him who set them and who appoints all things to converge when and where they do and who can use anything as a sign, even that which is a sign already."

"Why are you telling me this?"

"The erez tree fell to the ground on the eve of Passover. On that same night, the moon was darkened. The harbinger fell to the earth, and the moon was darkened…and turned blood red."

"So then there were three signs," I said, "three signs of judgment all on the same day."

"And yet another sign appears in the sky, another sign of judgment, different from the first but joined to it. So it is written:

> The sun shall be turned into darkness, and the moon into blood.[15]

"The darkening of the sun," said the prophet, "another sign connected to and reserved for the day of judgment. And yet this too has in part already appeared."

"A solar eclipse. But a solar eclipse can't take place at the same time as a lunar eclipse."

"No, it happens on another day. So we have two signs of judgment…two lights…two darkenings…two days. And how many harbingers of defiance remained?"

"The erez tree and the tower, two."

"The tower's ascent was completed on the day that the spire was placed on its top and it reached its full height of 1,776 feet. It was May 10, 2013. It was on that same day that the sun was darkened. So the tower touched the heavens on the same day the sun was darkened."

"Two signs of judgment, one for each harbinger. The one sign appeared as the one harbinger touched the sky—and the other sign as the other harbinger touched the earth."

"Yes."

"The seal," I said, "the circle around the tree—it stood for the moon."

"Yes."

"And in my dream, everything happened by the light of the moon…a changing moon, the moon of an eclipse. And the tree fell at the full moon.

"As the moon is full on Passover," he said.

"And the tree that fell in my dream was in the form of the Statue of Liberty because the Statue of Liberty is a symbol of hope, as is the Tree of Hope…and the erez tree was the ancient symbol of a nation's defiant hope."

"Yes," said the prophet. "So then what would the fall of the erez tree mean?"

"The fall of hope...the end of a nation's defiant hope and its plans to come back stronger without God."

"But the Statue of Liberty," he said, "is not just a symbol of hope—it's a symbol of America itself. So too the erez tree is a symbol of the nation itself in its defiance of God."

"So then does the fall of the erez tree prophesy the fall of America?"

"What happened to ancient Israel in its defiance of God? How did it all end?"

"With the nation's fall."

He was silent.

"I have a question," I said.

"Ask."

"The fall of the sycamore is also a sign of judgment. But does the fall of the erez tree speak of something bigger? A greater judgment, a greater calamity?"

"Yes," said the prophet, "and why do you think that is?"

"The sycamore is weaker. So it's easier to uproot. But the erez tree is stronger. So it would take a greater force to strike it down. So the judgment foreshadowed by the fall of the erez tree would be greater than that of the sycamore."

"Yes. When the Assyrians invaded Israel in 732 BC and struck down the sycamores, the invasion was a national calamity, but of shaking, of warning. So Israel vowed to plant the erez tree in place of the sycamore. But there would come another calamity. And this one would not only shake the nation—it would destroy it. So the fall of the erez tree speaks of something much greater than the fall of the sycamore."

"Then the fall of the sycamore is to 9/11...as the fall of the erez tree is...to a greater calamity to come?"

"The destruction of the erez tree warns of the fall of a great nation. It warns of the day when, as it is written...

> Its branches have fallen on the mountains and in all the valleys; its boughs lie broken by all the rivers of the land; and all the peoples of the earth have gone from under its shadow and left it."[16]

"And all the peoples of the earth have gone from under its shadow," I repeated, "…and left it…"

◆◆◆

"After receiving back the seal, he handed me the next."

"And what would it lead to?"

"An ancient valley, a prophet, a clay jar, a house of faces, a nation's darkening, and the harbinger that marked them all."

Chapter 25

Tophet

"S o what was on the seal?"

"Letters," said Nouriel, "as in the seal before it—but just three let-ters that I took to make up one word. And that's what it turned out to be. Around the letters were curved markings."

"And what did you make of it?"

"I made of it, as I often made of it, that I had no idea what to make of it. But since I was sure that it was a word, and since the script looked, again, like Paleo-Hebrew, I decided to bring it to an Orthodox Jewish scholar who could tell me what it meant."

"Wait," said Ana, "the man from Brooklyn, the man who owned the bookstore. You went to him years ago to interpret one of the seals the prophet gave you."

"Yes."

"But he didn't give you the right interpretation back then. So what made you think…"

"His interpretation was off, but he knew how to read the script, and he was a Hebrew scholar. This time it was just one word, so I didn't think he could go off track."

"So you went to Brooklyn."

"And to the bookstore. He welcomed me in, locked up his shop, and led me to the back room, where we sat down at the same bare wooden table as last time. Nothing in that room had changed, at least nothing I noticed. I handed him the seal. He put on his reading glasses and began examining the letters. He looked up at me, then back down at the letters, up again, and back down. He looked troubled."

————◆◆◆————

"Where did you get this?" he asked.

He had never asked me that when I came to him the first time.

"Someone gave it to me," I answered.

"Do you have any idea what this is?"

"No, or I wouldn't have come here."

"It is a dark thing," he said.

"What do you mean?"

"A dark word."

"What word?"

"*Tophet.*"

"*Tophet*?"

He looked at me as if I had said something wrong, even though I was just repeating what he had just said.

"What does it mean?"

"It comes from a root that has to do with striking...as in striking a drum."

"That doesn't sound so bad."

"You must have nothing to do with it."

"With the seal?"

"With that of which it speaks."

◆◆◆

"Quite a strong reaction," said Ana. "So what did you do?"

"He wouldn't tell me anything more. I went back home, collapsed on my bed, and fell asleep...and had a dream."

"I saw a bearded man, dressed in a robe and carrying a large clay jar or pitcher. He was walking toward a strange-looking building, sort of a cross between a house from a horror movie and a building from the Kremlin. I followed him inside.

"Its interior was dark, lit up by scattered lamps. We came to a large wall that appeared to be made of sandstone. Within the wall were faces."

"Faces?"

"As if they had been sculpted out of the stone...a multitude of faces. The man with the clay jar came to a stop maybe twenty feet away from the wall and began to speak as if addressing his words to the faces in the wall...not as if...he *was* addressing them."

◆◆◆

"And so this is where it happened," said the man. "This is where it began... where the door was opened to the dark."

At that, the faces began to move and then speak.

"We did," they said, "what we believed we had to do, what we saw as right."

"But woe," said the man, "to those who call evil good, and good evil, who put darkness for light, and light for darkness. You opened the door to darkness."

Then he looked upward toward the ceiling, but I knew he was looking beyond it, as if to heaven. He then let out a loud shout of agony.

"Tophet!" he cried out. Then he lifted the clay jar up over his head and smashed it down against the stone floor, where it shattered into what seemed to be hundreds of little pieces. Then he collapsed to the floor and there, on his knees, began to weep. And the dream ended."

"So what did you make of it?"

"The word he cried out was the word from the seal... and it didn't seem to be a good thing... just as the man in the bookstore had warned. But I was determined to find out what it meant. I had a Bible, in the back of which was a concordance."

"A concordance?"

"It tells you where specific words appear in the Bible. So I looked up the word *Tophet*. It led me to the Book of Jeremiah. With one exception, it's the only place in the Bible that the word appears."

"Jeremiah—was he the man with the clay jar?"

"Yes."

"And what did you find?"

"Tophet was a place just outside the city of Jerusalem in the Valley of Hinnom, a place of great significance. And the Lord would speak of it through the prophet Jeremiah:

> 'For the children of Judah have done evil in My sight,' says the LORD. 'They have... built the high places of Tophet, which is in the Valley of the Son of Hinnom, to burn their sons and their daughters in the fire.'"[1]

"To burn their sons and their daughters!"

"That's why God condemned it. Tophet was the place where they killed their own children."

"Why would they do such a horrific thing?"

"It was required in the worship of their new gods to which they turned when they turned away from God. They offered up their children as sacrifices, believing that by doing so they would obtain favor, increase, and gain."

"But why was it on the seal that the prophet gave you?"

"I had no idea. Later that day I went for a walk in Central Park. I sat under the shade of an oak tree. In front of me were children playing in the grass. It turned my thoughts all the more to the children of Israel and Tophet. I was lost in those thoughts until I noticed a silhouette, the figure of a man standing in front of me, blocking out the sun—the prophet."

◆◆◆

"So, Nouriel, have you decoded the seal?" he asked.

"I believe I have," I replied. "*Tophet.*"

He sat down beside me.

"Tophet," he said, "represented the depth of Israel's fall from God. It was all part of the progression. What did we say takes place when a nation turns away from God, from absolute truth, and its people worship the gods of their choosing and the idols of their hands?"

"It cuts itself off from its foundation. It loses its purpose and meaning."

"Yes. And so as Israel fell away from God, it fell away from its purpose and meaning. And when life loses its purposes and meaning, then you can do with it what you will. Then it can be abused, sacrificed, and disposed of. So when a civilization turns away from God, it can then blot out those created in His image. And so it did. The people of Israel began sacrificing their own children. And for the blood of its most innocent, the nation would stand in judgment."

"But why was it on the seal?"

"If America has followed the template of Israel's fall, then would it not follow in this as well?"

"Child sacrifice?" I replied. "That was part of the ancient world; it's not part of today."

"Or is it?" he asked. "As America followed in the footsteps of Israel's fall, as it turned away from God, the same dynamics were set in motion.

It lost its purpose and values. And so life lost its sanctity. And so life became disposable.

"And so the ancient sin was replayed on American soil. The nation gave its blessing and sanction to the sacrificing of its most innocent. It legalized the killing of its unborn children and celebrated the act. Those who should have been its most protected, its most defenseless, were put to death. It all followed the ancient progression. The same years that saw the progressive driving out of God from the nation's public squares also saw the return of the ancient sin. Israel killed thousands of its children—but America has killed millions."

"I see the parallel, but I don't understand how it relates to what I saw in my dream, the house of faces."

"Then there must be more for you to find."

And with that, he stood up.

"But I have faith that you will," said the prophet. Then he began walking into the field of grass, passing the children at play and gradually disappearing into the distance.

◆◆◆

"So the unexplained mystery," said Ana, "was the house of faces."

"Yes," said Nouriel. "I believe I understood the rest of it. The man with the clay jar was Jeremiah. I even found the place in the Book of Jeremiah where he brought a clay vessel to the elders of Israel and confronted them over the sacrifice of the children.[2] He was to smash the jar in their presence—just as in my dream. I got all that, but the house of faces remained a mystery. I went on for weeks without having any idea what it meant. And then the breakthrough came."

"In a supermarket?" she asked.

"No," he replied. "But if you must know, it happened in a convenience store."

"What is it about these breakthroughs?"

"I was on the road, starving. So I stopped in at a convenience store to pick up a snack. I was at the door, about to leave, when I glanced over to my left at the newspaper stand. That's when I saw it."

"Saw what?"

"A photograph on the front page—the building in my dream."

"The one that looked like something out of a horror movie and the Kremlin?"

"Yes. It was a real building. And I knew I had to go there. So the next day, I went on a road trip. It took about two and a half hours to get there. And by the time I did, the sun had set, the sky was darkening...and the building now had a distinctly ominous appearance."

"So what was it?"

"It was the capitol of New York, the house of its legislature. I was in Albany. It was the New York State Capitol building."

◆◆◆

As I stood there in front of it, I heard a voice from behind me.

"Is this how it looked in your dream?"

I turned around. And there he was.

"How did you know it was this building in my dream?"

"I had a hunch," said the prophet. "Come, Nouriel, let's go inside."

So he led me to the building and over to one of its side doors. He opened it up, went inside, and motioned for me to follow.

"Are you sure this is all right?" I asked. "We're not trespassing, are we?"

"I'm sure."

The building's interior was dark, lit up with scattered light fixtures similar to what I had seen in my dream. He led me over to a massive stone staircase....It was filled with faces, carved faces everywhere, in the stone framing the stairway, in the vaulted ceilings, peeking out of the stone ornamentations, faces everywhere."

"So this is the house of faces," I said. "But why did I dream of it?"

"Because," said the prophet, "this is where it all began."

"Where what all began?"

"The darkness," he replied, "the ancient sin, the horrific act..."

"The killing of the unborn."

"It began here in the house of faces. It was from here that it spread across the land."

"That's what the man said to the faces in the dream...that it was there that the door was opened to the darkness. But wasn't abortion legalized in the Supreme Court?"

"Yes, in 1973. It was that decision that made it the law of the land. But it didn't begin there. It began three years earlier, here, in the house of faces. It was here in these chambers, in 1970, that the first law to sanction the killing of unborn children, abortion on demand, to anyone who requested it was begun."

"It began in New York?"

"1970, a handful of states began moving in the direction of legalizing abortion. But it was New York that led the way passing a law that would turn the state into America's abortion mecca. So it was from here that the darkness began spreading, ultimately to the entire nation. In the year after the New York law was passed, the American Bar Association drafted the Uniform Abortion Act for the purpose of legalizing abortion throughout the nation and, the following year, voted to approve it. The Uniform Abortion Act was based on what sanctioned in this house. The following year, the Supreme Court voted to legalize abortion across America. Writing on behalf of that ruling, Justice Blackmun cited the Uniform Abortion Act, which was seen as a precursor of the Supreme Court decision. And regarding that act, Blackmun wrote:

'This Act is based largely upon the New York abortion act.'

"Soon after New York legalized the killing of unborn children, it began drawing women from across the country into its borders to take part in the act. Thus it rapidly emerged as the nation's undisputed epicenter of abortion. And so years before it was legalized throughout the land, New York served as the dark wellspring through which abortion spread to the rest of the nation. More abortions would be performed in New York than in any other place in America. And of all the abortions that took place in New York, the overwhelming majority were performed in New York City.[3] And thus when it comes to the killing of children, New York is America's capital city."

I took out the seal and gazed at it. It was then that I finally understood.

"The curved lines around the letters," I said, "they represent water."

"Yes."

"It's an island. The Tophet of the seal is an island."

"Yes."

"Tophet...is New York City."

He didn't say a word. He didn't disagree but appeared to change the subject.

"The meaning of towers," he said, "what did we say it was?"

"A tower stands as a symbol or embodiment of the nation or kingdom that erects it, a monument to its power and glory."

"Yes," he replied, "and often to its pride and arrogance...to its sin. So the World Trade Center stood as the embodiment of America and a monument to its glory and power. But it also stood as the embodiment of its sin and a monument to its darkness."

"What do you mean?"

"Do you know when the rising of the first tower was completed?"

"No."

"In 1970...the same year that abortion on demand as a universal right was voted into law. And in what state did those towers rise?"

"New York State."

"The same state that passed that law. And in what city?"

"In New York City."

"In the abortion capital of America. The towers crowned that capital. And the same hand that signed the paper to begin the rise of those towers—the same hand signed the paper that began the killing of children on demand.

"And do you know what year it was when both towers were completed?"

"No."

"1973, the same year that the darkness reached its completion—when the killing of the unborn became the law of the land. So it all came together—the towers and the darkness; the two were joined together from the beginning, the one marking the other.

"The prophet Jeremiah spoke of '*the high places of Tophet*.'[4] So it was in Tophet that they built the high places. And if New York City is the Tophet of America, then it must also be where the high places are built."

"The Twin Towers," I said, "the World Trade Center, the high places of America—the high places of Tophet."

"And as the high places of Tophet marked the place where the nation killed its children, so the Twin Towers marked the place where America killed its children, and the time when the killing began."

"I just thought of something," I said. "On the high places of Tophet, they would have had images of the gods that they sacrificed to."

"Yes."

"So it was on the high places of New York City that the image of a god appeared, the image, Kali, the goddess of death, dripping blood…over America's city of death."

"Come," he said as he resumed guiding me through the building.

"Do you know, Nouriel, the place where the Twin Towers began?"

"No."

"Here," he said, "in this house, in the house of faces. It began in the same house that began the killing of the children. The two began not only at the same time but in the same place, the same house."

"So this house was linked to the harbingers from the beginning."

"Yes," said the prophet, "and to the end."

"What do you mean?"

"Nearly half a century after New York led America into the ancient sin, it led the nation again…into a still deeper darkness."

"How?"

"The governor of New York demanded that the state legislature pass a law to exceed the law that had been passed in 1970, a law that would expand the practice of abortion in every direction. Despite the denials that were issued in response to the resulting controversy, the law legalized the killing of children up to the point of birth. The line between the two ancient acts, abortion and infanticide, began to disappear."

It was then that he led me into one of the building's legislative chambers.

"It was here," said the prophet. "It was here in this chamber where they passed that law. And do you know what they did here when that law was passed?"

"No."

"They cheered," he said. "They stood up and cheered…just as they did in ancient times. And do you know what day it was that they passed it?"

"No."

"It was January 22, the same day on which the Supreme Court made it legal to kill unborn children across the land half a century earlier. So New York passed a still more bloody and gruesome law on the same day in celebration. And immediately after the law was passed, other states began attempting to do likewise, to expand the amount of blood to be shed. Once again, New York had led the nation into the darkness."

"It's a sign," I said.

"What do you mean?"

"A sign of deepening. It hasn't turned around. It hasn't stayed the same. It's all deepening. America's fall is deepening and darkening."

"Yes," said the prophet, "and it's all following the template."

"How?"

"When Jeremiah prophesied against his nation for the blood of the children it had shed, the hour was late. The prophecy was given on the eve of the nation's destruction. One of the signs that precedes a nation's judgment is not only that it partakes in the murder of its children but that it does so brazenly, even with joy—even to the point of celebration. It's a harbinger of calamity. It means the hour is late."

"And it's all replaying itself...in America."

"Yes," said the prophet, "and speaking of signs...we saw the connection between the high places of Tophet and the killing of Israel's children...and the high place of New York, the Twin Towers, and the beginning of abortion."

"Yes."

"So it was on the day that New York passed its gruesome law that the mystery continued—and was once again joined to the tower."

"What do you mean?"

"On that day, the governor of New York ordered the tower at Ground Zero to be set ablaze with light in celebration of the act."

"He lit up the harbinger?"

"The harbinger of a nation's pride and rebellion against God was now bathed in the light of its sin. The tower whose top touched heaven and was crowned with the words of defiance was now lit up; the harbinger was illuminated. And this, in and of itself, was yet another sign and prophetic warning."

"In what kind of light did they light it up?"

"Pink light."

"Pink?"

"The color they associated with women—but a color also linked to babies."

"They should have lit it up in blood red."

"So on the anniversary of the day that America began killing its children, and the day that its sin grew even darker, the harbinger was illuminated, the high place of Tophet lit up for the world to see."

"It's all so..."

"What?"

"Demonic...I can't think of another word to describe...Offering up your children as sacrifices? Killing millions and then celebrating it. It's all demonic."

"It *is* demonic," he said, "just as what drove Israel to do such things could only be described as demonic. So too with regard to America."

He led me down a dark corridor, came to a stop, and pointed upward.

"Tell me, Nouriel, what do you see?"

I had to use the light of my cell phone to make it out.

"It looks..."

"What?" he asked.

"Like...a demon. What is it?"

It was the face of a creature lurking in the shadows of an opening in the stone. It would have been more at home in a horror movie than in a house of legislation.

"Do you know what it's called?"

"No."

"*The demon*. It's also known as *the devil*. It's the hidden face of the house of faces."

"Let's get out of here," I said. I didn't want to stay in that place another minute. We left through the same door through which we had entered. When we were a good distance away, I stopped and turned around. The prophet did as well.

"I have a question."

"Ask."

"Jeremiah was not only condemning the nation's murder of its children; he was prophesying judgment. He was foretelling the calamity and death that would come to Tophet and the nation....So does this all mean that calamity and death will come to Tophet, to New York City...and America?"

"If," said the prophet, "by the cries of thousands, judgment came to Tophet...then what will come by the cries of millions?"

◆◆◆

Ana looked shaken as she sat on the bench and gazed blankly into the trees on the other side of the walking path.

"It's getting dark," said Nouriel. "Do you want to go back?"

"No," she answered without turning her gaze. "Go on."

◆◆◆

I was expecting the prophet to ask me for the seal and to give me another, but he didn't.

"We're coming to the end. Tomorrow," he said, "we'll meet at the place where it began, where we first met. I'll see you there midafternoon."

◆◆◆

"When it came to advance knowledge of our encounters, that was about as specific as it ever got. It was enough for me to know where I had to go."

"Where?"

"At the bench, by the river, where it all began. There was one more thing he had to show me."

Chapter 26

The Convergence

I ARRIVED AT THE bench just before three o'clock. That's what I took *midafternoon* to mean. I sat down and waited. And it wasn't long before he came and joined me on the bench.

◆◆◆

"The little girl who told you I would come—what was it that she said you were to be shown?"

"*That which came after.*"

"And what did you think she meant?"

"The continued manifestations of signs and harbingers, that which came after our first encounters."

"And so you've been shown. And what do you think?"

"It's a lot to take in. And I find these even more ominous and scary than what I was shown in our first encounters, years ago."

"And she said you would be shown that which manifested up until when?"

"Up to the present."

"And what you've been shown has taken up to this last year. So it would appear that we've come to an end."

He was quiet. But I didn't believe he was finished. So I kept silent as well, waiting for him to break the silence.

"But I do have something to share with you," he said. "A secret from the beginning, as we bring things full circle. I told you of the scrolls that are opened up each week by the children of Israel and the words appointed to be read on each Sabbath day, the parashas. But what if there were a series of appointed words with regard to America?"

"What do you mean?"

"A calendar of ordained readings appointed for specific days."

"Parashas for America?"

"In a sense. Not that the words were appointed to be read only in

America, but rather that they were released in America and would be read by more people in this land than in any other."

"What if…"

"It exists," he said.

"How so?"

"In the form of what is known as *The One Year Bible*, a Bible that originated in America and is made up of appointed scriptures, each one ordained to be read on a specific day of the year. So for every date of the year is an appointed passage or passages of Scripture."

"Like the scrolls of the synagogue."

That's when he reached into his coat pocket and took out the book.

"*The One Year Bible*," he said, "another form of the parashas."

He opened it up, flipped through its pages, found what he was looking for, and handed it to me.

"Read it out loud, Nouriel," he said, pointing to the passage he wanted me to recite.

So I read it.

> "The Lord sent a word against Jacob, and it has fallen on Israel. All the people will know—Ephraim and the inhabitant of Samaria—who say in pride and arrogance of heart: '*The bricks have fallen down, but we will rebuild with hewn stones; the sycamores are cut down, but we will replace them with cedars.*'[1]

"It's the vow," I said, "Isaiah 9:10."

"The words that identify the beginning of a nation's judgment," he said, "which speak of a calamity that strikes a nation in the form of an attack.

"Now, look on the top of the page. You'll find a date. It's the date for which this word was appointed. Tell me what it says. Tell me the date."

"September 11!"

"9/11."

"This was the word appointed for 9/11! The Bible itself marked the exact date when America's progression of judgment was to begin?"

"The exact date," said the prophet. "It was to fall on September 11. Thus the day when the enemy strikes the land is identified as 9/11. It was all there. America would be struck by its enemy on September 11."

"That's beyond real!"

"And yet it is real. It was all there."

"And *The One Year Bible* is read all over America."

"Yes. Do you realize what this means? It means that all over America believers have been opening up their Bibles to this scripture, which speaks of the enemy striking the land—every year on September 11."

"The people who put this Bible together—how could they have known? Did they know the mystery?...Did they know about the harbingers?"

"They had no idea. They simply appointed the beginning of the Hebrew scriptures for the beginning of the year, Genesis 1:1, the first verse of the Bible, for the first day of the year, January 1. And the end of the Hebrew scriptures was appointed for the end of the year, Malachi 4 for the last day of the year, December 31. Going by that basic and fundamental algorithm, it ended up that Isaiah 9:10 was the appointed scripture for September 11...another manifestation of the dynamic working through the mystery, the convergence of all things to the exact time and place."

"So for that to happen, the Bible had to be the length it was and had to contain the number of words that it did so it would all end up converging on that particular day."

"He weaves all things, all events and realities together."

"When did *The One Year Bible* come out?"

"Before 9/11."

"So then it revealed the date of when it would happen before it happened."

"Yes. In fact, it revealed the date as far back as 1985 when it first came out. And every September 11 since then, believers were opening up their Bibles to that scripture, of the enemy coming to the land to bring destruction. Not only did it reveal the attack but that which would take place on that day—the bricks would fall, buildings would collapse—and it would be connected to and appointed for the date of September 11."

"And the tree," I said. "It spoke of the sycamore tree being struck down and connected it to September 11, the day the sycamore was struck down."

"Yes, all those things were marked for September 11. And then it happened. On the morning of September 11, believers all over America opened up their Bibles to the scripture that spoke of the enemy who would strike on the land.

"Before the nation's government, Defense Department, and intelligence agencies had any idea, believers across America were being shown that morning of the coming of the enemy to bring destruction.

"And before the first brick had fallen and the first building had collapsed, before the first building had even been struck, they were reading of buildings collapsing, as the bricks would fall.

"And before the metal beam would shoot forth from the North Tower to strike down the sycamore tree, they had already read of the sycamore having been struck down."

"And the scripture went further than that," I said. "It revealed to them what the nation's response to the calamity would be…defiance."

"Yes," he replied, "and the context of the appointed word was also significant—that of a nation that had once known God but had turned away from Him. September 11 would be the day of the first calamity to inaugurate a nation's progression to judgment."

"And the beginning of the harbingers."

"Yes, and their continuing. Everything you've just been shown in our encounters has concerned the continuation of the harbingers, the signs, the warnings, the advancing of the progression, the template of judgment—the withering of the tree, the ninth of Tammuz, the image of the god, the inscription on the tower, the broken vessel, the fall of the erez tree, and the warning of Tophet—the signs of a nation falling from God, the same signs given concerning the last days of ancient Israel. You see, Nouriel, the progression has never stopped."

"And the template leads to judgment," I replied. "So where are we now in that progression?"

"Do you have the seal?" he asked.

So I gave it to him. He then handed me another. But it wasn't exactly another. It was the same seal that the little girl had given me and the one I had given the prophet when I first saw him again on the island—the seal with the image of the city on the hill.

"Why are you giving it back to me?" I asked.

"Because you gave it to me, and now we've come to the end."

"But you didn't answer my question. Where are we now?"

"Is that what you were told would be revealed to you?"

"No, but…"

"If that's what you're supposed to know, then I imagine you will."

And with that, he got up from the bench and began walking away.

"I know there's got to be some sort of prophetic protocol you're following," I said with a raised voice, "but you could answer the question. You're allowed to break protocol."

He turned around enough to glance at me with a slight smile.

"Stay well, Nouriel," he said. "Stay well," and not long after that he was gone.

It was the last time I saw him.

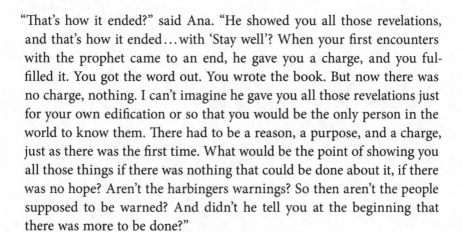

"That's how it ended?" said Ana. "He showed you all those revelations, and that's how it ended... with 'Stay well'? When your first encounters with the prophet came to an end, he gave you a charge, and you fulfilled it. You got the word out. You wrote the book. But now there was no charge, nothing. I can't imagine he gave you all those revelations just for your own edification or so that you would be the only person in the world to know them. There had to be a reason, a purpose, and a charge, just as there was the first time. What would be the point of showing you all those things if there was nothing that could be done about it, if there was no hope? Aren't the harbingers warnings? So then aren't the people supposed to be warned? And didn't he tell you at the beginning that there was more to be done?"

"But he never gave me a charge."

"So then maybe it was *an* end, but not *the* end. He showed you things that happened up to the present. So maybe it was the end for now, but not the end of what he has to show you."

"I couldn't tell you," said Nouriel.

"All right, but promise me something."

"What?"

"If the prophet should reappear, you'll let me know."

"Why are you so anxious about it, Ana?"

"Maybe because you're talking about life and death and the future of America... and the world. And maybe because I know it can't be the end. There's something more he has to show you. And I want to know it when it happens."

"You're very sure."

"Will you promise me?"

"Yes... if he should return."

Part IV

THE

COMING

Chapter 27

The Children of the Ruins

H E RETURNED!" SHE shouted. She knew he wouldn't have just shown up without letting her know in advance if it hadn't happened. "The prophet returned! And you saw him! And now *you've* returned."

"I told you I would."

"But with everything that's going on, with everybody so afraid to do anything, I didn't know you would even if he did return."

"But I made you a promise."

"How did you know I'd be here…and at night?"

"You never stop working, Ana. I saw the light in the office. I knew it had to be you."

"Come," she said.

There was nobody there but the two of them. Ana led him into her office, where she quickly set up two chairs facing each other, on which they sat down, six feet apart.

"So it wasn't the end," she said.

"You were right."

"So tell me how it began, about the encounter."

"It began with an encounter," he said, "but not with the prophet."

"What do you mean? With whom?"

"With one who came in a way I didn't expect. Months went by without anything, no leads, no clues, no signs, nothing. And then I had a dream. I was walking through the ruins of an ancient city. The air was filled with smoke and dust."

"You've seen that before…in your dreams."

"Yes, but this time it was different. This time the ruins were filled with children walking, playing, exploring. Others were sitting in the rubble or on broken walls and the remnants of fallen buildings. Since I was walking in back of them, I couldn't see their faces. One of them was sitting on the foundation of a broken pillar in a hooded robe of blue. I walked around to the other side of the pillar to see the child's face. It was a little girl…and she was wearing a mask."

"A mask?"

"A blue surgical face mask. And it wasn't only her. About half the children sitting in the ruins were wearing masks…ancient robes and yet with face masks."

◆◆◆

"Why are you wearing a mask?" I asked.

"Because of the plague," she replied.

"Do you have to wear it all the time?"

"No," she said. "I could take it off just for a little."

With that, she pulled back the hood and removed the mask. She had long wavy blonde hair. It was the girl, the little girl in the blue coat, only now the coat was a blue robe, and it was covered with dust.

"Nouriel," she said, "what is it that you see all around you?"

"The ruins of a city," I replied.

"What you see is the end of a kingdom that had known but turned away and refused to come back. What you see is a nation that deafened its ears to His voice…to His calling."

"An ancient kingdom?" I asked.

"No," she replied, "a kingdom you know very well."

"If this is its end," I said, "then it can't be changed. Then why am I seeing it? And why are all these things being revealed to me? What's the purpose?"

"So that this would *not* be its end."

"How could I change it?"

"It is for that purpose, Nouriel, that you've been shown what you've been shown."

"I don't see what I could do to…"

"And what is it that you will now be shown?"

"I have no idea."

"It will center on those things that are now and yet to come."

"The future."

"You will be shown that which concerns the future and what you need to do concerning it."

"I don't understand what I could do…"

"Therefore, you'll see him again."

"The prophet."

"And you'll need another seal. Do you have the last one, the one I gave to you and the one he gave you back?"

"I don't know," I replied. In real life I would have known, as I had always kept it with me. But I had no idea if I had brought the seal into the dream. So I reached into my pocket, and it was there. I handed it to her, and she handed me another. Except it didn't appear to be another.

"It's the same seal," I said. "You gave me back the same seal, the city on the hill."

"No," she said. "The seal will be different. But you'll have to look at it more closely. Then you'll see."

It was just then that I heard children calling her. I couldn't understand what they were saying, but I knew they were asking her to join them. She pulled the hood back over her head and the mask back over her face.

"Don't lose the seal, Nouriel," she said. "You'll need it if you're going to see him."

Then she ran off and joined the children who were calling her, running after them and disappearing into the ruins. And the dream ended.

———◆◆◆———

"As soon as I woke up, I went over to the drawer where I kept the seal, took it out, and began studying it in the hope of finding a clue or anything more I could go on."

"And did you?" asked Ana.

"Not *a* clue—but *many clues*. And they would lead me to the final mysteries…the mysteries of what was yet to come."

Chapter 28

The Shakings

"O K," said Ana, "what I'm not understanding is the little girl gave you a seal, but she gave it to you in a dream. So in reality she didn't give you anything."

"But she did," said Nouriel. "She gave me what I needed to go forward."

"But the seal you were looking at for clues was the seal you already had. It's what the prophet had given you back. So how could it lead you to anything new?"

"The dream was telling me that there was more to the seal than I had realized, clues I hadn't seen."

"So what did you see?"

"What I saw was the city on a hill. But when I examined it more closely, I saw it. Surrounding the image was what I had taken to be a decorative ring. But scattered around the ring in the midst of its decorative markings were tiny images. If you weren't searching, you'd never see them. And even if you saw them, you wouldn't be able to make out what they were without help. But I had help—a large magnifying glass I kept at home. With that, I was able to discern what they were or at least what they looked like. What they actually meant was another story."

"One seal with several images," she said, "all having to do with one mystery?"

"No, with several mysteries."

"Why all on one seal?"

"I don't know. Perhaps because it would be the bringing together of what had been shown me."

"What about the dreams? Would there be several dreams for several mysteries or one dream for all of them?"

"There would be no more dreams. The dream with the little girl would be the last. And the images on the seal weren't so much about the next revelation but the place where the next revelation would be given. So it wasn't that I was supposed to try to figure out the mystery, but rather the place where I was supposed to go to receive it."

"Why do you think that was?"

"Maybe because there wasn't time."

"So what was on the seal?"

"Since the images were arranged in a circle, I decided to begin examining them with the image that was just to the right of the top and go clockwise."

"So what was it?"

"A simple image: a circle within a square. The circle was a clock. The clock read half past nine. I struggled to uncover its meaning. I thought it might be pointing to a scripture, a Bible verse with the numbers 9:30. But nothing clicked.

"And then, when I wasn't trying to, I unlocked the meaning. I had the television going in the background. There was a news report. I heard the words *Times Square*. That was it. The clock represented time or times inside of a square, *Times Square*."

"What about the 9:30 on the clock?" she asked.

"I believe that was the time I was supposed to be there."

"But on what day?"

"As with everything else, I believed that everything would coalesce at the appointed time. I decided to go there that night, the night of the day it hit me."

"And what did you find?"

"I found the jarring spectacle of colored lights and giant screens and restless images for which Times Square is known. But the most striking thing was the absence of people. And of the few who passed through it that night, most were wearing face masks."

"Because of the crisis," she said, "because of the virus."

"Yes. Because of the virus, the entire city resembled a ghost town, a ghost city. And because of the scarcity of people, it didn't take long for me to see him. He was standing in front of One Times Square, the building from which they drop the ball every year on New Year's Eve."

◆◆◆

"So you have more to show me," I said.

"I do," said the prophet.

"And will this include the answer to my question—where we are in the mystery, in time, in the progression?"

"We've come to the place where time is marked," he said, "to speak of times and where we are within them."

He paused to look around and take in the surroundings.

"The *crossroads of the world*," he said, "and tonight there's virtually nobody crossing it."

"They're scared," I said.

Slowly we began walking the length of Times Square, occasionally coming to a stop while the display of moving images and colored lights played continuously above us, for no one.

"The mystery you've been shown involves the dynamic of recurrence, the replaying of a biblical progression of national judgment. It was there in America's fall from God. It was there in 9/11. It was there in the first harbingers you were shown and in the ones that followed. And it is there in everything that's happened to America up to the present hour. And so the question must be asked: What does the replaying of the template lead to? Where does the mystery end?"

"And so I've asked it."

"After the first shaking of ancient Israel, the nation hardened itself against God and turned further away. After 9/11, America did likewise. What then? In our last encounters, we've seen that the harbingers and signs of warning and judgment have not ceased but have continued to manifest. So what does that mean?"

"That America's fall from God has continued as well."

"Not only has it continued," he said, "but deepened and accelerated."

"Does that follow the ancient template?" I asked.

"It does. In Israel's last days as a nation, even after it was warned and shaken, its fall from God, likewise, deepened and accelerated."

"So the replaying has continued according to the ancient template—even up to now."

"Yes."

"Then is there a choice?"

"If there was no choice, there would be no warning, no signs, and no harbingers. But that there have been all these things is for the purpose of averting the template's end. In each case, the nation is given a window of time, years of grace, in which to turn back. The window for America began after 9/11 and has been until now."

"Has there been any turning? Has there been any return to God in the days since 9/11?"

"Since those days," he replied, "there have been those who have turned to God, and the rising of movements for the purpose of turning, and pockets of revival—but as for a massive return or a national turning—it has not happened. And America's mainstream culture has turned only further and more brazenly away. And in this, as well, America is following in the ominous path of ancient Israel."

"So what happens?" I asked.

"I really think you should read your own books, Nouriel. It's there in your first book."

"I'm sure I was just quoting what you told me."

"And I was just quoting a commentary on Isaiah 9 concerning ancient Israel and its vow of defiance. It was this:

> As the first stage of the judgments has been followed by no true conversion to Jehovah, the Almighty Judge, there *comes a second.*[1]

"In other words, if the nation refuses to turn back to God after its first shaking, its first calamity, there will be more."

"More shakings…"

"Yes. And I quoted another commentary on the ancient vow in Isaiah. You included it in that same chapter. It was this:

> That which God designs…is to turn us to himself and to set us a seeking him; *and, if this point be not gained by lesser judgments, greater may be expected.*[2]

"Seven years after 9/11 came the shaking of the American and world economy."

"The financial collapse."

"But there isn't to be only one shaking. There will come others, other calamities, greater than the first. When we first spoke of these things, you asked me what form the shakings and calamities would take. You recorded what I told you in the chapter called 'Things to Come.' It was this:

> They may take the form of economic disintegration or military defeat, disorder and division, the collapse of infrastructure, manmade calamities, calamities of nature, decline and fall. And, in the case of a nation so greatly blessed by God's favor, the withdrawal of all such blessings."[3]

"What about the timing of these things?" I asked. "Where are we now in the progression? How much time is left in the window?"

"The prophets gave warnings of coming events, immediately before those events came to pass. On the other hand, the prophets also gave warnings years, decades, even centuries before they came to pass. One cannot put God in a box or contain His ways within a formula. Whether it be days, years, decades, or centuries, God is sovereign; each case is its own, and the timing of all events rests in His hands.

"But you asked me years ago to tell you of a specific time period given in the ancient template—you asked me to tell you how long it was between the nation's first shaking and the coming of greater calamity and shakings. In the case of Israel's northern kingdom, I told you it was ten years. Then you asked me what it was in the case of the southern kingdom. You put that question and the answer I gave you in your book as well, in the same chapter on things to come. It was this:

> 'And what about the southern kingdom, Judah, did it follow the same pattern—an initial attack, a harbinger, and then destruction?'
>
> 'Yes, the same pattern. First came the Initial invasion in 605 BC, this time by the Babylonians. Later, the same army would return to destroy the land, the city, and the Temple.'
>
> 'When?' I asked.
>
> '586 BC.'[4]

"So the time span between the first shaking and the great calamities is 605 BC to 586 BC. How long is that?"

"About twenty years."

"How long is it exactly?"

"Nineteen years."

"Nineteen years," said the prophet. "It was nineteen years after Babylon's first invasion of the land that the judgment fell. Nineteen years after the initial invasion of the land that destruction came. Nineteen years…the time span of judgment."

He was silent, as if waiting for me to respond. I stopped walking and turned around to face him.

"2020!"

"2020."

"Nineteen years from 9/11, from 2001, the first shaking, comes out to 2020, the year of shaking, the year that the plague came to America, the year of the coronavirus…the year of disorder, of collapse, the year of greater shakings."

"Nineteen years," said the prophet, "the time span of judgment."

"And what was it again that the commentary said about greater things?"

"If we aren't turned to God '*by lesser judgments, greater may be expected.*'"[5]

"Everything that's happened," I said, "it's the greater shaking."

"It is a greater shaking," said the prophet, "but that doesn't mean it's the only one…that there aren't more or greater shakings to come."

"A shaking that spreads fear to every city and town in America and around the world, that causes millions to hide themselves inside their homes, that paralyzes much of the nation's economy and the world economy, that causes a declaration of disaster to be issued in every one of America's fifty states, and shuts down most of the planet for the first time in world history…I would think that's enough."

"Yes, but still, it doesn't mean there isn't more."

"I remember something else I put in that same chapter. When you spoke to me about the coming shakings and calamities, you said that in the case of a nation that had reigned at the head of nations, the coming judgments would ultimately mean the removal of its crown.[6] You connected the coming shaking to the *crown.*"

"And?"

"The word *crown*…it's the English form of the Latin word *corona*…*corona* is the name of the virus. And so the shaking is connected to *corona*, the crown."

"Yes," said the prophet, "the plague is called corona. And what is its official name?"

"COVID-19."

"Nineteen," he said, "the number of judgment. They named it that for an entirely different reason, of course. Nevertheless, it bears the number given in the template of judgment, the number of years from the first shaking to the greater one."

"Is that why you've returned," I said, "because of the shaking?"

"It's possible," he replied.

"And is there more to the mystery behind what's happening now…that you're going to show me?"

"That too is possible…and more."

Chapter 29

The Plague

"I THINK WE SHOULD sit down for this," he said.

We had just then come to a plaza within Times Square with empty chairs set up for pedestrians. But no one was there but us. We sat down.

"Look at all the lights, Nouriel, the glitter and glory of a city, a nation, and a civilization. And yet behind all that is darkness."

I didn't know then what exactly he was referring to. I didn't, at that moment, press the point. I had another question on my mind.

"America and the world have been brought to a near standstill because of a disease, a pandemic. Why? Why the plague?"

"Behind any phenomenon," said the prophet, "there are a multitude of causes, reasons, and purposes. And behind a solitary event, one can find causes both natural and transcendent, coexisting and acting in unison, occupying the space and moment. Why are there diseases? Because we live in a fallen world, a world of sin and evil, decay and destruction, wars, plagues, and disasters. Evil happens, calamities happen. And yet the fact that behind any given event are natural causes does not negate the fact that there are also transcendent and supernatural causes, or the fact that an event of evil may have redemptive purposes. The one does not nullify the other.

"Do you remember in our first encounters, when we read the words of Lincoln's second inaugural address, in which he spoke of the Civil War as the judgment of God upon slavery, a judgment in which the riches gained by oppression would be lost and every drop of blood drawn by the whip would be matched by the blood drawn in war?"[1]

"Yes."

"He was speaking of the war's transcendent causes and purposes, the judgment of God on the evil of slavery and the bringing of that evil to an end. Lincoln wasn't proposing that this was the only reason or cause for the calamity or that there wasn't a countless multitude of natural causes behind it. But the fact that the war had natural causes did not, in any way, nullify the transcendent purposes of judgment and redemption that were working through it. Both and all were taking place in the same place and time.

"In the same way, when judgment fell upon ancient Israel, it came through evil and brutal empires. Behind the rise of those empires were a multitude of causes, political, military, social, cultural, economic, and countless others coalescing with another multitude of turns, quirks, and twists of human events. And yet at the same time, all those factors converged to fulfill the judgments foretold by the prophets. Why did the calamity come? For all those reasons at once.

"When judgment came to ancient Israel, the destruction and calamity touched not only the unrighteous but the righteous. It even extended to the surrounding nations. It even touched the prophets. Perfect judgment does not belong to this world but to the next. And thus the striking down or sparing of any individual in the midst of such calamities did not, in and of itself, signify that the victim was, in any way, more or less guilty than anyone else. The calamity was not centered on the individual. It was the judgment of a civilization. So too when Lincoln spoke of the Civil War as a judgment from God, he was not suggesting that any individual struck down in that war was being judged, but rather that a civilization was being judged for the sin of slavery."

"I understand. So how does this relate to the plague?"

"In the same way, the fact that behind a plague is a multitude of causes does not mean that there are not also transcendent purposes. And the fact that there are transcendent purposes does not mean that any individual touched or struck down by such a plague is being judged. The question, rather, concerns the judgment of a civilization, of nations, and an age."

"So a pandemic can be a judgment?"

"Not that it *must* be," he replied, "but it can be. And if it is, there will be signs of it. The principle is revealed throughout the pages of the Bible where judgments can, at times, manifest in the form of pestilences and *plagues*. Though plagues would be seen then, as now, as evils and calamities, God used them for the purposes of redemption. How were the Hebrews saved out of Egypt?"

"By a plague."

"Yes, and by more than one. But it wasn't only then. The Scriptures record the coming of plagues as judgments against evil and the pride of man, to shake kingdoms, to cast down false gods and idols, to wake up the sleeping, to call back the lost and fallen, and to turn back nations to God."

"A plague used for the purposes of redemption?"

"Yes, Nouriel. It is not only that the natural and the supernatural can occupy the same space and time, but so too can good and evil, even judgment and mercy. Just as God can allow the strike of an enemy for the purpose of waking up and calling back a nation…that it might, in the end, be saved from destruction—so too can He allow a plague for the same purpose."

"So could that be part of what's happening now?"

"Yes," said the prophet, "that could be part. That which has come upon the world has certainly shown how quickly the certainties of life and the foundations on which a society stands can be shaken and removed. And sometimes they must be…in order that we might find the one certainty and the one foundation that cannot be shaken or removed—that we might find God."

"Then is the global pandemic a judgment?"

"If it was a judgment, there would have to be something being judged. The plague has touched the entire world. So is there anything unique about this generation, the modern world, as touching judgment?"

"Is there?"

"There is. No generation has so turned away from God or so massively overturned His ways as this one. But is there any *specific* sin or act that could call forth such judgment?"

"I can think of many."

"There *are* many," he said, "but there is one that especially calls it forth."

"Which?"

"The shedding of blood," he replied. "It is an ancient law that evil must be answered in kind and the taking of human life by the taking of human life."

"It's what Lincoln said, the blood drawn in slavery would be answered by the blood drawn in war."

"So can you think of any such sin that this world and generation are guilty of? A sin involving the shedding of blood and the taking of human life?"

"The killing of unborn children, the taking of human life, the slaughter of the most innocent, abortion."

"Where was it, Nouriel, that the prophet Jeremiah stood with the clay jar prophesying the coming judgment of his nation?"

"At the gate overlooking Tophet and the Valley of Hinnom."

"It was the ground on which the nation's children had been sacrificed to the gods. It was a prophetic pronouncement and a prophetic act, the foreshadowing of judgment. He was prophesying the judgment that would come for what they had done in that valley:

> ...(they) have filled this place with the blood of the innocents (they have also built the high places of Baal, to burn their sons with fire for burnt offerings to Baal)...therefore...this place shall no more be called Tophet or the Valley of the Son of Hinnom, but the Valley of Slaughter....I will cause them to fall by the sword.[2]

"Because they had shed the blood of their children in that valley, so in that valley, their own blood would be shed."

"The ancient law."

"It is the blood of children, the most innocent, that especially invokes the judgment of God. Jeremiah was prophesying the destruction of his nation. Their children's blood would bring about their destruction, the destruction of the entire kingdom. Now would you think that the sacrifice of their children was their only sin?"

"I'm sure it wasn't."

"No. The land was filled with sin, and all of it would be brought into judgment. But the killing of their children was the most gruesome of their sins, their defining sin, their epitome of sins, the graphic manifestation of the depths to which they had descended. And so, in the judgment of that sin would come the judgment of all their sins, the judgment and destruction of an entire civilization. Now listen carefully to the words Jeremiah spoke of the judgment that would come upon the nation because of its children's blood:

> I will make this city desolate and a hissing; everyone who
> passes by it will be astonished and hiss because of all its
> *plagues.*"[3]

"Plagues!"

"Yes...plagues, as in epidemics, pandemics, diseases, and viruses. The original word used to speak of the coming judgment was the Hebrew *makkeh*. As with other words used for *disease*, it can refer to a stroke or wound, an epidemic, a plague."

"A pandemic?"

"Yes," he replied. "Now listen to a second prophecy given through Jeremiah concerning the same sin and judgment:

> And they built the high places of Baal which are in the Valley
> of the Son of Hinnom, to cause their sons and their daughters
> to pass through the fire to Molech....Now therefore...this
> city of which you say, 'It shall be delivered into the hand of
> the king of Babylon by the sword, by the famine, and by the
> *pestilence.*'"[4]

"*Pestilence,*" I said, "another word for an epidemic, a plague."

"Yes. Again, the blood of the children would be answered by judgment, and one of the ways that the judgment would manifest would be in the coming of a plague, a pestilence, an epidemic. The second prophecy speaks of the plague by using the Hebrew word *dever. Dever* is the same word used in the Book of Exodus of the plagues that fell upon Egypt. And what was the first of those plagues?"

"I don't know."

"The turning of the Nile River into blood. The Nile was the place where the children, the baby boys of Israel, were killed by the Egyptians. It was their Tophet, their Valley of Hinnom. So again, the blood of little children calls forth the judgment of nations, and again, the judgment takes the form of a plague."

"So the plague that's come upon America and the world...does it have anything to do with blood?"

"Egypt murdered thousands of Hebrew children in the Nile. The Kingdom of Judah to which Jeremiah prophesied sacrificed thousands of its own children in the valley of Tophet. How many children do you suppose have been killed by our own civilization?"

"Killed by abortion?"

"Just in America."

"I wouldn't know."

"Not thousands," said the prophet, "not tens of thousands…not even hundreds of thousands…but *millions.* Over sixty million! Over sixty million children! Would you say that a civilization such as Nazi Germany should be brought to judgment for the Holocaust? Then what do we say of a civilization that has committed the equivalent of ten Holocausts? How much blood cries out from that?"

"I would imagine…rivers," I said.

"And how many children do you suppose have been killed by the nations of this age?"

"I don't know."

"Over *one billion children!*"

"One billion," I repeated.

"Each one a life, each one a child…torn apart, burned alive with chemicals, murdered before it had the chance to breathe its first breath or to cry out for its parent's comfort. How much blood is that? The gruesome truth is that this generation has killed more children, far more children, than any other in human history. Never has any generation had its hands covered with so much innocent blood. The loss of one life is a calamity. And the heart of God weeps over each life lost…but over one billion children…"

"It's hard to fathom," I said, "much less take in."

"And who was it in ancient Israel that committed the act, who offered up the little children?"

"I would imagine the priests of the gods."

"Not only the priests. They didn't take the children; the children were placed in their hands. So who was behind the sacrifice of the innocents?"

"It would have had to have been the parents."

"And so the act was all the more horrific, as it was the crime of the parents against their own children, the ones they should have most protected from harm. It was a crime of the strong against the weak, the older against the youngest and most defenseless. The judgment that came upon Israel for the children offered in sacrifice was the manifestation of the principle of inversion and reciprocity. As they had taken the lives of their children, so their own lives would be taken. The judgment becomes the inversion of the sin.

"So if a judgment was to come upon the world for such a massive and colossal evil, how would it manifest? What would be the judgment, the inversion, for the sin in which the older takes the life of the younger?"

"It would be a judgment," I said haltingly, almost trembling, "that strikes down...the older...a judgment that focuses its fury on the older, that strikes down the older of that generation."

"And?"

"And spares the younger...the youngest of that generation."

I was speechless for several moments. The prophet was silent as well, allowing me a moment to ponder what I had spoken. And then he spoke.

"And if one of the central consequences for the sin of shedding the children's blood is the judgment of the *dever*, or *'makkeh*, the pestilence, or plague, then what could we now expect to come upon the world? A plague that would especially strike down the older of our generation and especially spare the young...We would expect..."

"We would expect the pandemic," I replied. "We would expect COVID-19!"

"It is one of the unique properties of this particular plague that though the young may contract and carry the virus, its destructive power is overwhelmingly focused on the old."

"Like an ancient judgment," I said, "like a biblical plague passing through the land, its power is focused; it overwhelmingly strikes down the old."

"Tell me," said the prophet, "how long has abortion on demand been legal in America and in much of the world?"

"It was legalized across the nation in 1973, but it began in 1970."

"And for most of the world, from around that time or thereafter. That means that most of those responsible for the killing of the over one billion children would still be alive in the year 2020 and so too would be the multitudes who stood by and never acted or spoke a word to prevent it. And those who championed its legalization half a century earlier would be among the oldest of those still living. 2020 would

mark the closing of an era. It was then, in that year and to that generation, that the plague, with its strange properties, came upon the world.
The generation that had robbed millions of their first breath was now
struck by a plague that would require of them their last."

He paused again to allow me time to grasp what I was hearing. This
time it was I who broke the silence.

"So it is as it was then," I said, "the sins of the civilization under judgment are many, but the killing of its children is the epitome, the defining
evil."

"Yes, the most graphic witness to the depths of its darkness."

"And so in the judgment of the one evil is the judgment of an entire
civilization, the judgment of all its sins and evils."

"Tell me," he said, "what nation is it that performs more abortions
than any other?"

"I don't know."

"China. And where did this plague begin?"

"In China."

"And what nation, by its example and influence, has led the governments of other nations to sanction the killing of their children?"

"I don't know."

"America, the city on the hill, the exemplary nation. And when the
plague came upon the world, what place did it strike most severely?"

"America."

"Yes."

"But other nations have done likewise."

"Yes, and the blood of children can be found in every land. And in
ancient times, far more children were sacrificed outside the borders
of Israel than within them. But Israel was consecrated from its birth
to the purposes of God. It had known more, been blessed more, and
thus fallen more. And to whom much is given, much is required. And
so Israel was more accountable, and thus its judgment more severe.
America was likewise consecrated from its foundation to the purposes
of God. And America has, likewise, been given more and so has more
greatly fallen. And thus had it done nothing more than what other
nations had done, for that reason alone, we would have expected its
judgment to be more severe.

"But America has not only, by its example, led others into this practice but has killed more children within its borders than have the vast majority of nations. And beyond that, the laws it passed concerning the killing of unborn children are among the most permissive in the world and allow for the even more gruesome killing of children in the latter stages of pregnancy.

"America was founded after the pattern of ancient Israel. And so if it turns away from God and repeats the ancient act, then judgments that came upon ancient Israel will reappear. And so of all nations of the earth, the plague centered its wrath on America.

"Now let's go deeper. Within America, what state above all other states has the blood of children on its hands?"

"New York State," I replied.

"Far more than any other. So then what might we expect of the plague?"

"We might expect that it would focus its fury on New York."

"And where in America, of all its states, did the fury of the plague center?"

"New York."

"So the same state that had led the nation in the shedding of blood, the same state that killed more of its children than any other...now became the state in which more of its people were killed by the plague than any other...far more people...far more even than were killed in most nations."

"The ancient law of judgment," I said.

"Let's go deeper still. On what ground in the state of New York were more children killed than on any other?"

"New York City."

"Then what might we expect of the plague?"

"We would expect it to focus its fury most specifically on New York City."

"And what city did the plague actually strike most specifically and most severely?"

"New York City."

"More unborn children had been killed within that city than in any other city in America, far more, with numbers dramatically disproportionate to the numbers of those killed outside the city. So when the plague came upon America, it struck down more people within that one particular city than in any other city or place in the nation, far more people, and, likewise, with numbers dramatically disproportionate to those struck down outside that city. Remember what Jeremiah prophesied of Tophet and the Valley of Hinnom."

"That those killed on the day of judgment would correspond to the children killed in sacrifice there."

"And so it did. Tophet, the center of child sacrifice, would become the center of judgment, of slaughter. So if New York City is the Tophet of America, then we would expect that, of all places, the plague would focus its fury there. And so it did. America became the epicenter of the global pandemic, and New York City became the epicenter of the American pandemic...and of the global pandemic. The law of judgment: the abortion capital becomes the plague capital."

"New York City, the central ground of 9/11, and of the harbingers, and of the global financial collapse, and now of the plague...city of judgment."

"And the gate," said the prophet.

"Judgment begins at the gate."

"And do you know how most of America was infected by the plague?"

"No."

"It came from New York," he answered.

"Most?"

"Yes. Of all the cases of the virus in America, over half of them were traced back to New York. And what was it, half a century earlier, that also spread from New York to America?"

"Abortion."

"So the sin went forth from New York...and then the plague."

"Tophet."

"Was there anything significant that happened in New York just before the plague came upon the world, anything that happened in the preceding year?"

"The law!" I said. "The law that the New York legislature passed to legalize the killing of children up to the point of birth."

"The law that left many in shock and others calling it horrific and gruesome. The law that New York enacted with great joy and celebration. And others wondered if it would not call forth judgment."

"And it all happened in the year that led to the plague."

"Actually," said the prophet, "it happened in the same year. The act was passed at the beginning of that year; the plague began before that year was over. So they were both set in motion in the same year. In fact, the plague was named after the year in which New York enacted its law of death."

"The same year," I said, "that the governor of New York ordered the harbinger, the tower of Ground Zero, the high place of Tophet, to be lit up in celebration."

"Yes, they illuminated the harbinger of judgment."

"And judgment came."

"Much of the world was guilty of the ancient sin. But New York was at the forefront. And in 2019, it crossed the line. And then came the plague. Is it possible that the crossing of that line was the act that triggered what was to come? In any case, it would come to New York. And what was it that Jeremiah prophesied of Tophet? He prophesied that as Tophet had brought death to the nation's children, so death would come back to it. So in the year following New York's inaugurating and celebrating the death of yet more children, death would come to New York. And the governor who led that celebration of death now had to deal with the issue of death all around him. The one who had called for the disposal of human life was now forced to speak of the value of human life. And as the tower was illuminated in pink to celebrate that law of death, one year later, another tower would be illuminated in red, bearing witness to the plague of death that had come to the city."

"Which tower?"

"The Empire State Building."

"The Empire State Building," I said, "the same building that was illuminated with the image of Kali, the goddess of death. And now death had come to the city."

"There was another place," said the prophet, "from which the plague came to America, another gate."

"What place?"

"Seattle, Washington. It was there that the first official case of the virus was recorded. It is worthy of note that in 1970, Washington was one of the two states in America that followed New York in sanctioning the act of abortion and bringing it to America. Now, half a century later, it was from Washington that the news went forth that the plague had arrived on American shores. It was the case of Patient Zero. The day after the case was confirmed, newspapers around the country carried the headlines that the virus had come to America. Do you know what date appeared next to those headlines?"

"No."

"It was January 22. January 22 is the day America legalized the killing of unborn children. It was also the one-year anniversary of the day that New York crossed the line and passed its gruesome law—and exactly one year to the day that the harbinger, the tower of Ground Zero, was illuminated to celebrate that act."

"I have a question: Jeremiah prophesied the coming of a pestilence and a judgment that would answer to the blood of the nation's children. When exactly did that judgment come?"

"In 586 BC."

"586 BC was nineteen years after the nation's first shaking, the first invasion of the enemy."

"That's correct."

"Nineteen years after the nation's first shaking."

"So then, could it be that the mystery ordains that nineteen years after the first shaking of America, 9/11, there would come not only another shaking but a plague answering to the blood of the nation's children...in 2020?"

"What number is it that's contained in the name of the plague?"

"The number nineteen...COVID-19."

"And it was nineteen years," said the prophet. "And what happens if you open up the Book of Jeremiah and turn to the chapter marked by that same number, the number nineteen?"

"I have no idea."

"It leads you to Jeremiah's prophecy of the judgment and plagues to come upon the nation for the blood of its children...at the end of the nineteen years. It leads you to that very prophecy."

"The nineteenth year, a plague called *nineteen*, and the nineteenth chapter that contains the prophecy of the plague and judgment of the nineteenth year...It's too much to take in."

"And yet," said the prophet, "there's more. The word of Jeremiah concerning Tophet was connected to a prophetic act.

> Thus says the LORD: 'Go and get a potter's earthen flask....And go out to the Valley of the Son of Hinnom, which is by the

entry of the Potsherd Gate; and proclaim there the words that
I will tell you.'"[5]

"The clay jar."

"So as he exposed the nation's sin against its children and foretold the
judgment that would come because of it, he was holding the jar of the
potter. Then he smashed it as a sign of the coming calamity and said
this:

> ...and they shall bury them in Tophet till there is no place to
> bury.[6]

"So if New York City corresponds with Tophet, the ground of the slain
children, what would this mean?"

"That there would be so many deaths in New York City that they
would run out of room to accommodate them."

"And do you know what happened when the plague struck New York
City?"

"Tell me."

"There were so many deaths that the city that its morgues and funeral
homes could not accommodate them."

"So what did they do?"

"They took the unclaimed bodies to a place called Hart Island. Jeremiah's prophecy was linked to the potter. He issued it while holding
the potter's jar, then smashed it as the sign of coming destruction. The
place where he smashed it and over which he prophesied, the Valley of
Hinnom and Tophet, is identified as being near the Potter's Gate, which
is linked to the Potter's Field. So the prophecy foretelling the lack of
room to accommodate the dead in Tophet is linked to the potter, the
Potter's Gate and Potter's Field. So when New York City, unable to
accommodate the dead, took them to a burial ground on Hart Island,
do you know what that ground was called?"

"No."

"Potter's Field."

"No!"

"Yes, they buried them in Potter's Field, the field of the potter. And do
you know what that place on Hart Island and any such place identified
by those words is ultimately named after?"

"No."

"The very same field that sits by the Valley of Hinnom and Tophet, the same field over which Jeremiah prophesied and smashed the potter's jar in Jeremiah 19."

"It's too much."

"And yet," he said, "there's still more. There's only one other place in the Bible that speaks of what would happen in Tophet, the calamity and the burial of the dead. It's another one of Jeremiah's prophecies. It's found in the seventh and eighth chapters of his book. In the midst of that prophecy, Jeremiah cries out in mourning, seeking an answer to his nation's judgment. It's there that he speaks these words:

> Is there no balm in Gilead,
> Is there no physician there?
> Why then is there no recovery
> For the health of the daughter of my people?[7]

"The prophet is giving voice to his nation's pain and calling for its healing, for a cure. The Hebrew words used in that prophecy speak of health, soundness, recovery, doctors, restoration to wholeness, physicians...healing."

"It all sounds medical."

"Yes, that's the imagery being invoked."

"And the balm of Gilead," I said, "what was that?"

"Gilead was a place in Israel from which came a healing substance, an ancient medicine known for its curative powers. So in the wake of the calamity, Jeremiah was seeking a cure to heal and restore the brokenness of his people and wondering why it seemed that none could be found.

"So in the midst of the plague that devastated America, the nation and its leaders likewise desperately sought a cure. Pressure was placed on the medical industry to find an answer as quickly as possible—a medicine, a drug, a vaccine that would bring protection and healing from the pandemic. The first glimpse of hope came at the end of April when an American biopharmaceutical company announced that it had seen positive results in the testing of an antiviral medication on the virus.[8] Though the initial results suggested a minimal effect, the news made headlines around the world, led the Food and Drug Administration to issue an immediate emergency authorization for the medication's distribution, and caused the stock market to rally five hundred points. The nation was desperate for a cure."

"For a balm of Gilead."

"Yes, for the balm of Gilead, for that over which the prophet cried out—the hope of a nation that had turned from God and shed the blood of its children, the balm of Gilead…a cure for judgment."

"I remember hearing the news."

"And do you remember hearing of the company that was offering the cure?"

"I heard something about it."

"Did you catch the *name* of the company that was offering the cure?"

"No."

"The name of the company…was *Gilead*."

"No!"

"The balm that was offered for America's sickness came from *Gilead*."

"That's too…"

"Its full name was Gilead Sciences. And the purpose of its existence was to produce cures, *balms*. And so America was placing its hope in a literal *balm of Gilead*."

"And the balm of Gilead," I said, "was part of the prophecy that had to do with Tophet and a nation under judgment for the killing of its children."

It was as if I was stunned by my own words, or the reality behind them. I was silent after that, staring into the lighted signs and emptiness of Times Square but lost in thought.

"And yet there's more," said the prophet.

"I don't know if I can take more."

"One more thing."

"Go ahead."

"You know what the Jubilee is?"

"A celebration that comes from the Bible."

"It was the year when that which was lost was restored to its original owner. It was the year of restoration and restitution."

"It was a good thing."

"Yes. But there was another side to it. If you had taken the land that belonged to another, in the year of Jubilee, that which you had taken was taken from you. The Jubilee was the reversal of what had been done since the last Jubilee. What about life?" he asked.

"What do you mean?"

"What about a generation or nation that has taken life, life that belonged to another, life that belonged to God?"

"I don't know."

"Would life not be taken from that generation or nation?"

"I don't understand."

"When was it, Nouriel, that America first legalized abortion on demand, when it began within its borders?"

"In 1970."

"The Jubilee comes every fifty years."

"2020!"

"2020 was the Jubilean year of abortion in America."

"And what was taken…is taken back."

"In 1970, abortion on demand with no geographic limitations was initiated in New York, the act that would establish the state as the nation's abortion capital. Fifty years later, in the Jubilean year of that act, the wrath of the plague fell on New York. And do you know when, in 1970, it all began?"

"No."

"On two days," said the prophet, "it all began on two days…in the building to which I took you."

"The New York State Capitol building."

"It began there with a vote in the New York State Assembly and, the following day, with a vote in the New York Senate. By those two votes on those two days, the law was passed."

"When was it?"

"In April of 1970."

"And what were the two days?"

"The New York Assembly passed the law on April 9, and the New York Senate, on April 10."

"April 9 and April 10."

"Fifty years later, the plague struck America and, most specifically, in the state of New York. Do you know when its fury reached its peak in New York?"

"No."

"In April of 2020, the same month when New York legalized the killing of the unborn fifty years earlier."

"From April 1970 to April 2020, fifty years to the month."

"As to the peak of the plague's fury in the state of New York, the moment of its greatest impact, several organizations, including the *New York Times*, sought to pinpoint it. They charted the plague's infection rate in New York, the number of new people stricken through its seven-day average. It pinpointed a specific time period. Do you know what it came out to be?"

"Tell me."

"Two days...April 9 and April 10."[9]

"No!"

"The same exact dates on which the state had ushered in the ancient sin by voting for the killing of the unborn fifty years earlier."

"Fifty years to the same exact dates!"

"The dates that marked the completion of the Jubilee."

"It's too..." I couldn't finish."

I couldn't speak. The prophet allowed me to stay quiet until I was ready.

"What you're showing me," I said, "are the signs not only of a world under judgment but of a specific nation, a nation replaying the template of judgment with eerie and overwhelming precision. I'm looking for an answer for that nation."

"There is one," said the prophet.

"I don't see it coming."

"But there is one...even for those who have taken part in committing the ancient sin. For greater than any sin is His love...far greater. And far stronger than any judgment is His mercy. And for all who come to Him, His arms are open. There *is* hope. And it must be that darkness comes before the light...and that through the darkness the light would come."

"I'm not seeing the light in the darkness."

"But it's there," said the prophet. "*There is a balm in Gilead.*"

At that, he rose to his feet. But I couldn't move. So I just sat there in the middle of Times Square as the lights and colors displayed themselves, ceaselessly, restlessly, for no one.

Chapter 30

The Return

L ET'S GO SOMEWHERE," said Ana.

"Where?"

"I don't know; I just need to get out. I need some fresh air and space."

"It's nighttime," said Nouriel, "and we're in the middle of a plague. Virtually nothing is open, even if it wasn't nighttime. And I don't know how you feel about continuing this with masks on."

"I know a place," she said, "where it won't matter. My mother used to take me there when I was little, Brighton Beach. Let's go there, Nouriel. It's a nice night, and I doubt we'll find anybody there at this hour. I can get us a ride."

So she called for a driver. He took them down to Battery Park, through the tunnel to Brooklyn, and, from there, to Brighton Beach, where he let them out by the boardwalk. They made their way toward the shore, sitting down on the sand about thirty feet away from the water. In the darkness, they could hear the sound of the ocean more than they could see it. And, as Ana had thought, there was no one else there.

"So what happened," she asked, "after your time with the prophet in Times Square?"

"I took a few days to process what he told me there. Finally, I went back to the drawer, took out the seal and the magnifying glass, and began examining the next clue. It didn't take long for me to realize what it was."

"What was it?"

"An upright rectangle with something of a crown or spikes on its top."

"It sounds familiar."

"Yes," said Nouriel. "I had seen it before. It was on one of the seals the prophet had given me in our first encounters. So I knew what it meant and exactly where I had to go."

"Where?"

"To a place I had been to before—one of the most significant places in the mystery...St. Paul's Chapel."

"So I took a taxi down to Lower Manhattan. I got out in front of the chapel. I was standing there on the sidewalk when I heard his voice."

————————◆◆◆————————

"You've asked me if the future was sealed," he said, "if there was any hope for America, any way out of judgment. It was the day I first led you here that we spoke of that very thing…of hope."

"Yes," I replied, "but that was then. There was more time then. And this is the window in the template that's given for a nation to turn back. But the nation hasn't turned back, only further away. And everything you've shown me speaks of a nation racing to judgment."

"Tell me, Nouriel, of the mystery ground."

"It's in the book," I replied.

"I know, but tell me."

"Israel's most holy ground was that of the Temple Mount. It was there that its leaders gathered together with the people to consecrate the Temple to God. And it was there that King Solomon and the people prayed and committed the nation's future to God. But Israel would fall away from God, and after many warnings, shakings, and calamities, the judgment would come. The enemy would bring destruction to the Temple Mount, the nation's consecration ground, and leave it in ruins. The destruction of that sacred ground was a sign. The nation's ground of consecration, where it had been dedicated to God in prayer, had now become the ground of judgment. The nation's consecration ground became the ground of destruction."

"And what does that have to do with America?" he asked.

"America's first day as a fully constituted nation was April 30, 1789, the inaugural day of its first president, George Washington. After Washington was sworn into office, he led America's first government on foot to the place appointed for the new governments to perform its first official act—to pray and dedicate the nation's future to God. So on April 30, 1789, America's first government committed and consecrated the nation's future to God. The place on which they lifted up those prayers is the nation's ground of consecration."

"And it was in the nation's capital," said the prophet. "And what was America's first capital?"

"New York City."

"And where in New York City did they lift up those prayers?"

"In Lower Manhattan."

"And so America's consecration ground is…"

"Ground Zero."

"And thus," said the prophet, "on 9/11 the ancient mystery was fulfilled—the destruction returned to the nation's ground of consecration."

"The ground on which America was dedicated to God became the ground of its devastation; the nation's consecration ground became the ground of destruction—Ground Zero."

"And it still stands," he said, "the little stone chapel in which Washington and the nation's first government dedicated America to God— St. Paul's Chapel, in the back of which is Ground Zero. Nouriel, I don't believe you've ever been inside. Why don't we go in?"

"It must be closed. Everything in the city is closed because of the crisis."

"But we can go inside."

He led me to the front door, which, to my surprise, he opened, and led me in.

"How do you manage to get access to everything?" I asked. "Some sort of occupational perk that comes with being a prophet?"

"A trade secret," he replied.

There was no one there, just the two of us. It didn't look as I had expected it to. It was hard to say exactly what I expected it to look like, but it was bright and airy, with white columns and glass chandeliers, and full of light streaming in from its windows.

"It was here on its inaugural day as a nation that America was consecrated to God. It was here that its first president and Congress prayed."

He led me over to an oil painting hanging on one of the walls.

"What does it look like?"

It was of a bird with branches and arrows in its talons and a shield of stars and stripes over its breast.

"What does it remind you of?" he asked.

"The Great Seal of the United States. Only it looks more like a turkey than an eagle."

"That tells you how old it is. It was there from the beginning, before the bald eagle, one of the earliest of symbols to represent the United States, and it's been housed here on the corner of Ground Zero. Come," he said, now leading me to the front of the chapel, where a strange-looking sculpted piece rested against the chapel's central window. It was almost as if the entire building centered on that one object.

"It's called the Glory Altarpiece," he said. "It was created by the same man who designed Washington, DC."

At the bottom of the piece were the two tablets of the Ten Commandments. Above the tablets were rays, as if coming down from the sky, a sky of clouds, in the middle of which was what looked like a sun or radiant light...in the middle of which were four Hebrew letters.

"Do you know what it says, Nouriel?"

"Something significant?"

"I would say so. It's the tetragrammaton, the four letters that make up the Name of God. It's not only a depiction of the Ten Commandments but of the day the tablets were given and all that surrounded its giving...the glory, the clouds, the rays, and the Name of God. It's all the more striking in light of what happened here."

"What do you mean?"

"Do you know how many people perished on September 11?"

"About three thousand."

"As the Ten Commandments were being given on Sinai, the people of Israel turned away from God and worshipped a golden calf...the first instance of the nation falling away from God. It is recorded that the number of people who perished because of that was *about three thousand*[1]—the same that perished on 9/11. The perishing of the three thousand is linked to this object."

"And it was here in this building at the corner of Ground Zero..."

"As its centerpiece," he said, "for centuries. Come, Nouriel, let's go outside." He led me through the chapel's back door.

Once outside, I immediately recognized my surroundings. We were standing inside the chapel's courtyard, or graveyard. Enclosing it was the wrought iron fence through which I had looked in search of the Tree of Hope.

"The ground of the harbingers," he said. "Over there is where the Sycamore of Ground Zero was struck down and the Tree of Hope planted in its place...and where it withered away and was destroyed. And there, just beyond the fence, is the tower of Ground Zero...America's ground of consecration. Do you know what happened to Israel's ground of consecration?"

"The Temple Mount, after its destruction? Tell me."

"When the people came back to God, they returned to that ground. There they rededicated themselves to His purposes and were restored. The calamity of 9/11 turned the nation back to the ground on which it had been consecrated to God in prayer. God was calling America back to its ground of consecration and prayer. He was calling the nation to return. And people came here from around the nation and posted messages and prayers all over the gate of this ground. They were drawn here without fully knowing why."

"But even as the nation's eyes were turned back to this place," I said, "there was no turning back to God. And yet it was on the same day that America was dedicated to God on this ground that it was given a prophetic warning."

"Yes," said the prophet, "in Washington's inaugural address—that the blessings of God could never remain 'on a nation that *disregards the eternal rules of order and right, which Heaven itself has ordained.*'"[2]

"Yes. And from the time you first charged me to give warning until now, America has not only disregarded God's eternal rules of order and right but mocked them, broken them, and celebrated their breaking. It's not only disregarded them; it's warred against them."

"Yes, all those things are true. But do you not believe that His mercy is greater still, greater than all those things? Never forget, Nouriel, that the ending of darkness and the judgment of evil are what is required of the good, but compassion, forgiveness, mercy, salvation, healing, and restoration are the heart of good, the heart of God."

"But if, in the window of time given to America to return, America has turned all the more away, then..."

"Then perhaps it is all the more urgent now. You know that such things as repentance and revival often come only through shaking. And what has now come upon America...but a shaking? His voice still calls."

"Then perhaps His voice has to become louder."

"Do you remember the parasha, the ancient word appointed to be read just before the events of 9/11 began?"

"The calamities that come on the nation that turns away from God, the striking of the land, the invasion of the nation's enemies, the attack of its gates, the swooping eagle..."

"That was the scripture appointed to usher in the week of 9/11. But there was another scripture appointed to close the week of 9/11. Do you know what it was? It was a word to the nation on which calamity had fallen, a word appointed for the aftermath. It was this:

> Now it shall come to pass, when all these things come upon you, the blessing and the curse...*and you return to the* LORD *your God* and obey His voice, according to all that I command you today, *you and your children, with all your heart and with all your soul.*...The LORD your God will make you abound in all the work of your hand...and in the produce of your land for good....*if you turn to the* LORD *your God with all your heart and with all your soul.*[3]

"So as the week in which America was traumatized by the calamity of 9/11 came to its end, the word appointed for that moment was God's message to a nation traumatized by calamity. And what was that message? It was God calling that nation to return...and the promise that if they did return, He would restore them." that had turned away from His ways, that had fallen, that had suffered catastrophe...and now God was calling it to return. And if the people returned, He would restore them."

"Return," I said. "In our first encounters, you focused on that word."

"And it was all there," he replied, "in the appointed scripture that followed 9/11. Behind the word *return* or *turn* is the Hebrew word *shuv*. It also means to repent."

"Repentance, the one thing missing after 9/11. America never returned because America never repented."

"Yes, and without repentance, there can be no return. And without return, there can be no revival and no restoration."

We walked slowly along the courtyard path, through the grass and the aged gravestones and under the trees that had not yet blossomed.

"Do you remember the scripture," he said, "that was joined to the ground of consecration, the word God gave Solomon to answer the prayers he had prayed at the dedication of the Temple?"

"Yes, the word appointed for the nation that had turned from God and suffered calamity, the calling to a fallen and wounded nation:

> If My people who are called by My name will humble themselves, and pray and seek My face, and turn from their

wicked ways, then I will hear from heaven, and will forgive
their sin and heal their land."[4]

"It's the scripture of return," he said. "And it is now all the more critical. If there is to be national revival, healing, and restoration, then it
must come this way, through humbling, through prayer, through the
seeking of God's presence, through the turning away from sin, from all
that wars against the will of God, through repentance and return. And
the promise is that if this is done, God will hear that nation's prayers,
forgive its sins, and heal its land."

"It hasn't yet come."

"Do you know what leads up to that specific verse and promise?"

"No."

"The verse before it. And do you know what that verse says?"

"No."

"It says this:

> When I shut up heaven and there is no rain, or command
> the locusts to devour the land, or send *pestilence* among My
> people, if My people who are called by My name will humble
> themselves...[5]

"The last thing, the last event specified before that promise is the
coming of a pestilence on the land, a plague, a pandemic."

"The virus..."

"What leads up to the humbling, the praying, the seeking, the repentance, and the healing of the land...is a plague."

"Why is that?"

"Because shaking is often the only thing that wakes us up and causes
us to turn back to God...not only for individuals but for nations and
civilizations, especially those who have deafened their ears to His voice."

"The scripture also talks about locusts. I understand about the plague,
the pandemic...but locusts? How would that apply to the modern
world?"

"Do you know what year it is, Nouriel?"

"Aside from its number?"

"It's the year of the locusts."

"What?"

"A plague of locusts, hundreds of billions of locusts descending on the world, so massive that the United Nations called it a plague 'of biblical proportions.'"[6]

"Which plague came first?"

"First came the locusts and then the pestilence, two plagues of biblical proportions striking the world...the two plagues specifically mentioned in that verse leading up to 'If My people...'

"And the shutting up of the heavens?"

"That would be a drought or famine."

"Any sign of that?"

"In the year of the two plagues came reports of another, a mega drought, the most prolonged in centuries. At the same time, the United Nations sounded the alarm of a looming global famine, again of 'biblical proportions.'[7] And along with the scarcity of food, a drought or famine is marked by the withering of a nation's economy. The year of the plagues saw that as well. And yet that verse, 2 Chronicles 7:13, requires only one of the three. Thus we have more than enough."

"I had no idea..."

"But it was there in your book. First you wrote of the shaking that would come to America. Then you wrote of the template of years, nineteen years and thus to the year 2020. And then, after those things, you wrote of the promise in 2 Chronicles 7, '*if my people...*'—the promise that follows the time of plague and locusts. And all these things have now converged at the same moment."

"But it was *you* who said all those things."

"But you wrote them down for others to see."

"So what does it all point to?"

"The harbingers warn of coming judgment. They cry out that now is the time...and there may not be another. If there's going to be a return, a turning to God in prayer and humbling and seeking and repentance, now is the time."

"And He would still hear from heaven and forgive their sin and heal their land, even now?"

"Even with all that's been done against Him, even now...even to a nation and all who have warred against Him...His arms are open, and His heart longs to have mercy...to all who will come."

"And judgment?"

"The necessity remains. And without a return, it must come. And, thus again, the time is critical...and the hour, late."

"So then, what is it that lies ahead? Calamity and judgment or revival and restoration?"

"If America does not return, it will pass the point of no return. And America's light will be removed. But if it will return, then calamity may be averted, and revival may come. And yet, again, remember as well that it is through calamity, crises, and hard times that often come repentance, return, and revival. And so if these things must come, it is because they must and He must, in mercy, allow them that salvation might also come, that those who would, might return."

"How?" I asked. "How would America return? How would it happen if it could happen?"

"It already has," he replied.

"What do you mean?"

"The next time you see me, Nouriel, you will be shown the secret things, without which America as you know it would have ceased to exist."

Chapter 31

The Winds of April

A s soon as I got home, I took out the magnifying glass and began to study the next image on the seal."

"And what was it?"

"It looked like an ancient Greek temple, and yet it was familiar. I counted out the number of columns that lined the building's facade. There were twelve. I took out a five-dollar bill and compared it. It was as I suspected. It was the Lincoln Memorial."

"You had met the prophet there," said Ana, "once before in your first encounters."

"Yes," said Nouriel. "But it was a lot harder back then to know that I was to meet him there. This time the clue was much clearer."

"Why do you think that was?"

"I believe, because there was now less time. So I took a train to Washington, DC. It was a breezy spring day in the capital city. I checked into a hotel, unloaded my baggage, and took a cab to the Lincoln Memorial. By the time I got there, it was midafternoon. I ascended the steps, scanning my surroundings for any sign of the prophet. I reached the top of the stairs, passed through the massive columns of the colonnade, and entered the building.

"Because of the pandemic, I was mostly alone. But there, to my right, in his long, dark coat was the prophet. I could only see his back side, as he was turned away from me, gazing up at the words engraved on the memorial's northern wall.

"He didn't see me come in or approach him. It was the first time that that had happened. I was standing in back of him and to his left, thinking of what the most appropriate greeting would be. But I never had the chance to give it."

◆◆◆

"Nouriel," he said without turning his gaze. "This is where we stood the first time we came here. And this is what we read, the words of his Second Inaugural Address, in which he speaks of the Civil War as the judgment of God on the nation's sin of slavery:

> …until every drop of blood drawn with the lash, shall be paid by another drawn by the sword, as was said three thousand years ago, so still it must be said 'the judgments of the Lord, are true and righteous altogether.'[1]

"The war had turned farms into battlegrounds and cities into blood-covered devastations. As it approached its third year, the Union's prospects were looking grim. Its highest generals were failing and being replaced, one after the other. In the east, the Union was suffering defeat before the Army of Northern Virginia, led by General Robert E. Lee. In the west, its campaign to take the Confederate stronghold of Vicksburg was, likewise, suffering repeated failure. There was no end in sight. And with many in the North growing weary of the war, the danger of defection and the defeat of Lincoln's government, and thus the acceptance of the Confederacy's secession, was growing. And if that had happened, the United States of America as we know it would have ceased to exist.

"But then a stirring took place in the nation's capital. Based on the template given in the Scriptures of a nation suffering the consequences of its sins and the promise of healing and restoration, the United States Senate called on Lincoln to set forth a national day of prayer and repentance. Lincoln issued a proclamation calling the people of America to do what was set forth in 2 Chronicles 7:14, to humble themselves, to pray, to seek God's face, and to turn from their sinful ways, to repent. The proclamation ended in the hope of three blessings: that the nation's prayers would be 'heard on high,' that God would grant 'the pardon of our national sins,' and begin the 'restoration of our now divided and suffering country.'[2] They were the exact three blessings promised in that scripture and cited in the exact order in which they were given: 'then I will *hear from heaven,* and will *forgive their sin* and *heal their land.*'[3] So in the darkest days of that war, Lincoln called the nation to come in prayer and repentance before God."

"Historians are in agreement as to what year marked the turning point of the Civil War. Do you know what it was?"

"No."

"1863," he replied. "More specifically, July of 1863, with two battles: the most famous engagement of that war and the bloodiest ever fought in the western hemisphere, the Battle of Gettysburg, and the other—just as critical and decisive—the Battle of Vicksburg. They were both fought at the same time. The Battle of Gettysburg ended on July 3. The Battle of Vicksburg ended the next day. The turning point of the Civil War came in the first days of July 1863. It would determine the victory of the Union, the defeat of the Confederacy, and the survival of the United States.

"Do you know when the national day of prayer and repentance took place? In 1863, the same year. It happened at the end of April. And thus the turning point of the war came just over two months later. Gettysburg was the high-water mark of the Confederacy. General Lee's plan was to enter northern territory and crush the Union Army so decisively that the North would give up the war. Thus the battle threatened to bring about the dissolution of the United States, but instead, it became the turning point of its preservation. Gettysburg was Lee's greatest disaster. From that point onward, he would never mount a major offensive against the Union but would fight a war of defense. Gettysburg would begin the Confederacy's decline and lead to its destruction.

"Then there was the Battle of Vicksburg. The city of Vicksburg gave the South control of the Mississippi River and was known as the nail that held the Confederacy together. Lincoln saw its defeat as the key to ending the war. The Confederacy had attempted to divide the United States in two. But with the fall of Vicksburg on July 4, 1862, the Confederacy itself was divided in two, and its end was now only a matter of time.

"The man responsible for the fall of Vicksburg was Ulysses S. Grant. The victory would constitute the turning point not only of the war but of his career and would ultimately lead to his being placed in charge of all Union Forces and bringing the war to its end.

"The campaign to take Vicksburg had been underway since the winter of the preceding year. Grant had made five attempts to take the city. All of them had failed. But in the spring of 1863, everything changed as Grant led his men across the Mississippi River and, the next day, won the first victory of the entire campaign. It was called the Battle of Port Gibson, the first of five victories that would lead to the taking of Vicksburg. It was at Port Gibson that everything turned around. It was thus the turning point of the turning point of the Civil War."

"When did it happen?"

"It happened on May 1, 1863. The national day of prayer and repentance took place on April 30, 1863."

"It happened the next day!"

"Yes. The turning point of the turning point of that war, the day that led to the ending of the war and the healing of the land, took place on the day after the day of national prayer and repentance. In other words, April 30 was the day of '*If My people...will humble themselves, and pray...,*' and May 1, the day that set in motion 'Then I will...heal their land'[4]—the very next day."

The prophet then led me over to the colonnade, where we stood in between two columns.

"There are all together thirty-six columns here," he said. "Do you know why?"

"No."

"They stand for the thirty-six states that existed at the time of Lincoln's presidency. The names of those states are engraved over the columns. This one stands for Pennsylvania."

"Pennsylvania," I said, "Gettysburg. You told me about the turning point that led to the fall of Vicksburg. Was there a turning point that led to the Battle of Gettysburg?"

"Yes. It was the Battle of Chancellorsville. On the surface, it appeared to be a great victory for Robert E. Lee. But the deeper picture was very different. It would ultimately prove catastrophic for the Confederacy and is considered by some to be the third turning point of the war. It caused four things to happen that would lead to disaster. First, it left General Lee depressed over its outcome, as he believed it accomplished nothing. It frustrated him, so much so that he became all the more determined to deliver a crushing blow against the Union on its own soil. Second, it bolstered his confidence that he could fully execute that crushing blow. Third, it gave the Confederacy the confidence to approve Lee's plan. The Battle of Chancellorsville would lead directly to the Battle of Gettysburg, the Confederacy's greatest disaster and the turning point of the war."

"You said there were four. You only told me three."

"When Lee entered Gettysburg, someone was missing—his greatest general and the man he referred to as his right hand: Stonewall Jackson. His absence at Gettysburg would prove critical."

"Why wasn't he there?"

"Because of the battle at Chancellorsville. It was nighttime. Jackson's troops spotted the approach of soldiers on horseback. Taking them to be riders in the Union cavalry, they opened fire. But the approaching soldiers were their own. One of them was Stonewall Jackson. He was struck down by their fire. The injury was fatal. Lee was said to have commented that for the sake of the South, he would rather have been the one shot than Jackson. The death of Stonewall Jackson crushed the morale of the Confederate army and of the South itself and bolstered that of the North. And it removed one of the most brilliant commanders in American history from the Confederate campaign.

"Historians have cited Jackson's absence at Gettysburg as decisive in bringing about the defeat of Lee's army and thus, in the end, of the Confederacy."

"And when was he shot?"

"On May 2, 1863...two days after the national day of prayer."

"The Battle of Chancellorsville set all these things in motion. So when did Chancellorsville begin?"

"The battle began on May 1, 1863—the very day after the national day of prayer. One of Lee's other generals, General James Longstreet, would mark Chancellorsville as the war's turning point, when 'the dark clouds of the future...began to lower above the Confederates.'"[5]

"So it was the turning point of the turning point, just as was Grant's first victory in the Vicksburg campaign."

"Yes. The two turning points, the Battle of Chancellorsville and the Battle of Port Gibson, each began on the same day—the day following the day of prayer."

"If My people humble themselves and pray..."

"And so they did. And the very next day, it all began to turn. And just over two months later, it would manifest to the world. It was all set in motion on that day, the end was sealed, and America would survive."

The prophet then led me back into the chamber and to the statue. We stood there gazing at the massive figure sitting on the stone chair, burdened down and lost in somber contemplation.

"He is known for many things," said the prophet, "but it was what he did in the spring of 1863, his calling America to prayer and repentance, that ultimately changed the course of world history. Think about it; what would have happened had he not issued that call and had they not humbled themselves and prayed and turned from their sinful ways and sought the face of God? What if Grant had not crossed the Mississippi that day and won his first battle, and taken Vicksburg, and cut the Confederacy in two? What if Chancellorsville had never happened and thus Gettysburg had never taken place? What if Stonewall Jackson had lived to fight at Gettysburg and the South continued its offensive wars against the North?

"All these things would have led toward the nation's dissolution. The United States of America, as we know it, would have ceased to exist. The South would have gone on as a slave nation. The North would have gone on as a remnant of what had once been the United States, with only a portion of its former resources and powers.

"And what then would have happened, when the evil of Nazism began to rise and spread across the European continent, if the United States, as we know it, did not exist or was not strong enough to vanquish it? And what would have happened, when the darkness of Communism began to engulf the world, if the United States did not exist to oppose and restrain it? All those things turned on a single day in April of 1863 with the prayers of God's people. All that darkness, all those evils, were, in the end, undone because of the prayers lifted up on that last day in April of 1863. The defeat of Nazism and the fall of Communism and countless other turns and repercussions of world history all began with the mystery of return and an ancient biblical promise given for a broken nation.

"And it all goes back to Ground Zero."

"What do you mean?"

"Second Chronicles 7:14 was given as an answer to the prayers prayed by King Solomon on Israel's consecration ground. America was consecrated to God at Ground Zero. And 9/11 brought the nation back to that ground. 'If My people who are called by My name'—it was crying out from the ruins of Ground Zero.

"Did you notice the date, Nouriel?"

"Of the day of prayer and repentance?"

"Yes."

"The end of April."

"April 30," said the prophet. "Do you know what that date was? It was the date that America was dedicated to God in prayer...on its inaugural day...at Ground Zero! And it was the day that America was given that prophetic warning by Washington. It's all connected...Lincoln's day of repentance, America's consecration to God, Washington's prophetic warning, 2 Chronicles 7:14, Ground Zero, 9/11. It's all joined together. And Ground Zero is the beginning of the harbingers, the warning, the signs, the progression. It's all part of the same mystery. And we're still in it."

"What did he say?"

"Who?"

"Lincoln. What did he say in that proclamation?"

"You want me to recite it for you?"

"Yes."

"Here?"

"Could you?"

Aside from the guards assigned to protect the memorial, there was no one there but the two of us. The prophet turned around so that he was now facing away from Lincoln's statue toward the colonnade at the memorial's entrance. His gaze grew intense and distant, as if he were looking through the columns into the landscape beyond it. And it wasn't as if he was reciting the words of a historic document—it was as if he, himself, was issuing the call, here and now, to a broken nation that had fallen away from God. I backed away toward the entrance so I could receive it as would an audience. He began to speak:

> Whereas it is the duty of nations as well as of men to own their dependence upon the overruling power of God, to confess their sins and transgressions in humble sorrow, yet with assured hope that genuine repentance will lead to mercy and pardon, and to recognize the sublime truth, announced in the Holy Scriptures and proven by all history, that those nations only are blessed whose God is the Lord;
>
> And, insomuch as we know that by His divine law nations, like individuals, are subjected to punishments and

chastisements in this world, may we not justly fear that the awful calamity of civil war which now desolates the land may be but a punishment inflicted upon us for our presumptuous sins, to the needful end of our national reformation as a whole people?

We have been the recipients of the choicest bounties of Heaven; we have been preserved these many years in peace and prosperity; we have grown in numbers, wealth, and power as no other nation has ever grown. But we have forgotten God. We have forgotten the gracious hand which preserved us in peace and multiplied and enriched and strengthened us, and we have vainly imagined, in the deceitfulness of our hearts, that all these blessings were produced by some superior wisdom and virtue of our own. Intoxicated with unbroken success, we have become too self-sufficient to feel the necessity of redeeming and preserving grace, too proud to pray to the God that made us.

It behooves us, then, to humble ourselves before the offended Power, to confess our national sins, and to pray for clemency and forgiveness.

Now, therefore, in compliance with the request, and fully concurring in the views of the Senate, I do by this my proclamation designate and set apart Thursday, the 30th day of April, 1863, as a day of national humiliation, fasting, and prayer. And I do hereby request all the people to abstain on that day from their ordinary secular pursuits, and to unite at their several places of public worship and their respective homes in keeping the day holy to the Lord and devoted to the humble discharge of the religious duties proper to that solemn occasion.

All this being done in sincerity and truth, let us then rest humbly in the hope authorized by the divine teachings that the united cry of the nation will be heard on high and answered with blessings no less than the pardon of our national sins and the restoration of our now divided and suffering country to its former happy condition of unity and peace.[6]

◆◆◆

And then there was silence. The prophet's intense and distant gaze was gone. He began walking away from the statue toward the columns to exit the memorial. I joined him. We began descending the steps.

"It's amazing," I said, "how much of what you just said could be said to America now. Could it happen again?" I asked. "Could there be a turning as there was then?"

"When we stood in St. Paul's Chapel, you asked me how America could return to God. It could happen this way."

"But that happened a long time ago," I replied. "It's a different America now. How would it happen today, in modern times?"

"The Scriptures are eternal. The promise was given to Solomon, and yet three thousand years later it changed the history of America and the world. The Word of God is not limited by time."

We continued down the steps.

"And it *has* happened," he said.

"What do you mean?"

"It *has* happened in modern times."

"How modern?"

"In your own lifetime, Nouriel. The mystery of return manifested—and again it changed history."

"If it happened in my lifetime, how would I not know it?"

"It belongs to the secret things of God, to the hidden realm that lies behind history. That's why you didn't know. But soon enough you will."

Chapter 32

The Western Terrace

U PON REACHING THE bottom of the steps, we walked across the square, down still more steps, and along the Reflecting Pool.

"Do you remember the first time we walked from here across the National Mall?"

"Of course."

"We're going to do it again. Have you studied the seal to see what's next?"

"Not in detail but enough to know that the next image is the Capitol Building. So that's where we're going?"

"Yes."

The National, like the Lincoln Memorial, was mostly devoid of people.

"So the Civil War ended, and America survived. It was in the next century that it would attain heights of power and prosperity no nation or kingdom in world history had ever known. It would emerge from the Second World War as the head of nations. But then, in its turning away from God, it would experience years of civil unrest, social upheaval, the assassination of its leaders, political scandal, military defeat, and a multitude of other phenomena and indicators that mark a civilization in decline and decay.

"By the late 1970s, many were speaking of the end of the American age. The nation was in the midst of an economic recession. And at the same time, inflation had exploded into double digits. And because of an oil crisis, Americans had to wait in long lines to find gas for their cars. And at the end of 1979, America's archenemy, the Soviet Union, invaded Afghanistan.

"At the same time, the United States embassy in Iran was taken over by radical Muslims, and fifty-two American citizens and diplomats were held hostage. Every night, Americans turned on their television sets to watch multitudes fill the streets of Tehran chanting, 'Death to America!' The crisis dragged on for days, weeks, and months. The world witnessed a new phenomenon, an America that appeared to be helpless. By the spring of 1980, the president had decided to free the hostages by military power. But mechanical failure, a dust storm, and the crashing of American helicopters would result in disaster and the death of eight American servicemen. Their bodies were taken by the Iranians and put on display in the square surrounding the American embassy. As news of the debacle and images of the dead Americans filled American television sets, a deep gloom came upon the nation.

"Four days after that disaster, something happened in Washington, DC. Believers came from all over the nation to the capital city for a sacred assembly. The event was based on a single scripture—2 Chronicles 7:14, 'If My people...' They came to humble themselves and pray, to seek His face, and to turn from their sinful ways."

"Again, that scripture," I said. "Did they come because of what had happened?"

"No, the sacred assembly was planned long before the catastrophe, even before the Americans were taken hostage. But everything converged on that spring day in 1980."

"Where in Washington?"

"Right here, Nouriel. They held the assembly on the National Mall, right here where we're standing. And they proclaimed that scripture, 'If My people...,' throughout that day over and over again. They even read Lincoln's call for prayer and repentance."

"And what did they pray for?"

"For the forgiveness of their sins and the sins of the nation, for God's mercy on the nation, and for His healing of the land. But there were two prayers lifted up during that gathering that stood out above the others. In the middle of the day, they joined their hands together and prayed that whereas the American military had been helpless to rescue the hostages, God Himself, by His own hand, would release them. That was the one prayer. The other took place near the end of the day and the gathering. It was then that they lifted up their hands...like this."

At that, the prophet lifted up his right hand and stretched it forward toward the Capitol Building at the end of the mall.

"Go ahead, Nouriel, join me. Stretch out your hand."

So I did.

"What do you see?"

"The Capitol Building."

"The *western side* of the Capitol Building. That's the West Terrace. That's what they saw that day. And as they stretched out their hands toward it, they prayed that God would bring to the nation's capital and into government those of His will."

"And what happened?"

"Less than a month after that gathering, the Republican nomination was, for all intents and purposes, won by the former governor of California, Ronald Reagan. The following November came the presidential election. On the eve of that election, Reagan gave a speech outlining his vision for America. He said this:

> ...for the first time in our memory many Americans are asking: does history still have a place for America, for her people, for her great ideals? There are some who answer no; that our energy is spent, our days of greatness at an end...[1]

"Then he spoke of what he saw as America's true strength:

> It is not bombs and rockets but belief and resolve, it is humility before God that is ultimately the source of America's strength as a nation. Our people always have held fast to this belief, this vision, since our first days as a nation. I know I have told before of the moment in 1630 when the tiny ship Arabella bearing settlers to the New World lay off the Massachusetts coast. To the little bank of settlers gathered on the deck John Winthrop said: *we shall be a city upon a hill.*[2]

"He spoke of Winthrop and the city on the hill!"

"Yes."

"A candidate for president speaking of the spiritual vision given centuries before..."

"As if to remind the nation of a sacred calling long forgotten. The night before that election, he repeated the admonition that Winthrop had also given, the warning against turning away from God:

> The eyes of all people are upon us, so that if we shall deal falsely with our God in this work we have undertaken and so

cause him to withdraw his present help from us, we shall be made a story and a byword through the world."[3]

"The warning of judgment... amazing that he said that."
"And then he closed that speech with this:

> And let us resolve they will say of our day and our generation that we did keep faith with our God, that we did act worthy of ourselves; that we did protect and pass on lovingly that shining *city on a hill*.[4]

"He was calling America back to God, to the vision of its founding. The very last words were '*city on a hill*.'"

We continued walking toward Capitol Hill.

"The day after he gave that speech, there was a revolution in the polls, a landslide that swept Reagan into office, along with others who had pledged to uphold biblical values."

"The prayer they prayed that day at the gathering."

"And then another change took place. Since the time of Andrew Jackson, the presidential inaugurations had always taken place on the east side of the Capitol Building, facing the Supreme Court. But in 1981 the inauguration was changed to the western side, to the West Terrace, to face the National Mall. So the new president would now be facing the ground on which the sacred assembly had taken place and where those prayers had been lifted up. And he would be standing on the site to which they stretched out their hands as they prayed for God to place in power those of His choosing."

"Was it because Reagan knew what had happened on the mall?"

"No," said the prophet. "Reagan had nothing to do with it. It just so happened that the Joint Committee on the Inauguration was led to break the 150-year tradition and hold the inauguration that year where it had never been held before. So in January of 1981, Reagan gave his inaugural address facing the same ground on which the believers had stood as they prayed that prayer... and on the West Terrace, to where they had stretched out their hands. It was as if God was placing His fingerprints on that moment, moving the inauguration to that site and letting those who had prayed on the mall know that He had heard their prayer."

"If My people...," I said, "...then I will hear from heaven."

We came to a stop. Before us was the West Terrace.

"And what about the other prayer," I said, "that God would release the hostages?"

"The first prayer was answered on January 20, 1981, on Inauguration Day at the National Mall. As to the other prayer, the hostages had been kept in captivity for 444 days. It all came to an end on January 20, 1981—the same day. The two prayers were answered on the exact same day—within one hour of each other... and joined to the same ground on which they were lifted up to God."

"The secret things that lie behind history... amazing."

"What happened on that inaugural day wasn't about a ceremony, a political agenda, an administration, or a man, all of which are imperfect. It was about an ancient promise. When the believers gathered on the National Mall and prayed for America, they were standing on the promise God had given King Solomon. It ends with the words 'I will... heal their land.'[5]

"The inauguration," he said, "was the beginning of a massive change and a restoration. The soaring rates of inflation that had crippled the American economy would soon disappear and a deteriorating economy would soon rebound and expand by trillions of dollars in an era that would be known as 'the seven fat years.' The inauguration day of 1981 would usher in an era of economic expansion and prosperity that would be among the greatest and longest in American history, and the effects of which would continue long after Reagan's presidency had come to an end. And the transformation would go far beyond the nation's borders. American military power would likewise experience a resurgence, as would American influence around the world.

"And then, what few people could have imagined happening, would happen. After nearly seventy years of existence, the stronghold of Communism over eastern Europe began to collapse, and then the Soviet Union, itself. America was left in the unprecedented position of being the world's only superpower. Had Reagan not been sworn into office that day, had things continued as they were going, with a declining America, it is questionable that all those things would have happened as they did.

"So it was not only American history that changed, but world history. And it all turned on that inaugural day and, specifically, on the moment Reagan raised his right hand and took the oath of the presidency. In that moment, it all began changing. When he took that oath, the world saw his right hand, which was lifted up, but not his left."

"Why is that significant?"

"Because the Lord works through the left hand of history as much as the right. And it is the unseen realm of human events that is often even more critical than the seen."

"I still don't understand."

"His left hand was resting on the Bible, on a specific page, and on a specific verse of Scripture that he had chosen beforehand. It was on that scripture that the history of America would be changed."

"And what was the Scripture?"

"The Scripture was this:

> If My people who are called by My name will humble themselves, and pray and seek My face, and turn from their wicked ways, then I will hear from heaven, and will forgive their sin and heal their land."[6]

"No!... That's..."

"Yes," said the prophet, "that was the verse on which everything changed...the ancient promise of national healing that God gave to Israel through King Solomon. Three thousand years later, that same verse changed the course of American and world history."

"Why did he choose that verse of all verses?"

"One of the quirks of history. The Bible on which he swore the oath belonged to his mother. And in the margin, next to that verse, his mother had written the words 'A most wonderful verse for the healing of the nations.'"[7]

"So it all just happened to come together at that moment," I said, "to match the verse prayed on the National Mall months before, the fingerprint of God, the sign that He had heard their prayers and would heal their land."

"And so everything that would come from that moment began with that single scripture, and that ancient promise, *'I will...heal their land.'* Everything that happened was the fulfillment of that verse—the healing of America, the fall of the Soviet Union, the collapse of Communism, the liberation of nations. The course of world history pivoted on that ancient promise beneath the president's hand."

"The history of the world...changed by the word and the prayers of His people...the secret story of history."

"The ultimate story," said the prophet. "The power of the word and the prayers of His people are stronger than those of kings and kingdoms. And by such things the history of the world is determined. So it was in the days of the Civil War, and so it was again in our own days. And not just the history of the world but of our lives."

"So it changed everything," I said. "But what about now?"

"With the president's hand resting on that scripture, it was as if the nation had been given another chance. At the end of his presidency, in his farewell address, he would again speak of the city upon a hill, reminding the nation of its first calling.[8] But the nation, in its resurgence, continued its departure from God. And then came 9/11, and then the window of time, during which the departure deepened.

"You asked me if there was still hope for America, if it could return and be restored, and if so, how it would happen. You've now seen both—the darkness and the light, the fall of the nation from God and the harbingers of its judgment on one hand, and the promise of mercy and hope of redemption on the other. The promise is just as real now as it was in past and ancient times. But so is the warning. And the time now is later, and the danger, greater, and the need for return, now all the more critical."

He turned around and began walking away from the Capitol Building. I did likewise.

"It is time now to bring it home...and to show you one more mystery. To do that, we must make one more journey."

"Where?" I asked.

"To the city on the hill."

Chapter 33

The Island

HE CITY ON the hill?" said Ana. "But the city on the hill is America. How could you go there if you're already there?"

"That's what I didn't understand."

"But you had the seal. So what was the next image?"

"The outline of an irregular shape. It looked something like a horn and something like a bouquet of flowers. Within the shape was a pair of glasses."

"What did you think it meant?"

"I had no idea until I took note of the markings surrounding the outline. They were made up of curved lines. I took them to be a representation of water. So it made me think that the outline represented an island."

"And the glasses?"

"I searched the web for *island* and *glasses, glass island, island of glass,* but I couldn't find anything that made any sense. Then I tried the word *spectacles,* and then *island of spectacles.* And that's when I found it."

"There's an island of spectacles?"

"No," said Nouriel. "But there is a place called Spectacle Island."

"Spectacle Island?"

"It had the exact same shape as the image on the seal."

"Where was it located?"

"In Massachusetts Bay, in the waters of the Puritans. It all fit together. So I set out once more for New England. I spent the night in a hotel on the outskirts of Boston and, the next morning, set out to find a way to get to the island. It was about four miles offshore. I found someone to take me there for a fee, an old man, heavyset, with a short-cropped white beard and a reddened weather-beaten face. We arrived at the island's marina, where he docked and agreed to wait for me until I was ready to leave. I went ashore in hope of finding the prophet or of being found by him. The island was largely deserted. Along its perimeter was a walking trail, which I decided to take. At the end of the island was something of a hill or mound. I ascended it. And there, standing on the summit, as if waiting for me, which, of course, he was, was the prophet."

———◆◆◆———

"We've come back, Nouriel," said the prophet. "We've returned."

"We've returned to the place we were reunited, Massachusetts Bay."

"No, we've returned to the beginning, to the foundation. Look over there," he said, pointing to the right. "If you journeyed in that direction, you would come to the shore where the Mayflower landed four hundred years ago."

"And John Winthrop—did he land there as well?"

"No," he said, pointing to his left. "Winthrop landed over there, to the north."

"After he had given his vision of the new civilization."

"The city on the hill."

"And that's where you said we would go."

"And that's why we're here...in search of the city on the hill."

"But the city on the hill is America."

"The city on the hill *became* America," he said. "But you didn't come here so you could find America. So what is the city on the hill? What was it in its beginning?"

"This?" I said. "All this? New England?"

"It was Massachusetts Bay, the Massachusetts Bay Colony, the civilization that was planted in the new world and governed by Winthrop himself. But it goes beyond that. Though the city on the hill is a metaphor of a people and a society lifted up and to which the world would look, there actually was a city. Winthrop and those who joined him in the journey across the Atlantic and in his vision of the city on the hill set out to lay the foundation of a city."

"Of an *actual* city?"

"Of an actual city intended to become the embodiment of the vision. And so they did; they founded a city."

"And what happened to it?" I asked. "Does it still exist?"

"I would say so. And I would think you've heard of it. Come."

At that, he led me around to the left side of the mound.

"Look, Nouriel."

So I looked.

"There," said the prophet, "there it is…the city on the hill."

Across the water stood a modern city, office buildings, skyscrapers, a skyline of steel and glass resting on the other side of the water.

"I believe you know the city.…It's called Boston."

"Boston? The city on the hill?"

"Yes. Boston was the first embodiment of Winthrop's vision, the center of the new commonwealth, the city on the hill that would become America."

"Boston?"

"The city on the hill is one of its names. Boston would become the capital city of the Massachusetts Bay Colony and the home of John Winthrop. He would live there, govern there, and be buried there. Boston was founded by John Winthrop."

He didn't say anything after that.

"Why are you quiet?" I asked.

"You don't yet see it," said the prophet, "do you?"

"See what? I see the city."

"America was founded for the purposes and glory of God, to be a light to the world, the city on the hill. It all began here. It all came from these shores. And this was the first embodiment of that calling and vision. But America turned away from its calling, away from God's purposes, and then turned against them. And then it all began, the shaking, the beginning of signs, the harbingers. And where did it all begin? Where did 9/11 originate?"

And that's when it hit me.

"It all began here…"

"Yes," said the prophet, "9/11 originated from the city on the hill. The first planes took flight…"

"From Boston. So the shaking of America came from the city on the hill."

"Remember the principle: in the days of judgment, the nation is brought back to its foundations. So on 9/11, America was brought back to the foundations of its powers, to Lower Manhattan on the day of its discovery, to the Pentagon on the day of its groundbreaking, and to Ground Zero, where it was dedicated to God on its first day. But the mystery goes back and beyond even that, beyond Ground Zero and beyond that first day, to the very beginning, to the foundation of the foundation, to here, to the city on the hill. America had fallen away from its foundations and, on a single day, was brought back to them."

"It was all about return," I said, "the call to return."

"And what was it that Winthrop's vision prophesied?"

"That if America followed the ways of God, the blessings of Israel would come upon it, peace, safety, prosperity, power, and preeminence. But if it turned against the ways of God, then the judgments of Israel would then come upon it."

"And what was 9/11 and the harbingers that came from it? What was it all replaying?"

"The judgments of Israel…So 9/11 is joined to the city on the hill."

"And the mystery," said the prophet, "is that it actually was. The mystery is that 9/11 itself began in the city on the hill. The planes that brought destruction took off from the city on the hill. It was from the city on the hill that the calamity came upon America."

"So the calamity that came to America began in the city of the man who had given America the warning of calamity."

"And the warning he had given America came from the warning Moses had given to Israel beginning in Deuteronomy 28."

"And what was the scripture appointed to be spoken in the days leading up to 9/11?"

"Deuteronomy 28."

"And what did it warn of?"

"The enemy coming from a faraway land as a swooping eagle to bring destruction."

"Thus it was one of the judgments of Israel of which Winthrop warned. And it would all begin on the day the enemy took off as an eagle flying from Boston, the city on the hill."

"Everything comes together."

"And yet there's more to the mystery."

"I don't know if I can take more."

"Winthrop had a special place he called his own. It was an island."

"Not this island?"

"No, but just about as small as this one. And it was on that island that Winthrop planted a garden, a vineyard, and an orchard. It was said that the first apple and pear trees in New England were planted on that island by John Winthrop. The island sat close to the mainland. So Winthrop could gaze out at his city on the hill to contemplate its calling and pray for its future. It would be called Governor's Island."

"Why?"

"It was named after Winthrop. He was the governor. It was another way of saying it was *Winthrop's island*."

It was just then that a particularly loud and low-flying plane passed over the waters in front of us. I had noticed many planes taking off and landing at the nearby airport throughout the day, but this one was impossible to miss.

"Do you know where all the planes are going to and coming from?" he asked.

"To that airport."

"And do you know what that airport is?"

"I didn't think about it."

"That, Nouriel, is the place where it all began. It wasn't just that 9/11 began in Boston. It was there, in that place, that everything started."

"That's the airport that..."

"That's Logan Airport. It was from that ground that the terrorists took off to begin their mission. That's where 9/11 began."

"Before the plane flew by, you were telling me about Winthrop's island. Why?"

"Do you know what happened to Winthrop's island, Nouriel?"

"No."

He paused for a moment.

"It became an airport."

"No!"

"Yes. The island of John Winthrop became Logan Airport...the place from which 9/11 began."

"Logan Airport!"

"The shaking, the signs, the harbingers...it all began on the island of John Winthrop."

"No..."

"The man who laid the foundation and gave the warning of what would happen if America ever turned away from God. And the calamity came...and came specifically from his land, from his island, where he dwelt and prayed."

"It's beyond..."

"It's the mystery behind the mystery," said the prophet. "On 9/11 the calamity struck Ground Zero, where America was consecrated to God on its first day—but it all began here, where America was consecrated to God before its first day...the mystery ground beyond the mystery ground.

"And speaking of grounds, look over there," he said, pointing just right of the airport. "It was a peninsula so close to Logan Airport that it almost seemed to be touching it. It's a town. Do you know what it's called?"

"No."

"*Winthrop*...it's the Town of Winthrop."

"All the pieces of the mystery...together."

"Yes," said the prophet, "they all came together. On that September morning, three days after the scrolls were opened to the word that prophesied the enemy coming on the land as an eagle, the terrorists took flight from the land of John Winthrop in the city on the hill. On that same morning, in New York City and around the nation, the ancient prayers of the selichote were lifted up and spoke of the enemy attacking land and leaving destruction in his wake. And on that same morning, a ship named the *Half Moon* readied to journey up the Hudson River in a re-creation of the voyage that represented the beginning of that city hundreds of years earlier on September 11.

"And on that same September morning, in bedrooms and studies and on kitchen tables throughout New York City, the East Coast, and the nation, believers opened their Bibles to the word appointed for that day—Isaiah 9:10—the prophecy that spoke of an enemy strike on the land, the collapse of its buildings, and the falling of the sycamore tree—all of which it identified as the beginning of a nation's judgment, and all of which would be set in motion on the morning they read it. And on that same morning, on America's east coast and throughout New York City, the sound of the watchman, the ancient alarm appointed to warn the city of impending calamity, began sounding. It was that morning that what John Winthrop had prophesied came upon America from the ground of John Winthrop."

"And so now we've returned," I said, "to the beginning of the beginning."

"It had to begin from the beginning," he replied, "because it all comes back to the return."

"It was the call to return....It was the wake-up call."

"A severe call," said the prophet, "as severe as an alarm for a deafened people. But the purpose of the alarm is not to bring judgment but to awaken the sleeping and save them from judgment."

"So all the returns to all the foundation grounds and all the foundation days...it was all about return; the call of a nation to return to the foundation from which it had departed."

"Yes, but the foundation isn't a place or a set of principles or moral precepts. The foundation is Him. The foundation is God, Himself."

"Did Winthrop give any indication of what the end would be for America, the blessing or the judgment?"

"He ended his vision of the city on the hill by alluding once more to the words of Moses. He said this:

> 'Beloved, there is now set before us life and death, good and evil,' in that we are commanded this day to love the Lord our God, and to love one another, to walk in his ways.... *Therefore let us choose life.*"[1]

"So which one will it be," I said, "life or death?"

"The answer to that," he said, "lies with us. For there is set before us judgment and redemption, life and death. It is His will that we find life. And it is only in return that we can find it. If the end is to be blessing and redemption, then it will have been the will of God. But if the end is to be judgment, then it will have been our own. So the voice of God is calling, 'Return to Me, and I will return to you.'[2] In other words..."

"In other words..."

"*Choose life.*"

We stood there for a time in silence, watching toward the city on the hill as a warm wind swept over us. And then I broke the silence.

———◆◆◆———

"So," I said, "we've come full circle. When I first saw you on the island of the two towers, you told me about the city on the hill. We began with that. And now we've returned to it. So is this our last meeting?"

"I believe," said the prophet, "that there's one more thing I need to show you."

"I thought this was the last mystery."

"What I have to show you...I would call it something else."

"What?" I asked. "What would you call it?"

"A secret."

Chapter 34

The Lamb

A SECRET?" SAID ANA.
"Something known only by a few, something that took place away from the eyes of the world."

"And known by the prophet."

"Yes, of course," said Nouriel, "one of the few."

"So what happened?"

"I took out the seal and began examining it. And there was the image, clockwise from the image that had led me to the island."

"You didn't know it was there before that?"

"I had noticed it before as I had the other minute images in the ring that circled the city on the hill. But I didn't think that they were all there for my sake. And I was so convinced that my encounter with the prophet on that island was going to be our last that I didn't see the need to decipher every detail on the seal. But that changed when he told me he had one more thing to reveal."

"So what was the image?" she asked.

"A gate, an ancient gate."

"That's how it all began," she said. "The first mystery was that of the gate."

"Yes, and it all began with a dream in which I saw a gate covered with engravings, the sun, the torch, the body of water, and the land of hills. It was the same image that I now saw on the seal, only it was a miniaturized version."

"So what did you take it to mean?"

"The same thing it meant in the dream. It was a representation of the nation's gate, New York City, and, more specifically, the passageway into the Hudson River, with the island of Manhattan on one side and the Statue of Liberty on the other."

"And where did it lead you?"

"I decided to get as close as I could to that gate, to where the New York

Bay and the Hudson River come together. I went to the southern end of Manhattan, to Battery Park."

"And you were trusting that you were led to go there just when you did and the prophet would do likewise?"

"Something like that."

"So what happened?"

"When I got to Battery Park, it was deserted, except for one person, one who was impossible to miss. In more normal times, it's not uncommon to find people in the park dressed up as the Statue of Liberty, posing with tourists and making a living out of it. And that's what I saw: a woman dressed up as the Statue of Liberty. She was wearing a robe of aqua blue, with her face covered in aqua-blue face paint, and holding in her outstretched right hand an aqua-blue torch. And over her aqua-blue face was a white medical mask—the Statue of Liberty wearing a face mask. It was a disconcerting sight. I wondered what she was doing there when there was virtually no one else in the park that day. She stood there frozen except she seemed to be following me with her eyes as I wandered through the park in hope of finding the prophet.

"And then, just as I was about to give up my search, she lowered her torch until it was pointing toward the waterfront. I didn't try to figure out what was happening, who she was or why she was doing it. But having, once again, nothing else to go on, I decided to take it as a lead and go with it. So I made my way down to the harbor. That's when I saw him, the prophet in a rowboat anchored to the dock, waiting for me to join him."

◆◆◆

"Come, Nouriel!" he said. "We have a journey to make. You don't want to miss the boat. There won't be another one for some time."

So I went down to the dock and joined him in the boat. It was the second time I had found myself in a rowboat with the prophet. The first was in the lake at Central Park during our first encounters. But this time he would be the one doing the rowing.

"The lady who pointed me here," I said, "is she an employee of yours?"

"No," he replied.

"Where are we going?"

"You'll have to see."

"You promised me a secret."

"And it will be revealed…and a mystery of two holy days."

We launched out from Battery Park, southward into the New York Bay. He didn't say anything at first. He was focused on navigating the boat away from the harbor. Only after achieving that, he spoke.

"Unprecedented days," he said. "For the first time in history, the world is brought to a standstill with billions of people hidden inside their homes, waiting until a plague passes through the land. Unprecedented…except once."

"When?"

"In ancient times when a people were told to go inside their homes and stay there because a plague was passing through the land. The command was given to them by their leaders. Those who failed to stay inside their houses during the appointed time were risking being struck down by the plague."

"I've never heard of anything like this happening before."

"I think you have," he replied. "It was called Passover."

"Passover!"

"The land was Egypt. The nation was Israel. And a plague was passing through the land. The Israelites were to go inside their houses. They had been instructed to do so by Moses. None of them were to *go out of his house until morning.* They were all to stay inside until the plague had passed through the land."

"So it was the first national lockdown," I said.

"And there had never been another like it—until now. In the year 2020, for the first time in over three thousand years, the people of Israel were told to go inside their houses and not come out. As in ancient times, it was a command given to them by their leaders. And as in Egypt, it was because a plague was passing through the land. And it was not only the fact that the ancient elements were again coming together—it was *when* they were converging together."

"When?"

"On Passover. It all came together on Passover. It was the spring of 2020. The Israeli prime minister issued the order that starting on the eve of Passover at 6 p.m., there would be a total national lockdown. Everyone was to stay inside their houses with their immediate family.

The lockdown was to last until 7 a.m. the following day. And no one was to '*go out of his house until morning.*'

"So the people of Israel stayed inside their homes because a plague was passing through the land—on the very night that commemorated the very night that the people of Israel stayed inside their homes because a plague was passing through the land. The ancient mystery replayed itself on the very night of its commemoration."

"But it didn't only happen in Israel."

"Yes," said the prophet, "that's the point. The mystery was manifesting all over the world. People throughout the earth were now being told by their leaders to stay inside their houses and apartments, their mansions, and palaces, and huts…the rich and the poor, the weak and the powerful…because a plague was passing through their land, a plague was passing through the earth. The entire world was brought into the mystery of Passover; the Communist world, the Christian world, the Muslim world, the Hindu world, the secular world, the whole planet was immersed into the mystery of Passover in the early spring, the season of Passover."

"A Passover of judgment," I said.

"You could say that."

"And what does it all mean?"

"What was the center of Passover?" he asked. "The lamb, the Passover lamb. In the first Passover, the people of Israel were told to sacrifice a lamb and mark their doorposts with its blood. When the plague or judgment came upon their house, if that house was marked with the lamb's blood, the plague *passed over* them and they were saved. The lamb was, in a sense, absorbing the plague, dying in their place so that those who took refuge in it would be saved from the judgment. It all centered on the lamb."

He was quiet for a few moments, continuing to row and giving me time to absorb his words.

"What does the Bible call Jesus?" asked the prophet.

"The Lamb."

"And so Isaiah prophesied that the Messiah would be 'led as a *lamb* to the slaughter.'[1] And so John the Baptist heralded Him with the words 'Behold! The *Lamb* of God who takes away the sin of the world!'[2] So why is He called the Lamb?"

"Because His life would become a sacrifice."

"Yes, and for more than that. He didn't come only as the Lamb—but specifically as the *Passover Lamb*. What day was it that He gave His life? It was Passover. And what was the cross? Beams of wood as of a doorpost, marked with the blood of the Lamb—the sign of Passover. And what is the gospel? The message that says, 'The Lamb died in your place and took your judgment so you could be free, so you could be saved.' It's the message of Passover. It is, from beginning to end, a Passover faith.

"And what have we now witnessed, Nouriel? A nation, a civilization, a world culture turning away not only from God but from the Lamb, from the faith that centers on the Passover Lamb. And now, upon that world comes a plague, and the people of that world are told they must stay inside their houses until the plague passes over them. And it all comes upon the world in the season of Passover.

"So the world that had turned away from the Lamb of Passover is now drawn back into its mystery. And what does Passover reveal as the only answer?"

"The Lamb."

"The only answer to the judgment…but not merely the judgment of Egypt but the judgment that must fall on all sin and evil."

"So the world was being called back."

"And what was the global epicenter of the plague?"

"New York."

"And the harbinger that grew in New York at Ground Zero, the erez tree, the Tree of Hope…on what day was it struck down?"

"On Passover."

"And do you remember the two days on which the plague reached its peak in New York?"

"April 9 and April 10."

"And do you know what April 9 was?"

"No."

"It was Passover…the first day of Passover!"

"So the peak moment of the plague passing through the land fell on the Hebrew holy day that commemorated the plague passing through the land!"

"Yes," he answered, "And what is New York? It's the center of the

Jewish population in America. So on the day when the plague was ravaging New York, the Jewish people were observing Passover, the holy day that commemorates the overcoming of the plague by the blood of the lamb. And it was just after that day that the plague in New York would begin decreasing, passing over."

"That was April 9," I said, "but the peak took place over two days. What about the other day, April 10? Was that significant?"

"I would say so," said the prophet. "April 10 was Good Friday. Good Friday is, in reality, another reckoning of the same day, Passover, the day that commemorates the sacrifice of Jesus on the cross on Passover as the Passover Lamb...that the plague might pass over our lives."

◆◆◆

The dawn was just beginning to break over Brighton Beach. Ana was staring toward the ocean, but at nothing in particular.

"What are you thinking?" asked Nouriel.

"I don't know."

"You do know. What are you thinking?"

"It all goes back to Him," she said. "It all went back to Him the first time, when you first came to me."

"Jesus?"

"Yes."

"That's what it tends to do. That's what everything tends to do—go back to Him. The entire age is timed to the reckoning of His birth, every human event, every moment of our lives. Even America—it was founded because of Him and dedicated to His purposes. Even the city on the hill, America's founding vision—it wasn't Winthrop who came up with it; it was Jesus. It's the image He gave His disciples as to what they were called to be. As Passover centers on the lamb, so the world centers on Him—history itself is divided by his life...and not only history. In the end, it's not about history or nations."

"Then what?"

"In the end, it's about us, Ana, each of us. The judgment of nations belongs to *this* world. But this world is only a small part, the smallest part of eternity. Ahead of us lies eternity, an eternity with God or an eternity without Him. Remember what the prophet said: it is the necessity of God to bring evil into judgment. The light must overcome the darkness, and the good must bring evil to an end. And so every sin must be brought into judgment, and just one evil is enough to separate us from the good, and just one sin, enough to separate us from God, infinitely and forever."

"Eternal judgment."

"We're all appointed to stand in the light on the day of judgment."

"But nobody's without sin," she said. "So then no one can be saved."

"And that's the mystery of Passover. The judgment is coming. It's coming to everyone. But for those who take refuge in the Lamb, the judgment passes over them. Everyone who comes to the Lamb is saved."

"The Lamb being Jesus."

"The Lamb being Jesus, who died in our place, who took our judgment so that we could be saved...as it is written, 'For God so loved the world that He gave His only begotten Son, that whoever believes in Him should not perish but have everlasting life.'"[3]

"But perhaps some of us are too far away from God."

"You're not any farther away than I was. And how far away you are doesn't matter. On the night of Passover, it didn't matter who you were, what your past was, how good or evil, how holy or sinful. None of it mattered. No one was saved or lost because of their past, or because of what they had or hadn't done. Whoever entered through the door and took refuge in the lamb was saved from judgment, and whoever did not, was not.

"It's no different now. It doesn't matter who you are, what your past has been, your religion, or what you were born as, or how far away from God you find yourself. Look at me, Ana; I was the least likely person, the farthest from Him. But it's not about who we are. It's about who *He* is. In the end, it's all about His love. The door is open to everyone...the door that bears the markings of the Lamb's blood...now in the form of a cross. And whoever enters through that doorway is saved. And whoever does not, is not.

"The justice of God is found in judgment—but the heart of God you find in the cross, in the Lamb. God is love, and the greatest love is that which gives itself, puts itself in our place, bears our pain and sorrows, takes our hell and judgment, that we would never know it, that we would be saved. That's the heart of God. So when we speak of judgment, remember, God is the One who bears all judgment on Himself that we would never have to. God is the love...and love is the Lamb."

"You've become quite an evangelist, Nouriel."

"No," he replied. "I'm just sharing the most important thing I could share with someone I care about. He's not far from you, Ana. And it's not hard. All you have to do is come to Him who is love...who died for your sins, who took your judgment and overcame death so you could have eternal life...to receive Him, to receive His love, His forgiveness, His cleansing, His presence, His resurrection, His power, His Spirit, His peace, and His blessings...into your heart...and let it touch every part of your life. And then you follow in His footsteps. It's as it was on Passover...you walk through that doorway, you leave everything old behind, and when you come out of that doorway, everything becomes new."

"Like being born again," she said.

"Like being born again."

"I know I should but..."

"Don't wait, Ana. Don't put it off for tomorrow. Tomorrow never comes. All these things are reminders of how short, how fragile, and fleeting this life is. We live our lives just one heartbeat away from death. Every moment we have is separated from eternity by a single heartbeat. Every breath is borrowed, a gift from Him who gave us life and the only One who can give us life again. And no one knows when that last heartbeat and last breath will be. And then comes one of two eternities. But then it's too late to choose. The only time we have to choose is now. As long as we have that heartbeat, we can choose. So He calls out to all of us and says, 'Choose life,'[4]...and to each of us...to you, Ana, and says, 'Come to Me.'"[5]

She was silent for a time. And then she spoke.

"They were to stay in their houses until the morning. And in the morning..."

"They were free. Everything was new."

"A new birth?"

"Yes, a new birth, a new beginning...the resurrection of the nation. Passover ends with a resurrection. From death comes life, and from night, the day. So the night was over; morning had come. And now they began their journey home to the Promised Land."

"And do you know what, Nouriel?"

"What?"

"It's morning."

"So it is."

———◆◆◆———

The two sat there for a time without a word, watching the dawn come over the ocean.

Finally, Ana broke the silence. "So you're in the boat with the prophet. Where did you go? And what was the secret?"

Chapter 35

The Day of the Watchman

H E NAVIGATED THE boat in a southwesterly direction until we were in the middle of the water just about halfway between New York and New Jersey.

"All these things," he said, "the mystery, the signs, the harbingers, the warnings—they all began on the day of the first shaking."

"9/11."

"But it is written that before the day of calamity, God gives warning. Is it possible then that before that day, before all these things began, a warning was given? And if so, is it possible that within that warning was a revelation and a message for this present hour?"

"Is it?"

"In ancient times, God revealed the coming of calamity through prophetic acts."

"Prophetic acts...meaning...?"

"Acts that foretell in symbolism what is yet to come. The prophet Jeremiah smashing the clay jar, foretelling the destruction of Jerusalem; the prophet Ahijah tearing his garment into pieces, foretelling the dividing of the kingdom; the prophet Ezekiel carrying out his luggage in the sight of the people, foretelling their coming departure into exile.[1] A prophetic act could even be performed by those unaware that they were performing it—like the potter in the Book of Jeremiah who mars his vessel and then reshapes it, a sign to signify the sovereignty of God over the nation of Israel.[2]

"Prophetic acts occur throughout the Bible, often preceding and foretelling a day of calamity. Thus is it possible that a prophetic act took place before it all began, before 9/11? And if so, is it possible that it foreshadowed it?"

"I wouldn't know."

"It lies in the realm of the secret things. I never asked you for the last seal. Did you bring it with you?"

"Of course."

So I handed it to him. I didn't expect him to give me another, as I knew we were at the end, or beyond the end—but he did. On the seal was the image of a robed and bearded man sounding a ram's horn.

"The watchman!" I said. "This is the first seal I was given. It was to tell me there was more to be revealed. It was the seal that started it all. So everything's come full circle. But it was the little girl who gave it to me. And I gave it back to her. How did you get it?"

"Does it matter?"

The wind began picking up and the sky was growing increasingly cloudy, as if a storm was coming.

"And what did the watchman do?" asked the prophet.

"He kept watch on the city walls for the first sign of an enemy attack, and if he saw it, he sounded the alarm."

"And where specifically on the walls? At the gate. The watchman at the gate. Where are we, Nouriel?"

"In New York Bay," I replied.

"Look to your right. That's Ellis Island, through which millions of immigrants came to America. This is the passageway. This is the gate of America. And in back of me is Liberty Island, on which stands the Statue of Liberty, the first thing the immigrants saw as they approached their destination. This is the gate. Even the poem on its pedestal proclaimed that the statue would stand at 'our sea-washed, sunset gates.'[3] Who was it, Nouriel, that was first to see the attack of the enemy?"

"The watchman."

"Yes, because he stood at the edge of the city, on its walls, at its gate, and looked into the distance. And here we are at the edge of America, at the nation's gate...at the place of the watchman."

We were now approaching Liberty Island and the statue that was now towering over us.

"You're taking me to the Statue of Liberty."

"Yes."

"Why?"

"To show you where it happened," he said, "the prophetic event that took place before the calamity."

"When did it happen?"

"It happened two years before the calamity...on the day a watchman came to the gate."

"What do you mean, a watchman?"

"One called to see what was coming and to sound the alarm."

"So somebody came here two years before 9/11."

"He didn't come alone. Others came with him, and others joined him here. They all had come for the same purpose."

It was then that the boat arrived at the dock. The prophet used a rope to secure it to one of the wooden posts that was sticking out of the water.

"Can we just do that?" I asked.

"We just did."

"I mean, do we have the authority?"

"We do," he replied, "of a kind."

We got out of the boat, walked along the dock, and came onto the island. Like most of the other public places of our recent encounters, it was largely deserted. We stopped on the walkway by the water's edge.

"So who was it that came here with the same purpose?"

"People of God, believers," he replied, "warriors of the spirit."

"Where did they come from?"

"From the city, from the surrounding regions, and from all over the country."

"And why did they come?"

"For most of them, it was because they knew a calamity was coming upon the nation."

"How could they have known that?"

"They knew it by the Spirit. They knew that a calamity was coming to the nation and specifically to New York City."

"What did they see as the reason for the calamity?"

"America's departure from God had placed it in danger. They saw the nation's hedge of protection lifting."

"Did they know how the calamity would come?"

"They knew it would come in the form of a terrorist attack and it would be focused on New York City. So in view of that knowledge, they came here to pray for the city and the nation."

"And what did they do on this island?"

"Come," said the prophet, "I'll show you."

At that, he began leading me to the statue. As we approached the pedestal, I saw two security officials. I expected to be stopped. The island wasn't open for tourists. But the prophet approached the two officials as if he knew them. They responded as if they knew him as well. I don't know what the story was or what it was that he said to them; I never asked. All I know is that after looking me over, I presume to make sure that I didn't pose a danger, they let us through. We went inside the pedestal and began ascending the stairs. You wouldn't think it, but the pedestal is about as high as a ten-story building. Before reaching its top, the prophet led me outside onto something of a balcony and then to one of its four corners.

"And this is where the watchman led them that day, to the pedestal's northeast corner."

"It's kind of like a rampart," I said. "I can picture a watchman standing here."

"What do you see from here, Nouriel?"

The corner was facing the city, the bottom of Manhattan, and particularly the bottom of the city's west side.

"I see the harbinger," I said, "the tower, the World Trade Center."

"Yes, but *they* didn't. They saw the Twin Towers of the World Trade Center. They had come to the city because they knew an attack was coming. But now the watchman led them to this corner."

"So they could see the site where the attack would take place."

"What is it, Nouriel, that the watchman does at the gate when he sees the danger coming, the first glimpse of the coming attack?"

"He sounds the alarm; he blows the trumpet."

"Yes. And so the watchman came here that day and brought with him the watchman's alarm, the trumpet, the shofar. He led those standing at that corner in proclamation and prayer for America and for the purposes of God. Then he lifted up the trumpet, pointed it to the city, toward the two towers of the World Trade Center, and blew. And the sound of the watchman, which, from ancient times, warned of a coming attack, now went forth from the nation's gate to New York City toward the towers, the focal point of the coming attack. And so it was written:

> The sound of the trumpet...destruction is cried.[4]

> ...when he sees the sword coming upon the land and blows the trumpet...[5]

I set watchmen over you, saying, 'Listen to the sound of the trumpet!'[6]

If a trumpet is blown in a city, will not the people be afraid?"[7]

"Was this a prophetic act?" I asked.

"If it foretold that which was yet to come, then it was. The prophet Ezekiel was told by the Lord to perform a prophetic act involving an image. He was to create a representation of Jerusalem onto a clay tablet, an engraving. Then he was to 'lay siege against it.'[8] It was a prophetic simulation of the attack that would come against the city, a prophetic image foreshadowing the calamity that would come upon Jerusalem."

"Don't tell me they had a clay tablet on the Statue of Liberty."

"No. But they had something else on which images are created—a camera. As the watchman sounded the trumpet, they took a picture of it. And from this came a prophetic image."

"Which was what?"

"An image in which the trumpet was sounding to the World Trade Center. But it was more specific than that. In the image, the shofar was actually touching the World Trade Center, or rather, one of the Twin Towers."

"Which one?"

"The tower that would mark the beginning of 9/11, the North Tower, the first to be struck and the first sign of the calamity."

"Where?" I asked. "Where on the North Tower?"

"The shofar touched the top of the tower. It marked the exact spot where the calamity of 9/11 would begin. The trumpet and the tower. And so it was written in ancient times:

A day of the trumpet and alarm...against the high towers.

"In the image, the trumpet was literally set against the high towers."

"So as in the days of Ezekiel, it was a symbolic representation," I said, "of the attack that would come to the city...in this case on 9/11."

"And from where in ancient times would such attacks first be seen?"

"From the watchman's post, from the wall, from the gate."

"And so it was from the gate of America that the attack was first revealed…and not only the place and focal point of the attack—but the attack itself."

"What do you mean?"

"After the watchman sounded the trumpet, he lifted up his hands to chant an ancient prayer in Hebrew. As he did that, one of the others standing behind him decided to record it. When they later looked at what had been recorded, they saw something they didn't notice in the midst of his chanting. The image would reveal how the attack would manifest. It would come from the sky."

"How would it show that?"

"As the watchman prayed, an object appeared in the sky, coming from the left side of view and flying rightward."

"Rightward, meaning…?"

"Meaning the object was heading for the World Trade Center. And it would mark out the same path that would be taken by the first plane on 9/11. It would head to the North Tower and would intersect with that tower at the same point at which United Airlines Flight 11 would strike that tower on the day of calamity. The image was a foreshadowing of what the entire nation and the entire world would witness two years later in that same place. As it was written of the enemy's attack:

Set the trumpet to your mouth! He shall come like an eagle."[9]

"So the first glimpse of what was going to happen was given to those standing at the gate."

"As in ancient times."

"And what happened after that?"

"After that, the watchman spoke to them. He told them that something major was going to take place and that they were going to remember what happened there on that pedestal; they were going to remember that day."

"How do you know these things," I said, "if it wasn't made known? Do you know the watchman?"

"You might say that."

"Who was he?"

"What matters is not who the watchman is but what happened. And two years later, it all happened. The enemy would come to the nation and to its gate, as an eagle flying in the path foretold on the day of the watchman, and it would strike the tower at the place marked out by the watchman's trumpet. But it was not only that it happened two years later."

"What do you mean?"

"They were told that they would remember that day. The day itself was a sign."

"I don't understand."

"It wasn't just what happened that day but when."

"When?"

"The day of the watchman, the day they stood at the gate, fell on a specific date."

"What date?"

"It fell on 9/11."

"No!"

"Yes," said the prophet. "It all took place on 9/11. Everything that happened, happened on 9/11: the prayers that focused on a coming strike of terror, the gathering at the gate, the sounding of the alarm, the images of what was to happen—everything that happened, happened on 9/11. Long before anyone ever connected that date with calamity, or with an attack on New York, or the destruction of the towers, it was all connected, it was already revealed."

There was a pause as the wind swept through the balcony.

"But I promised you something," he said. "I told you I would share the mystery of two holy days. I've only spoken of one, of Passover. Passover comes in the spring. Judgment comes in the autumn."

"Autumn?"

"Or in its approach, at the end of summer."

"What do you mean?"

"The end of summer and the beginning of autumn is the time on the ancient biblical calendar appointed for judgment. It is then when all eyes turn to God. And it's then when one must take account of one's life because the time is coming when one must stand before God, when all sins are brought into judgment."

"What does that mean?"

"At the end of summer comes Elul, the month of the early trumpets, the month of the preparing."

"The preparing for what?"

"The Days of Awe, the Days of Repentance, the Days of Return, the time given, in light of judgment, to repent and return to God."

"When, exactly?"

"It all begins with the Feast of Trumpets, the holy day known as Rosh Ha Shannah, an entire day marked by the sounding of the shofar, the alarm, the sound of the watchman."

"In what month?"

"It typically falls in September."

"A day of sounding the trumpets...what does it mean?"

"The sound of the trumpets is one of alarm...a sound that causes trembling. The Feast of Trumpets is a day of alarm, of trembling, of shaking...the day of warning...of the coming judgment. The Feast of Trumpets inaugurates the Ten Days of Awe that lead to Yom Kippur, the Day of Atonement. The Day of Atonement is a shadow of the day when all sin is judged and all judgement is sealed—a shadow of the Day of Judgment itself. Yom Kippur represents the sealing of judgment, but the Feast of Trumpets represents its beginning. In fact, the day when the trumpets are sounded is also known by the name *Yom Ha Din*."

"Which means...?"

"The Day of Judgment," he replied. "So the ten days from the Feast of Trumpets to the Day of Atonement are linked to judgment and make up the window of time when, in light of the judgment to come, one can still repent and be saved."

"So the message of the Feast of Trumpets is..."

"Judgment is coming. Prepare to stand before God. Get right. Repent. Do whatever you have to do to get right with God and man. The time is now to turn back and be saved. For the day will come when the time given will have ended....Return."

"And why are you telling me about the Feast of Trumpets?"

"Because there's more to the mystery. The day of the watchman, the day on which the warning of the coming calamity was given at the nation's gate, was 9/11, but it was something else as well."

"What was it?"

"It was the Feast of Trumpets."

"The day that says, 'Judgment is coming. Prepare. Repent.' So it was saying prepare for the coming calamity. It was warning...9/11 was coming."

"Yes," said the prophet, "and more than that. On that day of warning, two years before the calamity, 9/11 *was* the Feast of Trumpets, and the Feast of Trumpets *was* 9/11. But the Feast of Trumpets is not the end of the matter but the beginning of the days of judgment. And thus 9/11 itself was not the end of the matter but the beginning of a nation's judgment. It was the *warning* of what was not yet. The first shaking is the harbinger of greater shakings."

"Then the time following 9/11 would correspond to the Days of Awe, the time given to repent and come back to God, the days that are numbered and must end.... But we haven't come back."

"No."

"Was there any sign of hope given on that day?"

"The watchman didn't just sound the trumpet; he prayed for America, that there would be revival and a harvest of salvation. He prayed that America's lamp would burn again with the fire of God and again blaze with the light of heaven to the world. He did so knowing it might be that sometimes the lamp must go out in order for the torch to shine...and that darkness must sometimes come to bring forth the light."

"The time is late," I said, "isn't it?"

"It is," said the prophet, "but not only because of these things but because of what lies beyond them. You see, our days here are numbered. They must and will ultimately come to an end. And then comes eternity. But now are the days given in which we determine eternity, which eternity that will be. These are the only days we have in which to turn, in which to come to God, in which to repent, and get right, and be redeemed, and come to salvation. Eternity is forever. But these days are not. They come but once in an eternity—and yet, by them, is eternity sealed. How awesome are these days! These," said the prophet, "are the Days of Awe.

"You see, we live our lives in between the trumpets and the Day of Judgment, when we will each stand before Him and eternity. And so the trumpets are sounding even now and calling out to us to say, 'You don't have forever. For your days on earth are numbered and ending. So whatever you would do, you must do it now. If you would ever turn to God, you must turn to Him now; if you would ever repent and come back, you must do it now; if you would ask for forgiveness, you must ask for it now; if you would ever be cleansed and made new, you must be so now; if you would ever make it right, you must make it right now; if you would ever be saved, you must be saved now; and if you would ever live the life you were created and called to live, you must live it now. For we will never pass this way again. And the time we have on earth…these are the Days of Awe.'"

The wind had now become even stronger and was relentlessly beating against us.

"So what do I do now?"

At that, he reached into his coat and took out a ram's horn.

"The shofar," I said. "You had another one that was filled with oil and with which you anointed me on the last day of our first encounters."

"And this is now the last day of our second encounters," he replied. "And this one is larger."

He placed it in my hands.

"It's the trumpet of the watchman. And now, Nouriel…it belongs to you. The time is now later than when we last parted. And it is now all the more urgent that you fulfill the calling of the watchman. Many will oppose you. Many will hate you for it. Many will turn the other way. But others will hear. Others will heed the sound of the trumpet, the sound of your warning, and will turn, and will come back, and will be saved.

"And for these, for all of these, you must sound the trumpet. For as long as they have breath, as long as their hearts are still beating, He calls to them, He calls them back. You must sound it for them. For these are the only days they have. These are their Days of Awe."

He then placed his hand on my shoulder and stared into my eyes.

"You've kept the charge," he said. "Now finish the course. Fulfill your calling. And the Lord…will be with you."

It was at that moment that I noticed the slightest smile, the slightest nod, and then the slightest closing of his eyes. He then turned away from me and walked back inside the pedestal.

◆◆◆

"I never saw him again. When I set out to leave the island, I would find the boat waiting for me at the dock, with no sign of him."

"How did he leave the island?"

"I have no idea, but I believe it was all planned to happen that way...that he would leave me standing there on that ledge where the warning had first been sounded."

"So he gave you the charge...a second charge."

"Yes. So I stood there on that ledge with the shofar he had placed in my hands. I lifted it up to look at it. It was this that the watchman was to sound in the face of danger so that the people could be saved. He had to do it regardless of the reaction, whether or not they woke up or kept sleeping, whether or not they found it disturbing, and whether or not they listened and heeded the warning. I knew what I had to do. I had to give warning; I had to sound the alarm."

"Yes, Nouriel," she said, "you were to give warning and sound the alarm through a book, a sequel to the first, a book that would take up where the other had left off, to reveal what the prophet had now shown you."

The sun was now beginning to set, and the wind was gusting even more strongly than before. And there I was, standing on that ledge, on the watchman's post, at the gate of America.

—————◆◆◆—————

I turned to the city, set the trumpet to my mouth...and blew.

—————◆◆◆—————

And now the trumpet has sounded.
    Let the one who has ears to hear,
    hear it...
    and return...
    and be saved.

About Jonathan Cahn

Jonathan Cahn caused a worldwide stir with the release of the *New York Times* best seller *The Harbinger* and his subsequent *New York Times* best sellers. He has addressed members of Congress and spoken at the United Nations. He was named, along with Billy Graham and Keith Green, one of the top forty spiritual leaders of the last forty years "who radically changed our world." He is known as a prophetic voice to our times and for the opening up of the deep mysteries of God. Jonathan leads Hope of the World, a ministry of getting the Word to the world and sponsoring projects of compassion to the world's most needy; and Beth Israel/the Jerusalem Center, his ministry base and worship center in Wayne, New Jersey, just outside New York City. He is a much-sought-after speaker and appears throughout America and the world.

To get in touch, to receive prophetic updates, to receive free gifts from his ministry (special messages and much more), to find out about his over two thousand messages and mysteries, for more information, to contact him, or to have a part in the Great Commission, use the following contacts.

Check out:
HopeoftheWorld.org

Write direct to:
Hope of the World
Box 1111
Lodi, NJ 07644 USA

To be kept up to date and see what's happening:

Facebook: Jonathan Cahn (official site)
YouTube: Jonathan Cahn
Twitter: @Jonathan_Cahn
Instagram: jonathan.cahn

Email: contact@hopeoftheworld.org

To find out how you can go to the Holy Land with Jonathan on one of his upcoming Israel Super Tours, write to: contact@hopeoftheworld.org or check online for the coming Super Tours.

The day of the watchman—the sounding of the trumpet to the World Trade Center, marking the North Tower and the place on the tower where 9/11 would begin. Sounded and recorded before it took place, two years to the day: September 11, 1999.

Notes

Chapter 4: The Gate

1.   Deuteronomy 28:52, emphasis added.
2.   Deuteronomy 28:55, emphasis added.
3.   Ezekiel 21:15, emphasis added.
4.   Lamentations 1:4; 2:9, emphasis added.
5.   Emma Lazarus, "The New Colossus," National Park Service, November 2, 1883, https://www.nps.gov/stli/learn/historyculture/colossus.htm.
6.   Deuteronomy 28:52.
7.   Deuteronomy 28:55.
8.   Isaiah 3:26.

Chapter 5: The Towers

1.   Genesis 11:4.
2.   Isaiah 2:12, emphasis added.
3.   Isaiah 2:17, emphasis added.
4.   Ezekiel 16:39.
5.   Isaiah 2:15, emphasis added.
6.   Ezekiel 26:4, emphasis added.
7.   Zephaniah 1:16, emphasis added.
8.   Isaiah 30:25, emphasis added.

Chapter 6: The Wall

1.   Deuteronomy 28:52.
2.   Deuteronomy 28:52, emphasis added.
3.   Deuteronomy 28:52, emphasis added.
4.   Isaiah 2:15, emphasis added.

Chapter 7: The Selichote

1.   Rabbi Abraham Rosenfeld, trans., *Selichot: Authorized Hebrew and English Edition for the Whole Year* (New York: Judaica Press, 1978), Day 3, 41–58.
2.   Rosenfeld, *Selichot: Authorized Hebrew and English Edition for the Whole Year*, Day 3.

3.   Rosenfeld, *Selichot: Authorized Hebrew and English Edition for the Whole Year*, Day 3.

4.   Rosenfeld, *Selichot: Authorized Hebrew and English Edition for the Whole Year*, Day 4, 59–76.

5.   Rosenfeld, *Selichot: Authorized Hebrew and English Edition for the Whole Year*, Day 4.

6.   Rosenfeld, *Selichot: Authorized Hebrew and English Edition for the Whole Year*, Day 4.

7.   Rosenfeld, *Selichot: Authorized Hebrew and English Edition for the Whole Year*, Day 4.

Chapter 8: Foundations

1.   Ezekiel 13:14.
2.   Jeremiah 45:4.

Chapter 9: The Night Address

1.   Henry R. Luce, "The American Century," *Life*, February 17, 1941, https://books.google.com/books?id=I0kEAAAAMBAJ&.

2.   Franklin D. Roosevelt, "Fireside Chat 18: On the Greer Incident," September 11, 1941, https://millercenter.org/the-presidency/presidential-speeches/september-11-1941-fireside-chat-18-greer-incident.

3.   "We Are in It; We Had Better Win It," *Bergen Evening Record*, September 12, 1941, 28, https://www.newspapers.com/newspage/491210602/.

4.   "At the Ready," *Canandaigua Daily Messenger*, September 17, 1941, 5, https://newspaperarchive.com/canandaigua-daily-messenger-sep-17-1941-p-5/.

Chapter 12: The Parasha

1.   Deuteronomy 28:1–2, 4.
2.   Deuteronomy 28:3, ESV.
3.   Deuteronomy 28:5.
4.   Deuteronomy 28:7.
5.   Deuteronomy 28:8.
6.   Deuteronomy 28:10.
7.   Deuteronomy 28:12.
8.   Deuteronomy 28:1, 13.
9.   Deuteronomy 28:44.
10.   Deuteronomy 28:49, emphasis added.
11.   Deuteronomy 28:52, emphasis added.

12.	Deuteronomy 28:16, ᴇꜱᴠ, emphasis added.

13.	Deuteronomy 28:17.

14.	Deuteronomy 28:23.

15.	Deuteronomy 28:24.

16.	Deuteronomy 28:29, ɢɴᴛ.

17.	Deuteronomy 28:25.

18.	Deuteronomy 28:49–50, author's translation from the original language.

19.	Deuteronomy 28:52, emphasis added.

Chapter 13: The Birds of Prey

1.	Hosea 8:1, 3.

2.	Ezekiel 17:3.

3.	Jeremiah 49:22.

4.	Luke 21:20, 24.

5.	Jeremiah 49:22, emphasis added.

6.	Jeremiah 49:22, emphasis added.

7.	Deuteronomy 28:49–50, author's translation from the original language.

8.	Deuteronomy 28:49, ɴɪᴠ, emphasis added.

9.	Deuteronomy 28:49, ɴʟᴛ, emphasis added.

Chapter 14: The Watchmen

1.	Jeremiah 4:19–20, 5–7.

2.	Amos 3:6, emphasis added.

3.	Zephaniah 1:16, emphasis added.

4.	Hosea 8:1, emphasis added.

Chapter 16: The Man on the Hill

1.	John Winthrop, "A Model of Christian Charity," The Winthrop Society, 1630, https://www.winthropsociety.com/doc_charity.php.

2.	Matthew 5:14.

3.	Winthrop, "A Model of Christian Charity."

4.	Winthrop, "A Model of Christian Charity."

5.	Winthrop, "A Model of Christian Charity."

6.	Winthrop, "A Model of Christian Charity."

7.	Winthrop, "A Model of Christian Charity."

8.	Winthrop, "A Model of Christian Charity."

9.   Winthrop, "A Model of Christian Charity."
10.   Winthrop, "A Model of Christian Charity."
11.   Winthrop, "A Model of Christian Charity."
12.   Winthrop, "A Model of Christian Charity."
13.   Winthrop, "A Model of Christian Charity."

Chapter 17: The Harbingers

1.   Isaiah 9:9.
2.   George E. Pataki, "Remarks: Laying of the Cornerstone for Freedom Tower" (speech, New York, July 4, 2004), http://www.renewnyc.com/attachments/content/speeches/Gov_speech_Freedom_Tower.pdf.
3.   John Edwards, "Remarks to the Congressional Black Caucus Prayer Breakfast" (speech, Washington, DC, September 11, 2004), https://www.presidency.ucsb.edu/documents/remarks-the-congressional-black-caucus-prayer-breakfast.
4.   "Senate Majority Leader Daschle Expresses Sorrow, Resolve," Washington File, September 13, 2001, https://wfile.ait.org.tw/wf-archive/2001/010913/epf407.htm.
5.   "Senate Majority Leader Daschle Expresses Sorrow, Resolve," Washington File.

Chapter 18: The Babylonian Word

1.   "Questions That Are Asked Frequently About the 9/11 Recovery…," Ground Zero Museum, accessed May 19, 2020, https://groundzeromuseumworkshop.org/faq.html.
2.   "Questions That Are Asked Frequently About the 9/11 Recovery…," Ground Zero Museum.
3.   Genesis 11:4, GNT.
4.   Genesis 11:3, GNT.
5.   Genesis 11:4, GNT.
6.   Genesis 11:1, GNT.
7.   Genesis 11:4, GNT.
8.   Isaiah 9:10, Brenton Septuagint Translation, emphasis added.
9.   Isaiah 9:10, Brenton Septuagint Translation.

Chapter 19: The Withered

1.   Psalm 37:2, emphasis added.
2.   Isaiah 1:30, NET, emphasis added.

3.   Jeremiah 8:12–13, NASB.

4.   Ezekiel 17:8–10.

Chapter 20: The Ninth of Tammuz

1.   Jeremiah 39:1–2.

2.   Jeremiah 39:4.

3.   Jeremiah 39:8–9.

4.   Jeremiah 39:2.

5.   Isaiah 5:20.

Chapter 21: The Hidden

1.   Isaiah 9:10.

2.   Isaiah 9:10.

3.   Josh Earnest, "Beam Signed by President Obama Installed at World Trade Center," White House, August 2, 2012, https://obamawhitehouse. archives.gov/blog/2012/08/02/beam-signed-president-obama-installed-world-trade-center.

4.   Earnest, "Beam Signed by President Obama Installed at World Trade Center."

5.   Earnest, "Beam Signed by President Obama Installed at World Trade Center."

6.   Charles F. Pfeiffer and Everett F. Harrison, eds., *The Wycliffe Bible Commentary* (Chicago: Moody Bible Institute, 1990), Isaiah, vol. 2, sermon III, https://books.google.com/books?id=r4lLCAAAQBAJ&pg.

7.   Richard Blanco, "One Today," in Mary Bruce, "'One Today': Full Text of Richard Blanco Inaugural Poem," ABC News, January 21, 2013, https://abcnews.go.com/Politics/today-richard-blanco-poem-read-barack-obama-inauguration/story?id=18274653.

8.   Blanco, "One Today," emphasis added.

9.   Genesis 11:4.

Chapter 22: The Image

1.   Winthrop, "A Model of Christian Charity."

2.   2 Kings 17:15–16.

3.   Ezekiel 8:3, 5.

4.   Ezekiel 8:10.

5.   Ezekiel 9:1, NIV.

6.   Deuteronomy 4:15–17, author's translation from the original language.

7.   Deuteronomy 5:7–9, author's translation from the original language.

8.   Isaiah 5:20, emphasis added.

Chapter 23: The Handwriting on the Wall

1.   Daniel 5.

2.   Ezekiel 1:26–28; Revelation 4:3.

Chapter 24: The Judgment Tree

1.   Isaiah 18:5.

2.   Ezekiel 31:12.

3.   Jeremiah 11:16.

4.   Isaiah 27:11.

5.   Psalm 46:9.

6.   Barack Obama, "Remarks by the President at the September 11th 10th Anniversary Commemoration," White House, September 11, 2011, https://obamawhitehouse.archives.gov/the-press-office/2011/09/11/remarks-president-september-11th-10th-anniversary-commemoration.

7.   Ezekiel 31:3, 12, author's translation from the original language.

8.   Jeremiah 22:7, author's translation from the original language.

9.   Zechariah 11:1–2, author's translation from the original language.

10.   Joseph S. Exell and Henry Donald Maurice Spence-Jones, *The Complete Pulpit Commentary*, vol. 5 (Harrington, DE: Delmarva, 2013), https://books.google.com/books?id=VjZcCgAAQBAJ&pg.

11.   Zechariah 11:2, author's translation from the original language.

12.   Jonathan Cahn, *The Harbinger* (Lake Mary, FL: FrontLine, 2011), 96, emphasis added.

13.   This was confirmed by two independent witnesses.

14.   Ezekiel 32:7; Joel 2:31, GNT.

15.   Joel 2:31.

16.   Ezekiel 31:12.

Chapter 25: Tophet

1.   Jeremiah 7:30–31.

2.   Jeremiah 19.

3.   Ryan Lizza, "The Abortion Capital of America," *New York*, December 2, 2005, https://nymag.com/nymetro/news/features/15248/.

4.   Jeremiah 7:31.

Chapter 26: The Convergence

1.   Isaiah 9:8–10, emphasis added.

Chapter 28: The Shakings

1.   Franz Delitzsch, *Biblical Commentary on the Prophecies of Isaiah*, vol. 1, trans. James Martin (Edinburgh: T&T Clark, 1873), 258, https://books.google.com/books?id=b0hGAAAAYAAJ&pg.

2.   Matthew Henry, *Commentary on the Whole Bible*, vol. 4, Christian Classics Ethereal Library, accessed May 24, 2020, https://ccel.org/ccel/henry/mhc4/mhc4.Is.x.html.

3.   Cahn, *The Harbinger*, 217.

4.   Cahn, *The Harbinger*, 220.

5.   Henry, *Commentary on the Whole Bible*.

6.   Cahn, *The Harbinger*, 217.

Chapter 29: The Plague

1.   Cahn, *The Harbinger*, 103. See also Abraham Lincoln, "Second Inaugural Address of Abraham Lincoln" (speech, Washington, DC, March 4, 1865), https://avalon.law.yale.edu/19th_century/lincoln2.asp.

2.   Jeremiah 19:4–7.

3.   Jeremiah 19:8, emphasis added.

4.   Jeremiah 32:35–36, emphasis added.

5.   Jeremiah 19:1–2.

6.   Jeremiah 19:11.

7.   Jeremiah 8:22.

8.   Gilead Sciences, "Gilead Announces Results From Phase 3 Trial of Investigational Antiviral Remdesivir in Patients With Severe COVID-19," press release, April 29, 2020, https://www.gilead.com/news-and-press/press-room/press-releases/2020/4/gilead-announces-results-from-phase-3-trial-of-investigational-antiviral-remdesivir-in-patients-with-severe-covid-19.

9.   "New York Coronavirus Map and Case Count," *New York Times*, updated June 7, 2020, https://www.nytimes.com/interactive/2020/us/new-york-coronavirus-cases.html.

Chapter 30: The Return

1. Exodus 32:28.

2. George Washington, "Washington's Inaugural Address of 1789" (speech, New York, April 30, 1789), https://www.archives.gov/exhibits/american_originals/inaugtxt.html.

3. Deuteronomy 30:1–2, 9–10, emphasis added.

4. 2 Chronicles 7:14.

5. 2 Chronicles 7:13–14, emphasis added.

6. Qu Dongyu, Mark Lowcock, and David Beasley, "Locusts in East Africa: A Race Against Time," World Food Programme, February 25, 2020, https://www.wfp.org/news/locusts-east-africa-race-against-time.

7. United Nations Security Council, "Senior Officials Sound Alarm Over Food Insecurity, Warning of Potentially 'Biblical' Famine, in Briefings to Security Council," April 21, 2020, https://www.un.org/press/en/2020/sc14164.doc.htm.

Chapter 31: The Winds of April

1. Lincoln, "Second Inaugural Address of Abraham Lincoln."

2. Abraham Lincoln, "Proclamation 97—Appointing a Day of National Humiliation, Fasting, and Prayer," American Presidency Project, March 30, 1863, https://www.presidency.ucsb.edu/documents/proclamation-97-appointing-day-national-humiliation-fasting-and-prayer.

3. 2 Chronicles 7:14, emphasis added.

4. 2 Chronicles 7:14, emphasis added.

5. Jennings Cropper Wise, *The Long Arm of Lee*, vol. 2 (Lincoln, NE: University of Nebraska Press, 1991), 557, https://books.google.com/books?id=KHSn_TeKbZIC&pg.

6. Lincoln, "Proclamation 97."

Chapter 32: The Western Terrace

1. Ronald Reagan, "Election Eve Address a Vision for America," Ronald Reagan Presidential Library & Museum, November 3, 1980, https://www.reaganlibrary.gov/11-3-80.

2. Reagan, "Election Eve Address a Vision for America."

3. Reagan, "Election Eve Address a Vision for America."

4. Reagan, "Election Eve Address a Vision for America."

5. 2 Chronicles 7:14.

6.   2 Chronicles 7:14.

7.   Michael Reagan and Jim Denney, *The Common Sense of an Uncommon Man* (Nashville: Thomas Nelson, 1998), https://books.google.com/books?id=bFriCQAAQBAJ&.

8.   Ronald Reagan, "Farewell Address to the Nation," Reagan Foundation, January 11, 1989, https://www.reaganfoundation.org/media/128652/farewell.pdf.

Chapter 33: The Island

1.   Winthrop, "A Model of Christian Charity."

2.   Malachi 3:7.

Chapter 34: The Lamb

1.   Isaiah 53:7, emphasis added.

2.   John 1:29, emphasis added.

3.   John 3:16.

4.   Deuteronomy 30:19.

5.   Matthew 11:28.

Chapter 35: The Day of the Watchman

1.   Jeremiah 19; 1 Kings 11:29–39; Ezekiel 12:1–16.

2.   Jeremiah 18:4.

3.   Lazarus, "The New Colossus."

4.   Jeremiah 4:19–20.

5.   Ezekiel 33:3, author's translation from the original language.

6.   Jeremiah 6:17.

7.   Amos 3:6.

8.   Ezekiel 4:2.

9.   Hosea 8:1.

Our FREE GIFT to You

Dear Reader,

We hope you found *The Harbinger II* to be as mind-blowing as *The Harbinger*.

If you aren't aware of how it all started, and would like to learn more about what caused a worldwide sensation, we have a **FREE GIFT** for you.

Link to stream
The Harbinger Decoded online
(video runtime: 62 minutes).

To get this **FREE GIFT**,
please go to:

www.booksbyjonathancahn.com/freegift

Thanks again, and God bless you,

Publishers of FrontLine books